The Worthy Soldier

The Gareth and Gwen Medieval Mysteries
The Bard's Daughter
The Good Knight
The Uninvited Guest
The Fourth Horseman
The Fallen Princess
The Unlikely Spy
The Lost Brother
The Renegade Merchant
The Unexpected Ally
The Worthy Soldier

The After Cilmeri Series:
Daughter of Time
Footsteps in Time
Winds of Time
Prince of Time
Crossroads in Time
Children of Time
Exiles in Time
Castaways in Time
Ashes of Time
Warden of Time
Guardians of Time
Masters of Time
Outpost in Time

The Lion of Wales Series:
Cold My Heart
The Oaken Door
Of Men and Dragons
A Long Cloud
Frost Against the Hilt

A Gareth and Gwen Medieval Mystery

The Worthy Soldier

by

Sarah Woodbury

The Worthy Soldier

This is a work of fiction.

www.sarahwoodbury.com

To Dan
as always

Cast of Characters

Hywel—Prince of Gwynedd; Lord of Ceredigion
Maurice Fitzgerald—Lord of Llanstephan, King Cadell's cousin
William de Carew—Castellan of Pembroke Castle, Maurice's brother
Cadell—King of Deheubarth
Maredudd—Prince of Deheubarth
Rhys—Prince of Deheubarth
Richard de Clare—son of the Earl of Pembroke

Gwen – Gareth's wife, spy for Hywel
Gareth – Gwen's husband, captain of Hywel's guard
Llelo—Gareth and Gwen's foster son
Dai—Gareth and Gwen's foster son
Meilyr – Gwen's father
Saran—Gwen's stepmother

Evan – Gareth's friend, Dragon member
Gruffydd – Rhun's former captain, Dragon member
Cadoc—Assassin, Dragon member
Steffan—Dragon member
Iago—Dragon member
Aron—Dragon member
Rhodri—Member of Hywel's guard
Goch—Member of Hywel's guard

Angharad—King Cadell's niece
Barri—Maurice Fitzgerald's man
Meicol—King Cadell's man
Alban—King Cadell's man
Caron—Alban's wife
Cadfan—Captain of Cadell's guard
Robert—Master swordsman
John—Captain of Maurice's guard

1

Wiston Castle

May 1147

Evan

Evan couldn't have been happier with his new companions and his new job—even if at the moment, he was struggling to remember that fact.

Hearts pounding loud enough to drown out the rain, the six men pressed their bellies to the wet grass, blending into the ground and the darkness above them. The weather would have been aggravating if it hadn't been the reason they'd chosen this particular moment in the first place to begin the attack on the Flemish castle of Wiston, owned by the improbably named Walter FitzWizo. Forty years earlier, King Henry of England had given Walter's family and his group of Fleming mercenaries this portion of southern Wales. In all that time, nobody had been able to evict them from it.

Until, hopefully, now.

Prince Hywel had entrusted his Dragons—Evan and his five companions—with the task of going over the wall first. Ahead of Evan was Gruffydd, once Prince Rhun's captain, now the Dragons' leader. Gruffydd nodded to Cadoc, the former assassin and preeminent archer of the group, who rose to his feet and directed his great bow towards the nearest sentry on the wall-walk. He could bring down a man from three hundred paces, though tonight his target stood only a third of that distance away on the nearest tower and was silhouetted against the sputtering and flickering torch behind him.

Cadoc loosed the arrow, which whispered through the air, audible over the rain only because Evan imagined he could hear it. It hit the soldier in the chest, and the power of the shot dropped him below the level of the wall. It was almost unfair how little the man's death taxed Cadoc's abilities.

Everyone held their breath, waiting for someone to raise the alarm, but no bell sounded, and the fallen soldier didn't call a warning—or at least not one they could hear from where they waited. His death had been instantaneous.

The last three squad members were young men in their early twenties, newly minted men-at-arms who'd distinguished themselves with their intelligence and physical skills: Steffan, who could do things with a knife Evan wouldn't have believed if he hadn't seen it for himself; Iago, whose bulk made Evan feel as small as a child; and Aron, Evan's favorite of the three and a son of Hywel's foster father, Cadifor. At first glance, Aron's open face seemed naive or even simple, but underneath that innocent exterior lay a sharp wit that had the power to leave Evan in stitches.

With the sentry down, the wall was free of watchers, and Gruffydd signaled that they should move forward. Steffan, as the knifeman, and Gruffydd, their leader, went first, moving at a low crouch. With the muddy ground and slippery grass, they had to concentrate on placing their feet carefully, so as not to fall and give the game away too soon.

A few weeks ago, Prince Hywel, Evan's lord, had chosen expediency and opportunity over caution and his better judgement. He'd allied himself not only with King Cadell of Deheubarth but a passel of Norman lords as well, all of whom were currently in rebellion against King Stephen, whereas Walter FitzWizo, their current opponent, remained loyal. It seemed the perfect opportunity to strike a blow for Welshmen and for Hywel to gain stature among his peers. The plain truth was that the prince's status as the future King of Gwynedd would be built less on his ability to govern than on his martial prowess—in other words, on opportunities like this.

Though it might not feel like it at the moment, they'd been lucky that the rain had come when it did, because they'd had a two-week dry spell that had threatened to undo the entire expedition. The bulk of FitzWizo's men had been lured outside the castle, convinced that they were facing a small party of Welsh raiders, who'd been burning Flemish holdings throughout this region of Wales—a bit too gleefully in Evan's opinion. Women and children had died along the way, and nobody but Prince Hywel and his men seemed to care—with the exception of Angharad, King Cadell's niece. How she'd heard about it, Evan didn't know, since up until yesterday, the alliance had put out that they were marching east to confront King Stephen's forces, not traveling west to Wiston.

Regardless, she'd come to the Dragons in tears about her uncle's activities, having already gone to the king himself. He'd dismissed her concerns like a man brushing a crumb off his sleeve, stating that she hadn't been on the receiving end of FitzWizo's depredations over the years nor among the families and villages displaced by the Flemings' coming. All of which was true, if callous. But it had fallen to Evan to tell her that there was nothing any of the men from Gwynedd could do about it.

Angharad appeared to be the only leak in Cadell's wall of secrecy. At any moment, FitzWizo would discover that he and his men were facing an army instead of a marauding band—and furthermore that they no longer had a fortress to retreat to.

That was where the Dragons came in.

Wiston was a typical motte and bailey castle. It consisted of a keep built on a forty-foot mound over the remains of an ancient Welsh fort. It was protected by a palisade five hundred feet in length on a side. In front of the wooden fence were a rampart and a deep ditch, which, for the Dragons' immediate purposes, simply meant the distance they had to scale to reach the top of the wall was greater than it would have been from level ground.

Because of the palisade, the castle was not nearly as defensible as it would have been had FitzWizo invested in stone.

Walter knew it too, and that was why he'd taken the news of marauders in his lands as a signal to march the bulk of his men out to meet them on better ground of his choosing, closer to the border of Deheubarth, rather than to wait for them to come to him. At dawn—an hour or so from now—Cadell intended to engage Walter's army. The Dragons had every intention of winning this fight here at the castle before the real battle began.

Gruffydd threw his grappling hook upwards, and it slipped easily between two of the palisade's slats and held. As part of their preparations, Aron had made knots in their ropes every foot to help in the scaling. Evan went up his rope quickly, and then held it for Iago, who followed last.

Huffing, the big man landed in a heavy squat on the wall-walk, his feet *thunking* onto the wood a little more loudly than Evan might have liked. Steffan and Gruffydd, who'd shared a different rope, had already killed a second man who'd come out of a nearby tower. Aron and Evan dragged him into the shadows to lie beside the man Cadoc had shot with the arrow. Such was the power of Cadoc's bow that the arrow had penetrated the man's chest to a depth of six inches, even through his mail.

Nobody had yet said a word, and they didn't need to now. Gruffydd indicated they should split up to their respective parts of the castle as they'd planned. Gruffydd, Iago, and Steffan would go to the main gate, kill whoever was there, and open the gate so that the men who were waiting outside could enter. Among this force would be Prince Hywel and a host of men from Gwynedd, but the company as a whole was led by a master swordsman from

Deheubarth, Sir Robert, who'd been Evan's first teacher. Evan hadn't seen any of the people he'd grown up with in the south in over ten years—since the 1136 war—which also happened to be the last time Gwynedd had allied with Deheubarth.

Meanwhile, Cadoc would keep watch from the top of the palisade, eliminating anyone who moved in the bailey or the wall-walk—anyone who wasn't one of the six of them, that is. In particular, he needed to kill any soldier who exited the barracks. Fortunately, because the castle was built in wood, its defenses didn't include a portcullis or barbican. Once the main gate was opened, there would be no stopping the attackers from taking the fort.

That didn't mean that it would be smooth sailing from that moment on, however. The genius of a motte and bailey castle lay in the construction of the mound upon which the keep perched. As the last defense of the castle, a ten-foot-deep ditch surrounded the motte at the bottom and a second palisade wall enclosed the keep on three sides at the top. On the fourth side, the wooden palisade ran down both sides of the stairway to an inner gatehouse that protected its entrance.

It was Evan and Aron's job to secure the drawbridge across the ditch and open this inner gate before anyone in the keep knew they were under attack.

Unfortunately, the gate could be opened only by the guard on the motte side. Thus, they first needed to subdue the guards on the bailey side, disable the drawbridge workings, get the key to the wicket gate that allowed the passage of one man at a time from one side to the other, and kill that last guard. Only then could they open the gate for the rest of their army and head up the stairs to the keep.

Leaping down the wooden steps to the courtyard, Evan and Aron raced towards the inner gatehouse, making sure they followed the curve of the palisade so as to stay out of Cadoc's line of sight. Their feet splashed through puddles that had formed in the few hours it had been raining, and Evan brushed his wet hair out of his face, wishing he'd had the foresight to cut it short like Gareth's.

Ahead of him, a man appeared from underneath the gatehouse on the other side of the ditch. He hadn't seen Evan and Aron yet, and at the same instant that he set foot on the bridge, an arrow hit his breastbone. He staggered, his hands grasping at the shaft protruding from his chest, and toppled backwards to lie flat on the ground.

"The man doesn't miss. I'll give him that." Aron ran across the drawbridge and crouched over the fallen guard. Just as with the first man on the wall-walk, the arrow had killed him as close to instantly as not to matter, so he'd had no chance to cry out. That, of course, had been the point.

The gate behind the drawbridge remained closed, as it should always be, even were the castle not under siege. Fortunately, the rain covered many sounds, and it seemed as if the rest of the garrison still did not know what was afoot.

Evan bent to the fallen soldier and patted him down, looking for the key to the wicket gate without which this entire endeavor would be a failure. He didn't find it, so with Aron's help, he rolled the dead man off the bridge into the ditch below. The body fell with a sodden thud, which could just be heard above the sound of the rain. In daylight, the body would be obvious, but in the dead of night, were someone to look outside any of the craft huts or the barracks, it was too dark down there for them to see anything.

"I don't see another guard." Evan was still crouched, trying to keep his profile low to the ground.

"He's inside his guardhouse, nice and dry." Aron laughed mockingly under his breath. "He should know better."

Evan had spent enough nights on boring guard duty to know that it was nearly impossible to stay alert all the time. The dead guard had probably drawn straws with his companion to decide whose task it was to take a turn around the bailey. "Don't get cocky, Aron."

"Never. But if it's too easy, it isn't fun."

"And don't say that either." Evan ran at a crouch to the gatehouse itself. Above the gate was the room that housed the workings for the drawbridge, though the winch itself was down below, where it was easily accessible. Breathing hard and perhaps as uncomfortable as Aron with how well things were going so far, he went to each of the chains that controlled the drawbridge and jammed an iron pike into the gears.

Disabling the drawbridge couldn't be done without making a little bit of noise, and it was probably that which finally drew the second guard out of his warm guardroom on the left side of the gatehouse archway. Aron had just pressed his back to one side of the door when it opened. "Edward, *wat ben je aan het doen*—"

Aron pivoted and met the newcomer's chest with his knife. The man collapsed over his hand, and, with Evan's help, Aron eased him down to the ground to sit with his back against the guardroom wall and his feet splayed out in front of him. While Aron cleaned his knife, Evan searched this man for a key as he'd done to his companion, who was now at the bottom of the ditch.

The key was on a chain around the man's neck, and Evan pulled it over his head and tossed it to Aron. The young man caught it in his left hand and immediately went to the wicket door, which was only four feet high: another precaution so that any opposing force that managed to make it through the rest of the castle's defenses could be stopped here. The only way to get through the door was in a hunched over position. The key fit the lock and turned easily, but Evan and Aron didn't yet enter.

"Edward?" a voice came from the other side of the gate.

Evan motioned towards Aron, knowing that the guard would know he wasn't Flemish the moment he opened his mouth.

Aron bobbed his head in a nod. "Ja." He had a facility for languages, which was yet another reason he'd been chosen as a member of the Dragons. If Evan hadn't known his own worth in battle, he might have started to feel inferior among so many skilled companions.

The man approached the wicket door. "Alles goed?"

"Ja," Aron said again—just as Evan drove his shoulder into the little door, putting his entire weight into the effort. The door hit FitzWizo's soldier full on from his knees to his chin, catching him completely by surprise. He fell backwards onto his rear, and by the time he realized the action wasn't a mistake and it wasn't Edward coming through the door, Evan had driven his knife into his chest.

It was only then, as they opened the inner gate and jammed another iron pike into the hinges so the gate couldn't be easily closed, that Evan looked to the main entrance to the castle. Their timing had been nearly perfect. Gruffydd had just opened the main gate and was signaling with a torch that the way was clear.

Iago arrived beside Aron. "I can't believe they don't know we're here."

"I guess we're just that good," Aron said.

Evan ignored him and spoke to Iago. "The barracks?"

Iago lifted one shoulder. "I barred the front door after I threw a burning taper inside. They'll notice it soon and come out the windows, which I could do nothing about."

"I say we get to the motte before the alarm is raised," Aron said. "It can't be much longer now."

Evan glanced again towards Gruffydd. Through the open gate, he could make out the figures of moving men, the first of whom had almost reached the castle.

"We were told to wait," Iago said.

Aron scoffed. "Did it make sense to you as to why?"

Iago's eyes narrowed. "No. And not to Prince Hywel either, though he didn't argue."

Aron started up the steps. "*It's better to die on the stage than to live your life in the wings.* Isn't that what Prince Hywel says?"

"Personally, I'd rather not die at all," Evan said under his breath, but he appreciated Aron's point and went up the stairs after him.

Iago took the steps three at a time. Even though he was a large man, he was puffing less than Evan by the time they reached the top. A last few steps took them up to the narrow doorway that was the only entrance to the three-story keep. Nobody guarded the outside, unsurprising given the lack of porch and the pouring rain.

Inside would be an anteroom with at least one guard on duty at all times. Beyond would be the great hall, such as it was—this was not a big keep—with the apartments for the lord on the floor above. Storage and armaments would be at ground level, but accessible only from the inside through a trap door and ladder. Finally, there would be a guardroom at the top for household guards.

It was only as the Dragons hesitated by the door that a defender on the top of the keep finally realized Wiston Castle was under attack. A bell clanged from above them, followed by a shout, which was immediately cut off. A moment later, a body hit the ground not far from the top of the steps, yet another of Cadoc's three-foot arrows protruding from the dead man's torso.

Iago hastened back down the stairs and dragged the body around the corner to the back of the keep to leave it in the shadows of the palisade. They didn't want it to be lying near the steps when whoever was guarding the front door to the keep opened it at their knock.

If he opened it.

He couldn't have missed the ringing of the bell, but the only way for him to know how much of the fort had been breached—or even if they were really under attack—was to open that door.

Aron knocked.

"Wie gaat daar heen?"

Evan prodded Aron and said in a harsh whisper, "Answer him!"

Aron shrugged. "Edward."

"Ja."

The door opened, and for the third time that night, one of Walter FitzWizo's men died from a knife to the chest.

"Stop!" The call came from behind them, at the bottom of the stairs, and the three Dragons turned, even Aron, who had wedged himself into the doorway with the body. A company of twenty men had surged through the lower gate and were heading up the steps towards the keep.

Evan frowned, but the three men from Gwynedd stepped back anyway, unwilling to openly disobey what was clearly a direct order. The man in the lead, the gray-haired Sir Robert, didn't deign to comment as he went by, just shot Evan a scornful look. Evan also recognized the man who followed right behind Robert. Alban was of an age with Evan, and the two men had known each other well many years ago. He was also the second-in-command of King Cadell's personal guard.

Alban's men charged through the doorway one at a time, though not before two of them pulled the body of the man Evan had killed out of the doorway and dropped him on the ground. Meanwhile, Alban put his nose right in Evan's face. "You were told to leave the keep to us!"

Evan couldn't deny it, but he wasn't willing to go down before Alban that easily. Evan was a knight now, same as Alban, and the order made as little sense in this moment as it had when it had been given. "You weren't here, and if we hadn't convinced the guard to open the door just as the alarm was raised, you wouldn't be entering the keep now."

Alban swept his gaze over Aron and Iago, both of whom gazed steadily back at him. Evan could hear shouts and fighting inside the keep. The twenty men Sir Robert had led inside were more than FitzWizo had left behind, and the remnant of the garrison at Wiston had been completely unprepared for attack.

Then Alban surprised Evan by bobbing his head. "No harm done." He clapped his hand on Evan's shoulder. "You did what you came here to do. You have the thanks of the men of Deheubarth, but you should find Prince Hywel now. Last I saw, he was on the wall-walk above the main gatehouse."

It was a dismissal, made all the clearer when Alban entered the keep after his men and closed the door behind him.

2

Dinefwr Castle

June 1147

Gwen

Two weeks later ...

The festivities were in full swing, and Gwen wished again that she hadn't come. Absurdly, she done this to herself, since she could have stayed at Aberystwyth with Mari and the children. But the look of utter panic on Hywel's face at the prospect of facing Angharad, Rhun's former betrothed, whom he would no longer be able to avoid, had softened her heart.

He'd looked imploring for only a heartbeat before clearing his face of all expression, but Gwen had seen his dismay. Probably his hasty rearrangement of his features had been calculated. She and the prince had known each other since they were children, and he knew exactly how to get her to do what he wanted.

"Gwen! You came!" Angharad spoke from behind her.

Gwen turned, holding out her hands to the girl. Since this was what she'd come here for, it was best to get the condolences over with. "I wouldn't have missed the celebration of such a victory—nor the opportunity to see you."

Angharad's expression didn't change, but a shadow entered her eyes, and she lowered her voice. "You don't have to pretend with me. I know how you must have dreaded this trip."

Gwen squeezed Angharad's hands, feeling bad now for her reluctance and fear. She should have known better. Out of all the girls in Wales, Rhun had chosen Angharad for a reason. "Then tell me the truth too. How are you?"

Angharad was all that a young noblewoman was supposed to be: dark-haired, only a year or two past twenty, with striking blue eyes. For her beauty alone, the girl should have been married long since, even before she met Prince Rhun. The fact that she wasn't married still, six months after Rhun's death, was an indication of the mettle behind her sweet exterior—and surely one of the many attributes that had drawn Rhun to her.

At Gwen's question, Angharad smiled sadly, not pretending to misunderstand. "Sad. As we all are. I've spoken already to Prince Hywel, though I have no doubt he would have preferred a night spent cleaning the latrines to speaking to me."

"His grief remains fresh," Gwen said, "though he has become more able to smile and put his anger aside for short periods of time."

"I remind him of what he's lost." Again, she smiled that sweet smile that had men all around the room turning towards her. "Someday, I hope reminders will be a cause for gladness, not grief."

"We can all hope for that," Gwen said, liking Angharad more and more. It was a rare woman of the court who spoke so straightforwardly. All of a sudden, Gwen was no longer fretting about the fifty miles home, or thinking to beg Gareth to take her back to Tangwen sooner rather than later.

"And you?" Angharad said. "I understand you are with child again."

Gwen ran her hand down her somewhat more rounded belly, though she was still not showing so much that she thought everyone could tell just by looking at her. "Did someone say I shouldn't be here?" A two-day journey in good weather wasn't yet beyond Gwen's capability, but she *was* in the middle stage of her pregnancy, due in the autumn, and people liked to criticize, thinking they knew what was best for everyone else. Most of the time Gwen ignored gossip, but as the wife of the captain of Prince Hywel's guard, she was often the object of discussion.

Angharad laughed. "Of course not. You are much admired. The only words I've heard have been pleased ones." But then she drew Gwen's attention to a woman sitting on a bench behind them. She had a long cane, almost a staff, resting against her shoulder, and she stared straight ahead, unseeing. "This is the woman I told you about, Old Nan."

The woman turned her head in Gwen's direction, though her eyes were focused on something far away. "Ah, the woman who solves murders."

Gwen's eyes widened. "You've heard of me?"

"Just because I'm blind doesn't mean I can't hear." The woman cackled. "My hearing is better than my sight ever was."

Gwen didn't know how to respond to that. *I'm sorry* just didn't seem appropriate. So instead she moved a few steps closer and bobbed a curtsy, even though Old Nan couldn't see that either. "I would never assume any such thing."

"I see you're enjoying yourselves."

Gwen turned to find herself facing yet another member of King Cadell's court, his younger half-brother, Rhys ap Gruffydd. The young man was dark-haired, dark-eyed, and fifteen years old last week, the same as Gwen's Llelo. And like Llelo, he looked as if he'd grown another inch since they were introduced an hour ago. His intelligence was also a palpable force in the room.

At their initial introduction, he'd given her a succinct summary of the state of political allegiances throughout Deheubarth and the March—after which he'd pumped her for information about Gwynedd. If the conversation had taken place with one of Cadell's courtiers or his steward, she would have thought Rhys's questions were to gain an advantage or for some nefarious purpose. But that wasn't Rhys. As she'd talked, he'd gazed at her with an intensity that indicated he was absorbing every word, storing each one to be taken out and examined later. He'd asked her because he'd wanted to know.

"I suppose we are," Angharad said.

Rhys grinned. "I can't say the same for some. We just killed three of FitzWizo's men on the road to Dinefwr."

Angharad didn't see the humor. "The war never ends." The pair apparently knew each other well, which made sense since they were both living at Dinefwr, though they weren't blood relations. Angharad was Cadell's niece through his dead wife. "I have been thinking that your brother's smile, and the celebration in general, seems forced. Maybe now I know why."

"He's my half-brother, and that's not the only reason," Rhys said.

At Rhys's arrival, Old Nan had pushed to her feet and departed, tapping her cane in front of her, so Gwen turned to face Rhys more fully. He sounded a bit like he was lording it over Angharad, but Angharad didn't take offense, instead smiling back. Gwen realized Angharad and Rhys were friends, this was an old dance between the two of them—and Rhys didn't much like his elder half-brother.

"I would love to know what is troubling everyone. I've felt it too," Gwen said.

Rhys pointed to where Gareth's friend, Evan, was standing with a well-dressed man, both eyeing a seated man-at-arms whose chin was sticking out in a way that didn't bode well for the peacefulness of the party. "Many of the knights and men-at-arms here, even if they are from other kingdoms, trained together at one time or another, those three included. Didn't you know?"

"I suppose I knew Evan had grown up at Dinefwr," Gwen said, "but even if I thought about it, I wouldn't have considered it a problem. Are you saying there's bad blood among them?"

"That's exactly what I'm saying," Rhys said.

Angharad eyed the young prince. "Aren't you going to tell us where the bad blood comes from?" She gestured to the three men. "Evan looks as confused as I am."

Gwen raised her eyebrows at the familiar way Angharad referred to Gareth's closest friend, but she chose not to tease her about it because Evan had put down his cup of mead and moved into a more ready stance. "It looks to me like he's starting to figure it out." She stood on her tiptoes, searching the crowd for Gareth. As a leader of men, he was used to heading off trouble before it started.

But before she could find him, the third man rose to his feet and stalked towards Evan and his companion, whose name Gwen didn't know. If the stalking man's glare had been a sword, both Evan and the man beside him would have been skewered through the heart, though it seemed most of the oncoming man's attention was directed at Evan's companion.

"This isn't good." Gwen grasped Rhys's arm. "Do you know those other two?"

"The man with your friend is Barri. I haven't seen him since I was a very young. He serves Maurice Fitzgerald. The other man is Meicol, a member of the garrison here at Dinefwr." Black-haired, with a pock-marked face and a nose that looked like it had been broken several times, Meicol's visage wasn't appealing, in contrast to Barri, who appeared far less menacing with his unremarkable brown eyes, a brown beard, and longish brown hair pulled back into a tail. He was well-muscled, as befitted a man-at-arms in a lord's retinue, and like Meicol, of medium height.

Gwen glanced at Rhys and then at Angharad. Neither's expression implied admiration of Meicol. "You don't like him?"

"He's a drunkard," Rhys gestured to him, "as you can see."

Angharad bit her lip. "And a bit of a bully. He isn't popular among the men, that's for certain."

"He's both drunk and unhappy today," Gwen said.

"It is my understanding that until this month, the last time many of these men were together was during the last war—though not all fought on our side." Rhys didn't need to elaborate on what war he meant. He'd been only four years old when the 1136 war began. At the end of it, both his parents, Gruffydd, the King of Deheubarth, and Gwenllian, sister to King Owain, were dead. It had been Gwenllian's death, in fact, that had spurred the Welsh forces into allying in the first place. That alliance between Gwynedd and Deheubarth had subsequently become strained when King Owain had claimed Ceredigion for himself, putting it under the authority of Gwynedd, rather than giving it back to Deheubarth.

With the loss of their father, Rhys's eldest half-brother, Anarawd, had taken the reins of Deheubarth. Then, after his murder, Cadell had ascended the throne. Gwen herself knew far more than she really wanted to about the intrigue that had put them both there, none of which she would dream of mentioning to anyone, particularly their younger half-brother.

For his part, Cadell had no sons, and it was to this much younger half-brother that the future of Deheubarth might ultimately fall. Gwenllian had given Gruffydd four sons. The eldest two had fallen in the 1136 war, leaving two remaining: Maredudd and Rhys, who were seventeen and fifteen. If either one inherited the throne, it would make Deheubarth more connected to Gwynedd again, as the brothers were first cousins to Hywel. But whether the brothers themselves felt that connection would greatly depend on how the next few years went and how long the current alliance lasted. Gwen herself had never met Maredudd, who wasn't even here: after the victory, he had returned to Pembroke, where he served as one of the Earl of Pembroke's squires.

And given that complicated history, perhaps it wasn't surprising to find Rhys more thoughtful than most boys his age. His prodigious memory was certainly more than equal to the task of keeping names and faces straight.

"They don't seem to be reconciled, do they?" Angharad said under her breath. Evan, Meicol, and Barri by now were looking at each other with hostility, which changed to open violence a moment later when Meicol took a swing at Barri.

Barri easily sidestepped the blow, so Meicol careened around to have another go. Before he could connect, however, Barri caught him by the shoulders and threw him to the floor. Meicol fell onto his right shoulder with a thud that made Gwen's own shoulder hurt. Grown men fighting like youths was always an ugly sight. She wanted to turn away, but like everyone else in the room, she was mesmerized by the scene before her. Meicol, grunting, pushed to his knees and then his feet. He stood there, weaving, but refusing to admit he was too drunk to continue fighting.

"That's enough, you two." Evan caught Meicol's arm before he could take another swing at Barri.

"It isn't nearly enough!" Meicol was in a rage and would have charged again towards Barri if Evan hadn't been holding his arm. "Traitor! Thief!"

"You should get out of here before you hurt yourself." Barri had a hand on the hilt of his sword. "You never were much in a fight."

"Better than the treacherous bastard you have proved to be!" Meicol clenched his fists and tried to pull away from Evan. As he twisted, however, he ended up looking straight at Gwen, so she saw the look of puzzlement when it crossed his face. Then the puzzlement turned to surprise—and then to fear. Instead of swinging back around to punch Barri, he grasped Evan's shirt, and he was a large enough man to force Evan to bend slightly forward. "Help me—"

Meicol sagged to his knees, and then vomited onto the floor at Evan's feet. Evan wasn't able to twist entirely away, though he managed to avoid the worst of the spray. For his part, Meicol ended up on his hands and knees, his head hanging, and then he slumped onto his stomach on the floorboards.

Barri gaped at Meicol, even as he twitched his dark green cloak out of the way so as not to mar the embroidered hem. "What happened?"

"I don't know. It isn't as if you hit him." Evan pushed at Meicol's shoulder, half turning him onto his right side. Then he slapped Meicol's cheek, but the fallen man didn't respond. "Get the healer!"

Instead of obeying, Barri backed farther away, horror on his face. His mouth opened and closed like he was a landed fish. Ignoring Barri's sputtering, Evan put a hand to Meicol's neck, looking for a pulse. But then he shook his head and said simply, "Never mind. He's dead."

3

Gareth

When the fight started, Gareth had been standing on the far side of the room, but by the time Evan declared Meicol dead, he was watching as raptly as everyone else. If this had been Aberystwyth—or anywhere in Gwynedd—Gareth would have immediately gone to Evan's side, knowing without being told that it was his job to begin the quest for answers. But Gareth had no authority here. More to the point, he wanted no authority here.

But then Evan straightened, and the first thing he did was search the room.

Gareth knew he was looking for him, and he resisted the temptation to hide behind Iago, who was standing beside him and could have easily blocked him from Evan's view.

Instead he allowed Iago to nudge him forward. "He wants you."

"I see that."

Iago laughed at Gareth's sour tone and added, "Go on. Cadell is sure to have someone else he'd rather have in charge, but Evan needs you now."

Comforted by Iago's reassurance, Gareth edged his way through the crowd of onlookers. Iago was right—Evan might need a staunch companion at his side in case someone decided to accuse him of killing the poor fellow. Gareth had been in Evan's shoes himself more than once, and it was not a comfortable place to be.

"Move back! Move back! Give the man some room." King Cadell himself could hardly have missed the commotion, and now he descended from the high table to approach the body. Cadell's voice was one nobody dared disobey, and the circle around the body expanded.

Gareth was one of the few who continued forward, however, and he stopped a pace behind Evan. He really did prefer not to become involved and resolved not to call attention to himself unless someone did it for him.

"I swear I barely touched him, my lord!" Barri gazed up at King Cadell imploringly. "I haven't seen him in years! Why would I hurt him?"

That was the question of the hour, and Gareth didn't know either man more than to greet in passing so he didn't know if what Barri said was true. He had encountered both men on separate occasions prior to the fight against FitzWizo. Gareth hadn't seen them again, however, since he'd been among those who'd traveled back to Aberystwyth with the bulk of Hywel's army, in part to disperse them in good order, but also to bring the news of the victory and to collect Gwen.

Cadell motioned with one hand to Evan that he should get to his feet. The King of Deheubarth was looking visibly older than the day he'd taken the throne over his brother's dead body, with lines on his face and gray in his hair that hadn't been there four years earlier. Gareth didn't know if the reason for the change was guilt at conspiring to murder Anarawd or simply that being king had proved burdensome enough that his cares couldn't help but be reflected in his physical state. Regardless, Cadell was not a happy man. He rarely smiled, and there was no joy in his heart.

That wasn't to say Gareth thought he was a bad king. For the most part, he seemed quite capable of managing his kingdom. Fields were sown, families were safeguarded, and the country quietly prospered, despite being almost constantly at war with its neighbors. Hywel viewed this competence as something of a pity, of course, since it made Cadell a real threat to Hywel's domain of Ceredigion.

"First of all, are we sure he's dead?" Cadell said.

Evan (the traitor!) answered that question by moving to one side and indicating that Gareth should take his place beside Meicol's body. With a sigh, Gareth did as Evan asked, seeing a degree of inevitability about the whole thing. Before crouching to the body, however, he glanced at Cadell. "May I, my lord?"

Cadell gestured again. "Please."

Gareth bent to the body and put two fingers to Meicol's neck, just as Evan had done earlier. He waited through a count of ten, knowing he would no more feel a pulse than had Evan—who was perfectly competent in such matters. And he was right. He twisted to look up at the king, though he stayed where he was, one knee on the floor. "He is gone."

Cadell made a tsk of disgust. "How?" He glared around at the onlookers, taking the death as a personal affront and implying that any one of them might have had something to do with it. Then his gaze fell once again on Barri, and his eyes narrowed in suspicion, apparently not believing Barri's initial denial. "It was you who shoved him, wasn't it? What else did you do to him?"

"N—n—nothing, my lord! I swear it."

Cadell made another gesture, this one indicating impatience, and turned back to Gareth. "What say you?"

"I can't say as to cause of death just by looking at him." Even though Gareth was inclined to agree with Barri that he'd done nothing wrong, he found the man's childish pleadings objectionable. Regardless, it was too soon to confirm or deny his claim to innocence. "Perhaps someone here who witnessed what happened could shed some light on the series of events leading up to it?"

Evan sighed. "I saw the whole fight, my lord. Barri threw Meicol to the floor, but all that happened was he fell on one shoulder. He didn't even hit his head."

Cadell pursed his lips. "Did anyone else witness the altercation?"

There was some nervous shifting among the onlookers, which puzzled Gareth, who'd risen to his feet, not feeling the need to spend any more time by the body than he had to. Gareth had wondered about the undercurrents he'd been feeling in the hall since they arrived, and he wished he'd asked someone, who might know more than he, about them earlier. It was as if, by supporting Barri's statement, the residents of the castle would be taking sides—but in what dispute, Gareth didn't know.

"My lord, we did."

Gareth jerked around abruptly at the sound of his wife's voice. She was standing a few paces away with the young Prince Rhys and Angharad, Rhun's former betrothed. At Cadell's encouraging wave, all three of them came closer, and in a show of unity, Evan moved to stand with them.

"We saw the whole thing," Gwen said. "Barri speaks the truth about what he did."

Beside Gwen, Rhys nodded vigorously, and Angharad added more fully, "From what we saw, Meicol started the fight, Uncle. He swung the first punch, which Barri avoided, and it was only when Meicol came back for more that Barri threw him to the floor." She gestured to Evan, who was standing beside her. "My lord Evan caught Meicol's arms when he got up to try again and prevented the situation from growing any worse."

Cadell frowned at her, but Angharad looked bravely back. Evan had told Gareth about her confrontation with her uncle over the way the attacks on FitzWizo's people had been carried out. He had to admire her fortitude, even as he would have advised against speaking her mind. This time, however, she was buttressed by Gwen, Rhys, and Evan, who had a hand to the small of her back, silently giving her support, and the king didn't choose to counter all those nodding heads.

Instead, Cadell turned to Prince Hywel, who'd arrived within the circle that had formed around Meicol. "The man I might normally task with heading up an inquiry was injured in battle and remains unavailable, and the second man—" he paused, and then after a moment added somewhat awkwardly, "—isn't here. May I borrow Sir Gareth, Hywel? He is well acquainted with untimely death, accidental or otherwise. If his skills are even half as good as his reputation says, then there is nobody better for the job."

Iago, who had mocked Gareth earlier but had followed him anyway, guffawed under his breath and poked Gareth in the back. Gareth ignored him, but at the same time barely managed to swallow down his own disdainful laugh.

He believed what Cadell said about the two men being unavailable, but what the king had left unsaid was that the second man who wasn't at Dinefwr was most likely Anselm, his spy whom Gareth had encountered a few months ago in St. Asaph. There, Anselm had masqueraded as a monk while spying for Cadell. Gareth hadn't seen Anselm since, and Hywel hadn't wanted to mar the current truce by bringing up past offenses. Better to husband the grievance until such a time as he could profit from bringing it out.

Undoubtedly realizing this, Cadell had been loath to say Anselm's name. Still, even if Cadell was short a trained investigator, Gareth was honestly surprised to learn Cadell would entrust him with any investigation. It wasn't that Gareth's reputation was unearned, but that Cadell himself had been implicated in three investigations Gareth had brought to a successful conclusion: the death of Anarawd, the murders last summer at Hywel's eisteddfod, and the recent incident in St. Asaph. Gareth wouldn't have thought Cadell wanted to be reminded of any of them.

Hywel might have been thinking all this too, but like Gareth, he hid his real thoughts and said obligingly, "Of course you may borrow Sir Gareth."

Gareth tipped his head, his eyes focused intently on Cadell, trying to read what was in his mind from what was on his face—which was nothing. "My lord, I will need a quiet place to work."

"I well remember." Cadell's tone was dry, revealing that Gareth wasn't wrong to think that, regardless of his complimentary words, he remembered past events as well as Gareth did. Then, sweeping out one arm, he turned to the crowd in the hall and lied, "Meicol was obviously unwell. It is unfortunate he didn't think to consult a healer. There is nothing more to learn here. You may return to your meal in peace." With a nod to Prince Hywel and completely ignoring the dead body, Gareth, and Barri, he strode back to the high table.

Hywel moved closer to Gareth and said in an undertone, "Sorry."

This time Gareth allowed himself a real laugh. "No, you're not."

Hywel grinned. "You're right. I'm not." The prince was ever one to gain any advantage if opportunity presented itself. "Cadell is not wrong, however. You are the best man for the job."

"I gather I should inform you of anything I find before I seek out Cadell?"

"Naturally you should. It would be absurd of you to do otherwise." He clapped Gareth on the shoulder, his eyes alight. "I *am* your liege lord after all."

4

Gareth

Hywel dimmed his good humor and returned to the high table to sit two seats down from Cadell in the same place he'd been sitting before Meicol died.

Most of the onlookers had also obeyed their king, realizing there wasn't anything more to see anyway. That was fine with Gareth, who sighed as he stared down at the body. It was just his luck he had to top off a war with an unexplained death that might well prevent him from going home tomorrow.

He undid his cloak and handed it to Gwen, who took it without speaking. It was warm in the hall with all the people, and Gareth, who was dressed more formally than he might have been at home, was sweating in his fine wool shirt and tunic. He'd left off his armor for the night, though he still wore his sword as a matter of course. A man had to leave his sword at the door in the presence of the English king, but Welsh kings had always been a bit more trusting, and in the history of Gwynedd, the only king who'd almost lost his life in his own hall had been Owain. In retrospect, perhaps that record should have been viewed less as a tradition than a miracle.

Barri remained close by, his hand gripped so tightly about the hilt of his ornate belt knife that his knuckles were white. His nervousness had Gareth wondering if perhaps he hadn't told the entire truth about what had gone on with Meicol. Meicol had certainly thought he'd known something about Barri, as he'd called him *traitor* and *thief.* Admittedly, they'd just fought together in battle, and it was perfectly possible something had happened out there that had carried over into the celebration in here.

Regardless, Gareth thought it was odd behavior for a seasoned soldier—especially for a man who'd spent a lifetime with a sword on his hip. Even if all soldiers dreamed of the horrors of battle, the unwritten code was not to show their fears to anyone else.

So Gareth raised his eyebrows at Evan, who was still standing with Angharad, and tipped his head in Barri's direction, asking without speaking for Evan to take him aside and question him.

Evan mouthed, "You're sure?"

Gareth motioned with his head again, this time asking Evan to come closer. Angharad came with him, which now that Gareth thought about it, might not be a bad idea. She knew Dinefwr better than any of the men from Gwynedd, and she had supported Barri's version of events. "You two would be doing me a great favor if you could get him to talk."

Evan blinked, and then he looked at Angharad. "Are you willing to give it a try?"

"Of course!" She paused. "If you really think I can help."

"I think you could," Gareth said. "A woman sometimes gets the best answers from a man—whether because her presence makes him boastful or because he doesn't realize he is even being questioned."

Evan grunted. "I suppose it's the least I can do, seeing as how it's my fault you were brought to Cadell's attention."

Gareth clapped a hand on Evan's shoulder. "You owe me one."

"That's sure to be something I regret." Now Evan laughed under his breath. "I've hunted with you before."

"And now you will again." Gareth paused. "I'm sorry. I know Barri is a friend."

"Not so close a friend. Not anymore." Evan pressed his lips together, his eyes going to Barri, who had seated himself on a bench at one of the nearby tables, though facing outward. He was talking to Alban, the second-in-command of Cadell's teulu. After Evan had told him about what happened at Wiston's keep, Gareth had made a point to find out who he was. From the expression on Alban's face, he was extremely put out, and Gareth wished he were closer so he could hear what they were saying.

"Was Meicol also?" Gareth said. "A friend, I mean."

"He was even less of one." Evan took in a breath. "Gareth, there's something you need to know. The last thing Meicol said to me was, *Help me*."

Gareth looked down at the body. "So he knew something was wrong. The question for us now is *what?*"

"I'll do what I can to help." Evan cleared his throat, and then added, with a sideways glance at Angharad. "As I know I told you once, my father served Gwynedd until Princess Gwenllian married Cadell's father. It was actually Prince Cadwallon, whom your uncle served, who asked my father to switch to her retinue, under circumstances similar to when King Owain asked you to serve Cadwaladr after the 1136 war. I was trained in this court, as were Barri and Meicol."

"You never speak of it."

"Those were some—" Evan paused, again with the glance at Angharad, who was looking at him with both interest and concern, "—difficult times. I haven't seen any of these men in ten years. I don't know how much bearing that experience can have on the present circumstances."

"That's why you have Angharad," Gareth nodded at the young woman, "who does know them and the situation."

"Maybe I do. What in particular do you want to know?" Angharad asked.

"I need to know about Barri's relationship with Meicol. Obviously they knew each other well. Why were they fighting?"

"It wouldn't be the first time they'd come to blows." Evan pursed his lips. "Still, Barri seemed genuinely surprised to find Meicol taunting him. I didn't see them together earlier, but then, I wasn't with the main body of the army."

"You were winning the war for us." Gareth's hand was back on Evan's shoulder. "And now I need you to do a little more. See what you can discover from him. Please. I could question him myself and probably will, but let's see what you two can get out of him first."

Evan held out his elbow to Angharad, who took it, and together they moved towards Barri, who at the sight of them coming towards him spun around on his bench so his legs were under the table. Evan walked Angharad around to the other side by the wall, and they both sat across from him, though not before Evan swiped two cups and a carafe of mead from an adjacent table on the way.

Gareth met his friend's eyes one last time, exchanging a mutual look of amusement. Good soldier that he was, Evan always sat with his back to the wall if he could. While it was true that in a room full of fighting men, not everyone could sit defensively, Barri had not chosen to do so even though the seat was available. That raised even more questions in Gareth's mind as to the kind of soldier he was.

Still, he could trust Evan with the questioning, no matter how friendly he had once been to Barri. Though as a rule Gareth didn't favor including people outside his immediate circle in an investigation, he was actively interested in what Angharad's perspective would turn out to be. He didn't know the girl well at all, but she'd proved to be loyal to Rhun and to Gwynedd in a way he wouldn't have expected from a woman from Deheubarth, and he hoped he could learn something from her about the way things worked here at Dinefwr. Angharad didn't trust her uncle and, in fact, had been at odds with him. That was definitely a mark in her favor in Gareth's eyes.

Meanwhile, Gareth knew where his current duty lay, and he returned to the body. Thankfully, a servant had cleaned up the vomit on the floor. Gwen was waiting for him, along with Prince Rhys, who spoke first. "Shall I find men to move him?" The boy's eager expression told Gareth he'd seen how Gareth had put Angharad to work, and he couldn't wait to be of some help himself.

"It would certainly be better if I didn't examine him here."

Rhys ran off, and Gwen laughed as she watched him go. "I like him."

"What's not to like?" Gareth smiled at his wife. "You do have a way with young men."

Gwen wrinkled her nose at him. "I am mother to three, as you may recall." She was referring to Llelo, Dai, and Gwalchmai, her younger brother, whom she had mothered from birth.

He held up one hand to show he hadn't meant to criticize. "I'm just teasing."

Gwen harrumphed, but she folded their cloaks and put them on the end of a bench. Then she crouched over Meicol with Gareth and gently put her hand over his eyes to close them. Meanwhile, Gareth adjusted the dead man's limbs into more seemly positions, rolling him more fully onto his back in the process and straightening his legs so he would be ready to be carried away to wherever Cadell designated.

"My man, Barri, did this?"

Gareth and Gwen had been so focused on Meicol that they hadn't noticed the arrival of yet another baron, this one Maurice Fitzgerald, Barri's liege lord. Gareth rose to his feet, in part to be respectful to a ranking lord of the March, and partly because Maurice might treat him with more respect if they were looking each other in the eye. "That remains to be seen, my lord. He is being questioned as we speak." He chose not to indicate where that questioning was taking place. "I would be grateful if you would leave this matter to me for now, as King Cadell indicated."

Maurice grimaced. "I'm not questioning your methods. I simply want to be kept apprised of the progress of the investigation."

"Of course, my lord," Gareth said.

"I saw the whole thing." Gwen straightened too, though she was many inches shorter than both men. "Barri did no more than fend off an attack from Meicol. As we told King Cadell, it was Meicol who threw the first punch—the only punch, really, since Barri never hit him at all, just shoved him a little to keep him away."

Maurice scratched the back of his neck as he studied the body. In his early forties, he was the second son of Gerald of Windsor and Princess Nest, who was herself sister to King Cadell's father, Gruffydd. That made Maurice and Cadell first cousins and could have explained the current alliance Maurice and his elder brother, William de Carew, had made with Cadell and Hywel. In these complicated Norman-Welsh families, however, blood wasn't always a strong tie. Only last summer, Cadell had raided Maurice's lands and taken his stronghold of Llanstephan from him.

But things had changed since then, not just in Gwynedd. Maurice and William were vassals of Gilbert de Clare, the Earl of Pembroke, an allegiance that superseded the family's loyalty to the King of England. From the moment Gilbert had rebelled against King Stephen a few months ago, William and Maurice had too. Because they were both opposed to Stephen's meddling in Wales, Cadell and Gilbert had become allies, under the principle that the enemy of an enemy is a friend.

Subsequently, Cadell had given Maurice back his castle, and since everyone was now acting as if they were friends, it seemed the perfect time to bring their armies together in a joint endeavor. Although they'd put out that they were marshaling their forces to retake Chepstow Castle, Gilbert de Clare's former holding, from King Stephen, they'd instead turned their attention to FitzWizo. That Cadell had invited Hywel to join the fun remained something of a mystery to Gareth. Hywel thought it was a way for Cadell to assess his mettle and resolve, but Gareth believed it to be more complicated than that.

Hywel was now the heir to the throne of Gwynedd and thus the future king of a rival kingdom. Nobody knew how long Hywel's father would live. If Cadell didn't want Hywel to attack Deheubarth as his first order of business once he became king, he was wise to court Hywel. Cadell didn't want a war between the two kingdoms until he himself was ready for it. Hywel, in turn, didn't either.

Gareth just hoped Meicol's death didn't have the power to end the truce right here in the hall within hours of the alliance's first victory.

Losing interest in the body, Maurice turned back to Gareth and looked him up and down as if seeing him for the first time, which perhaps he was. "You are Prince Hywel's man, yes?" But before Gareth could answer, he continued, "Why is it that Cadell entrusted you with this inquiry instead of one of his own men?"

Gareth hesitated, uncertain which question to answer first. "I'm afraid you'll have to ask him that, my lord. I am Gareth ap Rhys, and this is my wife, Gwen."

Maurice continued to study Gareth. "I feel we have met before."

"When I was younger, I was posted in Ceredigion, but I've—"

Maurice barked a laugh, stopping Gareth in mid-sentence. "You're the one who thumbed his nose at Cadwaladr." Again, before Gareth could answer the accusation, the Norman baron, eyes alight, clapped Gareth on the shoulder. "I know exactly why Cadell chose you. I'll leave you to it then. Keep me informed."

"Yes, my lord." For once, it was a good thing his reputation had preceded him.

Gwen was looking at him with an amused expression. "That's three lords who specifically asked for you to report any results to them."

"And they all want me to do so before I tell anyone else."

Gwen laughed under her breath. "Why do I keep thinking Cadell and Maurice know something we don't?"

Gareth looked towards Maurice's retreating back. The Marcher lord jerked his head at two of his men, and the three of them looked to be leaving the hall before the dessert was served. Gareth had seen it during a security pass through the kitchen: a magnificent multi-layered custard pie with a currant topping and a walnut crust. It was within Maurice's rights to leave while the night was still young, but it made Gareth think he wasn't enjoying this new alliance with his cousin as much as he was showing outwardly. In truth, in taking his castle and then giving it back in a magnanimous gesture, Cadell had made Maurice look the fool. That would sit well with few men, much less a man of Maurice's lineage.

"It's good to know you have allies even among the Normans." Gwen's eyes had followed his. "Cadwaladr has burned a great many bridges in his time."

"I don't know how many of these southerners approve of Hywel either, but at least they respect his abilities in battle," Gareth said.

"Or if not that, his ability to choose the men to fight them."

Gareth nodded. "The Dragons relieved FitzWizo of Wiston Castle easily."

Gwen gave him a sad smile. "Easy in the moment is not necessarily easy in the aftermath. I see it in Evan's eyes." She paused. "And in yours."

"Don't worry about me," Gareth said, though her not worrying was as likely to happen as snow in mid-summer.

He glanced towards where Angharad and Evan were still talking with Barri. He couldn't see what Gwen saw. They'd all killed many men long before this. And yet, maybe Gwen wasn't entirely wrong. Gareth had fought beside Hywel against FitzWizo's forces, but while this battle had been a long time coming, with enormous animosity on both sides, it hadn't been the great victory that the party tonight indicated. FitzWizo's men had been woefully outnumbered and unprepared for the fight. The trick to lure them from Wiston had been spectacularly successful, but the actual battle had been more of a rout, with little glory on either side.

Gwen had returned to her crouch beside Meicol's head, and since she was no longer looking at him or pursuing this line of thought, Gareth didn't continue the conversation. Since Rhun had died, she was less likely to ask for real details of battle, and that lack made him feel relieved rather than slighted. She did want to know, but she trusted him to tell her when he was ready.

Now, she gestured to Meicol's lips. "He vomited right before he died, Gareth. That's not a good sign."

Gareth lowered his voice in case anyone was near enough to hear it. "He was drunk, and he'd just fallen. A person can vomit for many reasons."

"It doesn't usually kill a man, though."

Gareth nodded. "Where exactly was he sitting, Gwen?"

She pointed with her chin to a table closer than the one at which Evan and Angharad were questioning Barri. "On the end there."

A family of five occupied that spot now, and the used cups and trenchers of previous diners had been pushed to the center of the table.

"I'll secure his drink and his belongings. We should have done it a quarter of an hour ago." Gareth pulled a cloth from his scrip and crossed the few feet to where the family sat. "Which of these are yours?"

The father, a man in his middle forties, eyed him uncertainly at first and then with growing concern as he rose to his feet. "We just sat down, my lord." He pointed to two empty trenchers and a cup in front of him. "Those aren't ours."

"Good." Less concerned about the food than the drink, since everybody was eating from the same dishes and nobody else was sick, Gareth wrapped the cloth around the cup and took it away. He was using the cloth in case what was in the cup had found its way to the rim and dripped down the sides, since some poisons could be absorbed through the skin. Meicol may not have been poisoned, but it was silly to take risks at this point in the investigation. If things went like they usually did, there would be plenty of time for risk later.

Some deadly poisons were slower-acting too. King Henry had died supposedly from eating too many lampreys, which Abbot Rhys had told them was untrue and people believed only because they couldn't bear to admit the alternative. Henry hadn't died right away, so a food taster wouldn't have done him any good.

Then Prince Rhys returned with a board and three eager companions, all his age. One was Llelo, Gareth and Gwen's foster son, and another was Gilbert de Clare's son, Richard, who was seventeen. Days before the battle with Walter FitzWizo, Richard and his father had escaped from Chepstow Castle by the skin of their teeth. Gilbert had ridden to Pembroke in order to shore up his forces there, but Richard had come here in the retinue of William de Carew, set on participating in a more immediate blow to King Stephen, no matter how minor, and to more completely sell the idea that they were about to attack Chepstow.

The young men put down the board and loaded the body onto it without any need of direction from Gareth. Then they stood, the board balanced on their shoulders. The residents of the hall had gone back to their merriment after Meicol had been pronounced dead, but now they quieted again, and as the body passed through their ranks, those who'd been sitting stood.

Gareth found himself walking beside Richard de Clare. His father was known as a great warrior, which was quite a reputation to live up to, but Richard had a bearing about him and a glint in his gray eyes that indicated the apple hadn't fallen far from the tree. "Is it you who will be finding out how he died?"

"It is," Gareth said.

Richard adjusted the board on his shoulder. "Barri isn't a good man."

"How so?"

"My own swordsmaster, Robert, trained him. And Meicol too as he tells it. Robert's here tonight. You should talk to him." He lifted his chin to point to where Robert stood with his left shoulder braced against the wall near the fire and his arms folded across his chest. He was ten years older than Gareth, tall and muscular, as befitted one of his profession. Evan had already told Gareth about the strange run-in with him at Wiston Castle, so Gareth wasn't inclined to think well of him, but interviewing him was a different matter.

"I will speak to him after I examine Meicol's body," Gareth said. "Thank you, my lord."

Richard nodded and continued walking. "Robert isn't one to speak ill of the dead or spread untruths, but he has said some things about his time at Dinefwr that might have a bearing on the events of tonight."

"Can give you me an example?"

Richard cleared his throat, suddenly looking uncomfortable, which was exactly why Gareth had asked him to elaborate. Richard may have intended merely to be helpful, but such behavior on the part of a Marcher lord was rare in Gareth's experience, especially one who'd grown up with intrigue from the cradle. "Barri wasn't one to put the needs of his companions before his own. And Meicol was a drunkard." Richard shrugged the shoulder that was not carrying the body. "I really can't say more than that." They exited the hall and started down the steps, and Richard used the moment to urge his companions to move faster.

Gareth didn't press him again, though as he followed behind the body to the room in the barracks Cadell had designated, the whisper of distrust that had been wafting through the hall all evening blew by him with a little more force.

5

Saran

Saran had seen Gwen and Gareth enter the barracks, following four boys who were carrying a body. One of the boys was Llelo, Saran's new grandson. To her utter delight, she and Llelo had come to an understanding almost immediately upon her attachment to Meilyr. Llelo was Gwen's foster son and Saran was Gwen's stepmother, but grandson and grandmother the two of them would be. Almost overnight, Saran had found herself with a family to care for, and she couldn't be happier about it.

Though Llelo and his brother, Dai, were ostensibly in the retinue of Prince Hywel's younger brother, Cynan, they'd come with Gareth first to Dolwyddelan Castle and then to Deheubarth. They were enmeshed now in Hywel's teulu, and it seemed likely to Saran, who'd spent a lifetime in one castle or another, that neither was ever going back to Denbigh.

It wasn't that they hadn't been learning what they needed to in Cynan's company, but Prince Hywel—and thus Gareth by extension—had decided he needed every man he could trust beside him, no matter how young. To that end, he'd also brought in all of the sons of Cadifor, his foster father, in one way or another, though the eldest remained in service to King Owain as the captain of his guard. Cadifor himself remained at Aberystwyth, personally responsible for Mari's safety and the safety of Hywel's sons.

From the beginning, Llelo had proved himself to be thoughtful and competent, and the fact that he was Gareth's son made him all the more trustworthy. While some not so favored might resent what they saw as premature advancement, family ties were an important bond. Hywel would be foolish not to exploit them.

Though Saran might have gone after Gareth and Gwen whether or not they were following a body, that there was a body at all meant something fairly disastrous had happened in the great hall during her short absence in the latrine. She hurried towards the barracks after them and just managed to stop herself from hurtling into the room.

By then, all of the boys but Llelo had left, and he, Gwen, and Gareth had their heads together over the body.

"Who died?"

"Come in! Come in!" Gwen, bless her sweet heart, beckoned Saran closer. "You're just the woman we were looking for. Where have you been?"

Saran blinked, more pleased than she could say that Gwen had welcomed her. When she'd arrived at St. Kentigern's Monastery a few months ago, she'd been surprised and overjoyed to discover Gwen not only alive but whole. Since then, Gwen, like Llelo, had included Saran in her family with hardly a break in stride. Saran had no intention of replacing Gwen's mother, but it would have been a shame for Meilyr and Saran to spend another year alone. They'd married soon after they'd arrived at Dolwyddelan—not so much in haste, as with purpose. "My stomach hasn't been happy for a few days."

That got Gwen's attention. "We think this man could have been poisoned! Are you sure you're all right—"

Saran put up a hand. "I'm fine. As I said, it has been a few days."

That got a different kind of attention from Gwen, who then said, her eyes widening, "You don't think—"

"Absolutely not."

Gwen wasn't convinced, as evidenced by the smile that hovered on her lips.

Saran put her mouth to Gwen's ear and spoke so the men couldn't overhear. "I'm too old for a child, and you know it."

"You're forty-eight," Gwen said flatly. "Not too old, and you know it."

Saran huffed out a breath, anxious to change the subject. She, of all people, having tended to women since she herself had become one thirty-five years ago, should know better than to deny what God had in store for her, and acknowledge that a healer was often most blind to her own health. Still, she wouldn't entertain the idea of a child until there was no other possible explanation. "Have you seen your father?"

"Meilyr was in the hall last I saw. Cadell asked him to sing again to distract from the untimely death." Gareth spoke absently while removing the man's boots and socks one at a time and dropping them to the floor. The dead man's feet looked nothing out of the ordinary, though he had thick yellowing toenails that might have been causing him some discomfort.

Saran gestured to the body. "Who is this?"

"His name is Meicol," Gwen said.

"The castle healer should be here too, Gareth," Saran said. "He will take offense if you examine the body without asking for his advice."

Gareth scoffed under his breath. "I would, but he's drunk." With Gwen's assistance, he worked to remove the dead man's cloak and jacket.

Saran tsked through her teeth. "He's a drunkard on his best day. I don't know what hold he has over the king to keep him on all these years."

Gwen looked over at Saran with a smile. "As I recall, that position was offered to you, once upon a time."

"Ach." Saran waved a hand dismissively. "I was happy at Carreg Cennan."

Meilyr's voice came from behind Saran. "I hope you're not reconsidering your changed circumstances."

Gareth threw up his hands in mock despair as his father-in-law appeared in the doorway. "Anyone else coming? Because we might as well leave the door open!"

Gwen patted Gareth's arm soothingly. "We're all family here."

Gareth subsided, and Saran smiled at her new husband. Gwen was right, and while Gareth and Gwen had been involved in many murder investigations over the years—and Llelo too, she understood—Saran and Meilyr were no stranger to them either, if only by association. And if bonding over a dead body was a little odd for a family to do, at least they were bonding. Saran and Gwen had first become friends at Carreg Cennan during a murder investigation that had implicated Meilyr, so it was really a matter of destiny.

Since they were all here now, and the evening was growing old, Saran moved to stand beside her new son-in-law. He appeared to be avoiding removing Meicol's breeches, so the next thing to come off was his shirt, which Gareth tugged off over his head with quick movements.

That left his torso exposed—and everyone recoiled at the sight of the man's purpling bruises.

"Ouch." Gwen's hand went to her own belly.

"That couldn't have been comfortable," Gareth said in gross understatement. Then he shook his head. "Meicol's last words to Evan were *help me.*"

Saran put her hand to her mouth, her own stomach rebelling at the pain the man had experienced. "He needed help, that's for certain, but—" She frowned as she looked more closely, "—I would have said whoever beat him did so before tonight."

"I agree. These bruises are far too pronounced to have happened an hour ago in the hall. Barri didn't do this—at least not today." Gareth gently touched Meicol's stomach. "This one in particular reveals the shape of a man's knuckles."

Gwen lifted Meicol's right hand. The body was newly dead, so it wasn't yet stiffening. It would be good to get the examination over quickly before it did. "And yet, his hands are unmarred—or as unmarred as a warrior's ever gets. He didn't fight back."

Meilyr frowned. "He *did* fight in a battle two weeks ago."

"That's too long ago for his skin to still be this color," Gareth said.

Nobody contradicted him. He'd fought in that battle too. By two weeks, bruises would be yellow or green, not this fresh purpling. These were two or three days old and had to have been paining Meicol badly.

"Could the beating be the cause of his death?" Gwen said. "Perhaps he has a broken rib and his lung was punctured when Barri shoved him to the ground."

"Maybe." Saran moved on to the dead man's right arm, and she lifted it to show Gareth the rounded burns on the tender skin that made up the inside of his upper arm. They were white, indicating they were old. "And what of these?"

Meilyr, who'd taken up a position against the wall, sighed. "Those are from a charred stick."

Everyone turned to look at him, so Meilyr sighed again and straightened, moving closer to look at the scars, though the sadness in his eyes told Saran he didn't need to see them more closely to know what they were. "You put a stick in the fire, burn the end, and press it to a child's skin. It's cruel. Evil, even. But that's where he got them."

Saran swallowed. "How do you know?"

"Because I have some just like it from my father." He shrugged his cloak away from his arms and rolled up his left sleeve to show the inside of his upper arm. "If I had to guess, this is Meicol's father's work. And he did it on the inside of his arm so it wouldn't show, and nobody would know."

"You never told me." Saran traced a gentle hand along Meilyr's scars. She had half-noticed them, but had thought nothing of them. If anything, she had assumed they were childhood burns from spattered oil.

Gwen said softly. "You never told me either."

Meilyr didn't look away from either of them. "It doesn't matter anymore. My father is long dead." He smiled sadly, and after placing a gentle hand on Saran's shoulder, moved past her to his daughter. "We can stop wondering what made Meicol belligerent."

"From what I saw in the hall, he was something of a bully," Gareth said.

Gwen blinked. "That's exactly what Angharad said."

Meilyr kissed Gwen's forehead. "Scars like these heal over in time, but only if a man is lucky enough to find love later in life. As I have."

Saran had lived all of her nearly fifty years in close proximity to families, good and bad, large and small, and she'd tended children of abusive fathers. She understood too that in this moment, Meilyr was apologizing to Gwen for the times he'd bullied her—and asking for her forgiveness and understanding.

Gwen, sweet child that she was, had forgiven her father long since.

To give the pair of them a chance to recover, Saran turned to Gareth and said straightforwardly, "What led up to his death?"

Gareth related what he knew so far, mentioning the vomiting last. Gareth was speaking to her, but his eyes kept flicking to his wife and father-in-law.

Saran frowned, and her hand went to her own belly. "Is anyone else sick?"

"Not that we know," Gareth said, "which is why I didn't raise a general alarm. How likely do you think it is that it was poison?"

"He died, which can't be a good sign. Many poisons cause vomiting. The herb garden outside the castle walls contains elderberry." She glanced up at Gareth. "There are more dangerous herbs, of course, but not grown at this castle. Aconite, for one—that's Monkshood to you—could have been administered in his wine. But the world is full of poisons. If people really knew how many, they'd never leave the hall." She barked a sardonic laugh. "They'd certainly never eat in one."

"He was drinking mead, as we all were," Gareth said.

Saran bent forward to sniff around the dead man's mouth, and then opened it, immediately recoiling at the half-dozen blisters that had formed on his tongue and on the inside of his cheeks. They had to have been painful.

"Could these have been caused by boiling liquid?" Gareth said.

"The clam chowder wasn't boiling when it was served, and who drinks boiling water unless he's being tortured? Even then ..." She frowned and put a hand to her head, thinking hard. "I have never seen anything like this. If this is poison, I'd have to consult my book to tell you which one."

Gwen kept an accounting of the murders she'd investigated in a little book. As a wedding present, she'd given Saran something similar to write in so she could keep track of herbs and treatments. Between the two of them, they might find some herb that would explain the blisters, though as Saran had said to Gareth, she could not think of any poison that caused blisters in the mouth.

Meanwhile, Gwen had moved to a side table and had begun to unpack the satchel they'd found next to Meicol. She laid out its contents one by one. "Doesn't Monkshood kill instantly?"

"Not always." Saran rubbed at her forehead, feeling a headache coming on. "Sometimes the symptoms are similar to drowning or asphyxiation, and it takes longer. Do we have the cup he drank out of?" She held her breath. It was really too much to ask.

Gareth's eyes lit. "We do." He tipped his head to indicate a clay cup on the table next to where Gwen was working. "That's how I know he was drinking mead. It's over there."

Saran leaned forward to smell the cup's contents, but all she could smell was fermented honey. "Monkshood has an unpleasant taste—or so I've been told—but it would be far less noxious in mead."

"Be careful, *cariad*," Meilyr said.

"I am," she said mildly, rather than retorting that she knew what she was doing, even though she did. He was expressing his love for her, something she hadn't had shown her often enough before this year.

"Oh." Gwen drew back slightly. "Look at this!" She showed Saran a clay vial, four inches high, stoppered and sealed, which she'd found in Meicol's knapsack. The vial could have come from Saran's own workshop, and was similar to ones she'd seen a hundred times in other healers' collections. Containers such as this were used to hold potions for ailments. Gwen herself had a box with many similar vials that Saran had helped stock.

And because she recognized the container, Saran didn't reach for it immediately, and she was pleased Gwen had handled it only after wrapping it in a cloth first. Saran sniffed around the edges without unstoppering the lid, but as with the cup, she couldn't name what was inside—if it contained anything dangerous at all. "Without opening it, I can't tell you more than it isn't elderberry, which has an extremely pungent odor."

"In fact, elderberry smells like cat piss," Meilyr said.

Saran shot him a look. They hadn't been married long, but he had apparently been paying attention. "More like rotting fruit," she said diplomatically. "With a crush of people in a hall, someone poisoned with it might not notice the—" she glanced at Meilyr again, "—fragrance."

Meilyr grinned. "Cat piss. The only way Meicol wouldn't have noticed if he was poisoned with elderberry was if he was too drunk to notice anything."

"Which he may have been." Saran narrowed her eyes at Gwen. "Is this the only vial you found? There are no others?"

Gwen shook her head.

"Open it, Saran," Gareth said. "We need to know for certain what we're dealing with."

Saran pulled her belt knife from the sheath at her waist, took in a breath, and pried the stopper out of the vial. First she poured a drop into the cup of mead. The reddish liquid spread out, coloring the surface of the drink for a moment, before becoming too diffuse to be noticed. Then Saran sniffed the vial, which only caused her to frown more, and she narrowed her eyes as she thought. "Reddish liquid, bitter smell."

"Bitter how?" Gwen said.

"Like I just tasted a dandelion." Saran held the vial away from her daughter-in-law. "Not for you."

"Do you know what it is?" Gareth said.

"Whatever it is, it isn't common in liquid form." Saran sniffed again. "Wild cherry, perhaps? We should assume it is poison until we are certain it isn't."

Gareth grunted his agreement. "What I don't understand is if Meicol is the one with a vial of poison, why is he the one who's dead? And does the fact that he begged Evan for help mean he knew he was poisoned, or was the quest for help about something else?"

Saran looked down at the body, but like everyone else in the room, she had no answer to those questions—though she did have one of her own. "Meicol was a warrior, wasn't he?" And at Gareth's nod, she continued, "Do you know a warrior who could prepare a poison on his own?"

Gareth eyed the vial. "Would he need a healer's hut to do so?"

"Most likely," Saran said. "I suppose there are a few instances of sap being poisonous and something you could collect in the wild, but liquid comes from berries, which have to be crushed and the juice extracted. Seeds have to be soaked, and roots mashed and combined with oil." She glanced towards the dead man. "If he did that without being an accomplished healer, he is a fool."

"Maybe he was foolish and ingested his own poison by mistake," Gwen said.

Saran picked up each of Meicol's hands in turn. "No discoloration, no oil splatters or burns, no scrapes, cuts, or rashes." She shook her head. "He doesn't work with plants."

"Do you have Monkshood in your collection?" Gareth asked.

"No, it's too dangerous, and anyway, this isn't that. Monkshood doesn't cause blisters in the mouth, and it's the roots and seeds which are the most dangerous. They're not red."

"What about elderberry?" Gwen said.

"Yes, I have that. Elderberry tincture can help heal wounds, and when ingested it aids coughs and sniffles. The berry must be well cooked, however. Cooking destroys the poison. I wear gloves when I gather the berries and immediately put them into a pot to cook." She gestured to Meicol's body. "But even uncooked, it takes a great deal of elderberry to kill a man."

"Could he be dead now because he handled the vial?" Gwen said.

Saran pressed her lips together as she thought. "You and I both know poison can be absorbed through the skin, but only the most potent ones: aconite, as I said; belladonna; hemlock. And they work fast."

"Could he have handled them this morning and died tonight?" Gareth said.

Saran waggled her head from side to side, not ready to say anything definitive. "I don't know the poison, Gareth—but two to six hours is possible if the dose was small enough. He could have been feeling ill all afternoon and evening."

"He was certainly belligerent." Gwen tapped a finger to her lips. "That he asked for help doesn't preclude him being responsible for his own death, only that he knew he was ill."

"He could have had an accomplice," Llelo said, speaking for the first time. He'd propped himself in one corner, looking on and absorbing what everyone else was saying. Saran had glanced at him once or twice, but he'd kept so quiet she'd almost forgotten he was there. "What if Meicol is an agent of King Stephen or of Walter FitzWizo, and he saw an opportunity to eliminate a host of enemies in one night without fighting a battle?"

Everyone turned to look at the young man. He'd been twelve when Gareth and Gwen had adopted him and was now a very mature fifteen.

"That's a terrifying thought." Gwen studied her son. "Normally, we worry about the *why* of murder after we figure out the *what* and *who*."

"Except this time, the body isn't telling us enough," Llelo said.

Gareth threw Meicol's own cloak over the body and headed for the door. "I've seen enough for now. If you're right, Llelo, we need to speak to Prince Hywel immediately. Everyone in the hall could be in danger."

6

Evan

Barri took a long drink from his cup, draining it completely. When he put it down, Angharad immediately refilled it without needing to be asked to do it.

Evan knew from experience—both in regards to himself and during his investigations with Gareth—that a full cup went a long way to loosening a man's tongue. As any priest could attest, it was man's nature to feel guilty when he sinned, and killing another human being was the ultimate sin. It was only the hardened killer who was the least likely to reveal himself under the influence of strong drink—and was also the man least likely to drink to loquaciousness. At first and second glance, a killer was the last thing Barri was.

But then again, he *was* a soldier, just like Evan. He had killed in battle, possibly many times. Maybe Evan was completely misreading him and the situation. Barri had always been the cleverest of their group.

"Why would Meicol attack you like that?" Evan asked him.

"I don't know! I swear it!"

If Evan's hackles hadn't already been up, they would have risen, and he had to reconsider his initial dismissal of Barri's culpability. Barri's choice of words, which Evan had heard many times from many different culprits, usually meant the exact opposite of the superficial meaning. *I swear it!* was synonymous with *I'm lying through my teeth!*

Evan didn't want to believe Barri was lying to him, and he prided himself on his ability to sense the truth in people. It was one of the things that made him helpful to Gareth. With Evan's change in occupation, Hywel had intended that Evan himself no longer be Gareth's right hand man in investigations. Faced with Meicol's death, however, Evan and Gareth had immediately fallen into old patterns, and Evan *was* the best one to speak to Barri.

It certainly appeared to Evan that Meicol's death was an accident, but if he'd learned anything from his years with Gareth, it was that assumptions were often wrong. "When did you last see him?"

Barri raised one shoulder and dropped it. "We were children together. You know that."

"I remember. I left the south, however, and you didn't. You're telling me you haven't seen him at all?"

"Not for years and years. Not until I arrived with Lord Maurice a few weeks ago before the battle." Barri looked at Angharad. "You can attest to that, I'm sure, my lady."

Angharad smiled sweetly. "Of course, Barri. It's true I've never seen you together."

Barri nodded at that and then took another long drink. When he put down his cup, Angharad was right there to fill it again. Evan leaned back against the wall behind him, studying Barri and remembering their youth together. As Evan had reminded Gareth, he'd been raised in Ceredigion because Evan's father had been in the service of Gwenllian, and thus her husband, the King of Deheubarth. In fact, Evan's own training as a man-at-arms had taken place in the courtyard of this very castle. "I haven't been to Deheubarth since the 1136 war. What happened to you and Meicol? Where have each of you been living all this time?"

"I've been in Lord Maurice's service. You know that. Meicol's been here. Though—" Barri frowned. "It isn't as if he ever moved up in service. He started as a man-at-arms at sixteen, and that's all he's ever been."

"Perhaps he would have been better served to have pursued a life as a craftsman," Evan said. "He was always whittling one thing or another."

Barri shrugged. "I wouldn't know."

"You fought against Deheubarth in the 1136 war," Evan said, seeing no reason to avoid the fact.

Barri scoffed. "Are you questioning my loyalties? I served Lord Maurice. I was given to him by the king! A man puts his sword where he is told. You know that."

Evan did know that, but it didn't make him trust Barri more. All these years of living in the south, serving a lord who thought of himself as more Norman than Welsh, could not be good for a man's soul. "Did Meicol resent his lack of advancement?"

"How could he not?" Barri slapped the table with the palm of his hand. "But as I said, you shouldn't be asking me. I didn't know him anymore."

Evan studied his former friend. "Who should I ask?"

"Lady Angharad, here, perhaps."

Angharad smiled blandly. Barri had made several similar assertions, and they were just a little too pat.

"Who else?"

Barri shrugged. "Alban is second-in-command of King Cadell's guard. He knew him." Then he smirked. "Not quite risen as high as *he* planned either, has he?"

Evan managed to tame his expression before he sneered too. Evan and Barri had been friends of a sort when they were younger, and neither of them had liked Alban much. Everyone had known he was destined for great things. Evan could admit now that they'd been jealous, and he was interested that Barri still seemed to carry that resentment. Evan hadn't given more than a passing thought to his upbringing in Deheubarth in years, and he certainly hadn't wasted a single moment hating Alban.

But the truth was, Evan didn't know what had happened with Alban. No one could deny his all-around good looks, muscular physique, and natural skill, which had stood him in good stead into adulthood. While Meicol had used his early growth to intimidate the other boys, Alban had needed no such false authority. He'd been the best of them—and everyone had known it, including Alban, of course. But still, Barri was right that he hadn't risen as he'd wanted and they'd all expected.

Regardless, Evan leaned forward, deciding to take advantage of Barri's casual dismissal of Meicol—and hoping he was drunk enough not to take offense—or not so drunk he would. "Meicol called you a traitor and a thief. Why?"

Barri scoffed. "I have no idea! As I said, I haven't seen him. I haven't spoken to him. Why don't you believe me?"

Now it was Angharad's turn to try a question, and it was a pointed one. "Was it because you fought for Lord Maurice?"

Barri's face reddened and puffed up, like he was holding his breath and would soon explode. "I. Don't. Know."

Evan hastened to intervene. "So you can't think of anything that would make him attack you?"

Instead of shouting or defending himself even more vociferously, Barri drank some more. He was already through three cups, each of which Angharad had calmly poured for him without comment. Evan wasn't sure if Barri was stalling or looking to regain control. Then Barri put down his cup, burped, and wiped at his mouth with his sleeve. "Not unless you include the incident with the rope swing."

Evan sighed. "That was twenty years ago."

"Some men hold a grudge."

As Barri's reaction to Alban had just indicated exactly that, Evan couldn't disagree. And then Barri elaborated without Evan having to prompt him. "I saw Meicol only twice after that before this month: once in the infirmary before I left for Lord Maurice's domain and then again in 1136—though that was only in passing."

Those were the two times Evan had seen Meicol too. "You can't blame him for being angry. You were the one who rigged the rope to fail."

Barri crossed his arms defensively. "It was a jest."

"A jest that nearly killed him." Even after all these years, the memory of that day stood out in sharp relief in Evan's mind. In the hot August sun, a crowd of young men—boys really, though they'd been men by law—had gone to the river to swim. The rope swing was a favorite plaything, and Meicol, at the time being bossy and bigger than everyone but Alban, browbeat the other boys into letting him swing first.

But that day, Barri, knowing Meicol's habits, had all but severed the rope so it hung by a thread. It had been a move that, in retrospect, was just like Barri. He wasn't the kind to take on a problem head on, but to look for a way to attack it sideways. True to form, Meicol had swung and then fallen prematurely—not into the pool for which he had been aiming, but onto rocks.

He'd broken two ribs and his arm, and King Gruffydd, Cadell's father, had been angrier than Evan had ever seen him. Both boys had been sent away: Barri to Gruffydd's sister's household and Meicol to recuperate at one of Deheubarth's more remote holdings. Furthermore, in the aftermath, the king had dispersed the group of young men-in-training, and Evan had asked Queen Gwenllian for reassignment to Gwynedd. It had been a transformative moment for Evan—to know what he wanted, to ask for it, and to have his wish granted. And he hadn't looked back.

Because Evan had positioned himself against the wall, he could survey the whole of the great hall from where he sat, and thus he saw the moment John, Lord Maurice's captain, returned to the room. He edged through the revelers, for all appearances heading towards Barri, so Evan stood to intercept him.

"Did he kill Meicol?" John pointed with his chin to Barri's back.

"I dare not say one way or the other as of yet." Evan glanced back to Angharad to make sure she was all right sitting with Barri alone, but all Barri was doing was staring into his cup while Angharad studied the top of his head. "But I saw the fight, and Barri shoved Meicol. That's all."

John nodded. "If you're done questioning him, Lord Maurice asks that you release him into my custody." He followed Evan's gaze. Barri was now lying with his head on his arms. "Let him sleep it off."

Evan canted his head. He didn't know John at all. He was a Norman, so not part of the Dinefwr cohort, and they'd played very different roles in the battle against the Flemings. "Is he a good soldier?"

"Barri?" John sucked on his teeth. "Good enough. He puts his sword where I tell him." Among the Normans that really could be good enough. Prince Hywel demanded more from the men in his teulu.

"But?" Evan let the question dangle.

John shrugged. "He's not a leader of men."

"Is he insubordinate?"

"I wouldn't have him among my men if he were, though I've always had the sense he thinks he's the smartest man in any room." John scoffed. "He should know that honor is reserved for Prince Rhys, who really is."

Evan couldn't argue with that, and, not finding a reason to deny John's request, which was really Lord Maurice's, he gestured towards where Barri still sat. "He's all yours."

"Thank you." John nodded, and Evan bent his head as a sign of respect for John's station. As John went to collect Barri, Evan motioned that Angharad should come to him.

"Will you tell me the story of the rope?" she said as she reached him.

Angharad knew so much more about him than she had an hour ago that Evan saw no point in keeping this bit of history from her, so he told her.

"Nobody has ever spoken of this directly to me," Angharad said, "but Meicol is not held in high regard." She glanced back to where John was getting Barri to his feet. "Nor Barri, truth be told." Then she fixed him with her gaze. "You, on the other hand ..."

He blinked. "I can't imagine why anyone would say two words about me."

She laughed. "You sell yourself short. You're one of the Dragons! I know what you did at Wiston."

"Alban didn't think much of it," Evan said before he thought to stop himself.

"Alban thinks one man's gain is another man's loss, instead of knowing we all rise, or fall, together."

Evan found himself admiring her precise assessment, which now that he'd heard it, exactly characterized why Alban hadn't made a great leader of men.

He held out his arm again to the girl. "Shall we find Sir Gareth?"

She took his elbow. "I think we should."

He didn't know what her uncle would say about her walking beside him, but Angharad was clearly her own person and thought herself old enough to make her own decisions. He wasn't sure why she'd chosen to continue in his company, but he certainly wasn't going to send her away if she wasn't ready to go.

They headed out the door into the courtyard. On the stairs down from the main doors, Angharad paused to take a breath. Evan stopped too, enjoying the cooler outside air, which felt good after the too-warm hall.

"Evan!"

At the woman's voice, Evan's eyes searched the courtyard but didn't immediately alight on the woman who'd spoken, though somewhere in the back of his mind he thought he recognized the voice even if he couldn't put a name to it. Then she passed through the light of one of the torches. Very conscious of Angharad still on his arm, Evan headed down the steps and across the courtyard to intercept her.

As she had in his youth, Caron still had the power to take his breath away, though perhaps less so than she might have if he hadn't been standing with Angharad. Even as Caron approached middle age, her red-blonde hair and green eyes were stunning, and he found himself pausing as if he was still that boy of fifteen who hoped she could be his.

"It's been so long! How are you?" Caron stopped in the act of reaching out to hug him, realizing at the last moment that his arm was linked with Angharad's. She curtseyed instead. "My lady."

Angharad smiled gently. "Caron."

Evan cleared his throat awkwardly. "I am well. How is it with you?"

"I am well too." She put a hand on her belly, which could mean only one thing. "Mostly."

Evan laughed at himself under his breath. Caron belonged to Alban—for of course she'd married the golden boy—and always had. "When is the child due?"

"Late in the year."

Evan indicated with his head that the three of them should move to one side, out of the direct path of the stairway. John was just coming out of the hall with Barri and two other men. They set off towards the stables. Maurice's men, like Hywel's, were not housed at the castle but in tents in a field at the base of the hill upon which the castle was built.

"Alban must be very proud," Evan said. "How many children do you have?"

Caron simpered, and Evan's emotions settled further. As a girl, she'd been a beauty, sought after by every man in the cantref, but she'd never been much of a thinker, unlike the other woman with him tonight, whose expression remained serene and her eyes thoughtful. Angharad seemed alert to every nuance of what was happening around her, and Evan hoped that later she'd tell him what she'd seen.

"It's been fifteen years now since we married." Caron rubbed her belly. "This will be our sixth. Our eldest two are already training to be men-at-arms."

"I would very much like to sit with you both, catch up on old times." And as he spoke, Evan realized he didn't have to fake his sincerity. While the memory of Alban's rebuke at Wiston Castle was still fresh in his mind, he had been following orders—something Evan and his Dragons had expressly not done. It didn't excuse the disrespect, but Alban wasn't the golden boy anymore, for all Caron had implied it just now. Evan's station was just as high as his.

Caron smiled. "I would like that. I will speak to Alban, and we'll make sure it happens before you go." She curtseyed again at Angharad. "You would be most welcome too, my lady." She turned towards the steps and started up them.

Evan looked carefully at Angharad. "That is an invitation you are under no obligation to accept, my lady."

"Call me Angharad, please, and I have every intention of accepting it." She paused. "You're the first person I've spoken to in months, other than Prince Rhys, who speaks to me as if he's actually interested in what I have to say. Is that a characteristic of all men from Gwynedd?"

"I-I don't know." Evan found himself stuttering. "Most of the women of my acquaintance speak their mind when it pleases them to do so."

"I really must visit your country sooner rather than later."

Bemused, Evan fought a smile as he directed their steps across the courtyard. He certainly wasn't going to object to her company. They were almost to the barracks, the place to which Meicol's body had been brought, and he stopped in the shadow of the porch, not ready to say goodbye to Angharad, but knowing it wasn't appropriate for her to see Meicol's body either.

But Angharad was frowning. "The more I consider that exchange you just had with Caron, the more confusing it seems."

"How so?"

"You were friends twenty years ago, so Caron hailing you across the courtyard isn't something to remark upon, especially since you hadn't seen her since you left for Gwynedd. But it's odd she chatted with you so happily."

"Why would that be odd?" Evan puffed out his chest. "Am I not a brave and handsome fellow?"

Angharad patted his arm. "Of course you are, but how can she be so unconcerned with Meicol's death so soon after it happened? Isn't it strange she never mentioned it?"

"You are absolutely right, and I should have thought of that." Evan gave himself a shake. "While Meicol was of a lower order and thus not someone Caron might have been close to, he has been a member of the garrison all these years. He didn't serve directly under Alban, but they all must have rubbed shoulders often over the years."

As he finished speaking, Llelo appeared at the entrance to the barracks, followed immediately by Gareth, who urged Llelo to continue towards Evan and Angharad. The rest of Gareth's family followed hard on his heels.

"What's going on?" Evan said, noting their tense looks.

"We may have been complacent in thinking Meicol was the only victim or even the intended target," Gareth said.

"What do you mean *target?*" Evan stared at his friend. "So Meicol was murdered?"

Gwen motioned to the bag slung over Meilyr's shoulder. "We found a sealed herbalist's vial that we have reason to believe contains poison."

Gareth was already two strides ahead of Evan, but he called over his shoulder. "We fear this one vial might not have been all there was and a second was discarded."

"Why would someone do that?" Angharad asked as she hurried beside Evan, hastening to catch up with Gareth.

"Because it was empty," Gareth said.

7

Hywel

"Catch him! He's going over!" Hywel spoke at the same instant he sprang towards the falling man, one Cadfan, who also happened to be the captain of Cadell's guard.

Then, all of a sudden, there were more sick people in the hall, holding their stomachs and vomiting, or simply moaning and calling for help. Those who weren't unwell were looking around in shock at their friends and companions. Hywel hadn't seen the entire series of events leading up to Meicol's death, but it looked to be what had happened to *him* writ large.

From across the room, Gruffydd grabbed one of Cadell's men around the middle as he toppled over. Hywel would have run to help too if the man right in front of him hadn't at that moment vomited the entire contents of his stomach onto the floorboards. Grimacing, Hywel caught his shoulders before he fell and laid him down more gently, where he writhed in obvious pain.

Hywel turned to look at Cadell. "Don't eat or drink anything more! We don't know what could be tainted."

Cadell had risen to his feet, gaping at the carnage before him, but at Hywel's words, he swept his arm across the table, knocking all of the food and drink within four feet of him to the floor.

Then the door to the hall swung wide, and Gareth, Evan, and Llelo leapt inside. At the sight of the chaos in the hall, Gareth, who was in the lead, broke into a run, ultimately skidding to a halt in front of Hywel. Such was his urgency that he actually grabbed Hywel by the upper arms so he could look him directly in the face. "Are you ill?"

"I'm fine." Hywel lifted his right hand awkwardly, trying to appease Gareth while at the same time encouraging him to let go of him. "Though I believed Gruffydd's strictures excessive, I obeyed them nonetheless. I drank only what we brought ourselves and ate only meat and bread."

"Cadell himself is sick." Gareth pointed to the high table, where Cadell was now bent over, a hand to his head.

Gareth's hand briefly touched Hywel's shoulder, in another rare gesture of familiarity from his captain. Even though he was not a member of the Dragons, Gareth had been one of the primary voices urging carefulness and caution in this rapprochement with Cadell and his half-Norman relations. To be constantly vigilant was exhausting but hard to argue against when anything untoward happened. Such as now.

"Others are still standing too," Llelo said, "our men among them."

Hywel glanced around the room. The boy was right. Along with Evan, who'd come in with Gareth and Llelo, Iago, Cadoc, Gruffydd, Aron, and Steffan were on their feet, giving aid to those who were ill. Others unaffected included Prince Rhys, Cadell's brother.

But at the high table, William de Carew had his arms around his belly. Then he leaned to one side and vomited. Meanwhile, the man at Hywel's feet moaned. "My mouth hurts."

"We have very little time, my lord." Saran bustled in, Gwen, Angharad, and Meilyr at her heels.

"Is there any treatment?" he said when she reached him. "So many are sick."

"Unfortunately, by the time a person becomes sick, it can be too late because the poison moves through the stomach too quickly. Everyone needs to drink as much water as possible, however, and, if they can keep it down, eat whatever is left of the clam chowder."

Hywel blinked at the oddly specific remedy. "Why?"

"Because it can help." Saran started towards the high table. "Do we know what was poisoned?"

Hywel stared after her. "No. It could be anything."

"It happened awfully quickly to be anything," Gwen said. "Besides, not everyone is affected."

"Maybe that's because they ate the clam chowder for dinner, and it diffused the poison." That answer came from behind Hywel, and he turned to find Rhys, Cadell's brother, staring at him, white-faced. "Like I did."

Saran gave the boy a curt nod, and then her eyes went to William, who now had his head on the table. She waved a hand at Rhys. "Hurry."

While Rhys knelt beside Pembroke's castellan, Saran went to Cadell and tried to get him to sit up. He wasn't dead yet and didn't seem to be in as bad a way as some of the others in the hall, so maybe he'd imbibed less of whatever had caused this. Gareth, meanwhile, crouched to put two fingers to the neck of the man at Hywel's feet and then shook his head.

"What was just served?" Gwen had taken a stewpot from one of the tables and began to move from person to person administering the chowder to whomever had the wherewithal to taste it.

"Dessert. A custard pie with currants." Hywel sent Evan to assist her and then turned back to Gareth. "Was it poison that killed Meicol?"

"Hard to think otherwise now, though why he died an hour ago and everyone else is ill only now isn't at all clear to me. We found an unexplained vial in his satchel, however, which could be the same poison."

"A liquid?"

"Yes. It is an unusual enough concoction that Saran didn't know immediately what it was, and the only way to know for sure is to test it on someone—or something. Meicol vomited, as these people are, and he had blisters inside his mouth, as it appears some of them do. We would have moved more quickly to warn you of the danger, but the vial was sealed, and it didn't occur to me until later that it could have been one of several others." Gareth ran a hand through his hair, his expression drawn and bleak. "Those few moments might have made a difference."

"You can't blame yourself." Saran was back, now with a stewpot of her own. At the high table, Rhys was carefully spooning chowder first into his brother's mouth and then into William's. "Our poisoner knew what he was doing; he didn't seem to care how many were harmed."

Gareth lifted his chin to point to a nearby table. "Cadell's men seem more affected than anyone else's."

"Some of the other lords may have had the same policy we did," Hywel said.

"Don't eat from the common dish, you mean?" Saran said. "Don't trust anyone?"

"Let this be a lesson to us all." Meilyr bent his head to Hywel. "I confess, I was skeptical of your command."

"But you obeyed it?" Hywel raised one eyebrow.

"Always, my lord."

Hywel didn't quite guffaw, seeing as how the circumstances were too serious and dire for that. Meilyr had a twinkle in his eye for a moment too, before his expression hardened. "This has gone far beyond the death of one man, my lord. Cadell has a traitor in his midst."

Gareth looked around the room. "There are no servants in this hall, my lord." Even as he added, "We should check the kitchen," both he and Hywel were already moving towards the door behind the high table.

This was a back door into the hall, fronted by an anteroom, which then opened into the rear of the bailey. The postern gate was nearby, and a covered walkway led to the kitchen, which was a large adjacent building within Dinefwr's palisade. Dinefwr, like Aber, was a royal palace, a *llys*, far more than a castle. As a motte and bailey castle, Wiston had been built with defense in mind and nothing else. It was small and uncomfortable—and a symbol of foreign rule meant to intimidate the populace and protect the invaders.

Welsh royal courts, on the other hand, were meant to house hundreds of people at one time, and the palisades that surrounded them often encompassed huge spaces. Unless a fortress was built in stone, however, it was only nominally defensible. That was why Welsh palaces also tended to be built on high hills or the tops of mountains rather than in the lowlands as the Normans preferred. Wooden palisades were also relatively cheap to build and could be constructed in a summer and expanded as necessary.

The door to the kitchen was open, as might be expected given the constant comings and goings to serve the great hall. But before Gareth and Hywel could cross the threshold, a young man with tousled brown hair crawled onto the flagstones of the walkway and collapsed, moaning, half in and half out of the door.

Gareth bent to him, but Hywel stepped over the body and entered the kitchen. None of the servants were on their feet. Several were vomiting into buckets, and the chief cook, a squat man with a large belly, was bent over the table, his head in his arms. A small boy lay near the fire, twitching and unconscious.

"Is he alive?" Hywel called to Gareth over his shoulder.

"No." Gareth spoke abruptly and left the dead man where he lay in the doorway.

"Get someone to help these people. There has to be something here that will tell us what was poisoned."

"Whatever you do, if you find it, don't touch it. Many poisons can be absorbed through the skin, and I'm thinking this is one of the more dangerous ones."

Hywel swallowed down the snide comment that rose in his throat. Gareth was speaking the obvious because he was protecting Hywel, not insulting his intelligence. He swung around to look at his captain. "Is it possible Meicol did all this but mishandled the poison—and died because of it?"

"I don't know. One moment he's the victim, then he's the perpetrator, and back again. I'll get Gwen." Gareth dashed for the hall.

Hywel turned back to the room, going first to the head cook. He put a hand on his shoulder, making sure he was still breathing, and then went to the stewpot that hung over the fire. Ladling out a cup of chowder, he brought it to the man and set it in front of him. "Eat."

"I can't." The man moaned.

"According to the healer, this will help."

The man was alive enough to scoff. "He knows nothing—"

"I meant Saran."

Such was her reputation that the cook immediately acquiesced and started to sip the chowder, even going so far as to swallow down a clam. Fearful the man would die before Hywel could question him, he pulled up a stool and sat. "What did you eat?"

"Everything."

"No—I mean from whose dishes did you eat? Every one of your staff is ill, but not everyone in the hall is. That means you consumed tainted food. When did you do so and for what table was the food intended?"

"I don't know." He moaned and laid his head back onto the table. "My mouth hurts."

Hywel looked around the kitchen. The workers had their own long dining table, which still contained the remnants of their dinner. If life at Dinefwr was similar to Aberystwyth or any other place Hywel had lived, during feasts like this, the kitchen workers ate in shifts, in bits and pieces when they could. Other meals might take place at odd hours when no official meals were being served. It looked like a dozen people had eaten well. Hywel went over to the table to look over what remained. It was the standard fare that had been served in the hall itself.

He sniffed the mead—no wine was served in the kitchen—but didn't dare drink it for fear of what it might contain. It occurred to him that whoever had poisoned the residents of Dinefwr had dosed the kitchen staff so there would be nobody to testify to what he'd done.

Finding nothing that stood out immediately as helpful, he went to the back door, which led to the well, and stood in the doorway to gaze out at the rear palisade wall. It was here firewood was chopped, and to the right was a walled herb garden, only one of several gardens that served the castle, with the larger vegetable gardens planted outside the palisade wall. Here also was the latrine, a long low building abutting the palisade. Waste fell into a deep trench, to which lime and ash were added weekly—daily in summer—to keep down the stench.

Hywel pressed his lips together. If he had a vial that had once held poison, he would have discarded it in the latrine. If that was the case, God help him, Hywel wasn't going after it.

The scrape of a boot sounded behind him, and he turned to see Gareth entering the kitchen. He'd brought a woman and a man from the hall to see to the workers, though Hywel feared there was little hope for some of them.

"I did a quick assessment of the state of our people. All obeyed the stricture not to indulge tonight—except for Dai. Llelo found him vomiting outside the hall. Gwen is with him now."

Hywel's heart clenched for his friend. "I'm sorry."

Gareth drew in a breath. "He is well enough to apologize for not obeying your orders. He said he had only one bite of the pie. He has a raging sweet tooth. Always has."

Hywel grunted. "It looked good to me too, but I am not thirteen."

"If I had been Dai's age," Gareth said, "I would have been tempted too."

"No, you wouldn't have," Hywel said shortly.

Gareth lifted his head. "I wouldn't?"

"You obey orders. That's what made your disobedience to Cadwaladr so memorable." Hywel returned to the head cook, who was still alive, if barely, and bent to him. "Who made the dessert, and what was in it?"

"Eggs, flour, cream, and honey in a nut pastry shell with a currant sauce topping," the cook said. "As always, I made it myself."

"Is there any left?" Gareth said.

"It would be in there." The cook gestured feebly to the right, indicating an open door to a subterranean pantry. Food that needed to stay cool was kept there, and a custard pie would qualify.

Once inside the pantry, Hywel gaped at the abundance of foodstuffs, which made his stores at Aberystwyth seem paltry by comparison. Cadell was doing *very* well for himself in terms of tithes.

On a small table near the entrance had been left various crocks containing food destined for immediate use. Gareth lifted the lid over a ceramic tray to reveal rows of sliced mutton. A second lid covered cheeses destined for later in the evening. Gareth lifted a third lid and recoiled. The dish contained the last half of a pie the width of Hywel's forearm—but also a dead mouse.

Hywel let out a wavering breath. "Cadell asked that the pie be served to distract everyone after the fight between Barri and Meicol."

"If not for the dead mouse, it would look delicious," Gareth said. "The liquid in the vial was reddish, but because of the currants, it wouldn't be noticed."

"Someone has it in for Cadell."

"Are you worried he's going to think it's you?"

Hywel barked a laugh. "That never occurred to me. I was ruminating along the lines of Maurice. You'll note his brother, William, is among the ill."

Gareth laughed mockingly. "Which makes Maurice an obvious culprit." Then he shook his head. "Several of Maurice's men are ill as well. It's just that Maurice left after Meicol died. Most of the men at Dinefwr are Cadell's people, and thus they comprise most of the sick. At least ten have already died."

"Poison." Hywel shivered. "Every lord's nightmare. A coward's weapon."

Gareth had his lips pressed tightly together, and when he didn't speak, Hywel looked at him curiously. "What is it, Gareth? It isn't like you to hold back your opinions."

"Cadell himself is no stranger to poison, my lord. We never determined what exactly was in that bottle of wine he gave to that merchant in Aberystwyth, but it killed him just the same."

"Are you suggesting this poisoning has something to do with that one? Revenge, perhaps?"

"No." Gareth gave a sharp shake of his head. "Not so much that, but Cadell is a poisoner himself. He got his poison from somewhere and someone."

"Are you thinking to ask him who was his supplier?" Hywel gave a low laugh. "That won't go over well. For now, I'm more concerned with stemming the tide of deaths tonight. We can worry about the who after we find the what."

Then Gareth lifted his chin to point beyond the wall. "There's more that concerns me here, my lord. What if this is the first wave of an attack? Does an army wait beyond these walls, biding its time until the moment of our greatest weakness?"

"You mean *now.*" As before in the hall, the two men surged at the same moment for the exit and the stairs up to the wall-walk. Hywel allowed Gareth to precede him to the top, as was his duty, and a moment later they stood together, looking down at the landscape below them and the campfires that dotted the fields along both sides of the road. These were the remains of the large army that had taken Wiston.

Because most soldiers in Wales were, in fact, farmers and herders, only great lords had the wealth to employ a permanent army. Even Hywel, as the edling of Gwynedd, had a force of only fifty that went everywhere with him. They were camped in the fields of the monastery located three-quarters of a mile away and not visible from this side of the castle.

"It seems quiet," Gareth said, "but I should send out the Dragons, along with our usual scouts, to discover if anything is amiss. Cadell's men killed three of FitzWizo's men on the road tonight. There could be more."

"Do it." Sometimes Hywel worried that the name he'd given his elite fighting force skated a little too close to *the four horsemen* for comfort, but he'd sworn when he recruited them that their service would always be honorable. The oath was a promise to them and a check on Hywel himself, truth be told—and given the carnage in the hall, he could hardly regret calling them into being. It was their suspicious minds, training every day to think more like spy than soldier, that had saved them all.

Before the poisonings and deaths had given the day new purpose, Hywel had been at war with himself as to whether he should have stayed at home in Aberystwyth rather than traveling to Dinefwr for the celebrations. He'd told himself he'd come out of obligation to the new alliance, but at the same time, he had to be honest with himself that there was more to it. He'd been absent from Ceredigion since his music festival last August, and the last time he'd been there, he'd been with Rhun. They'd spent the summer together, and everything about the place reminded him of what he'd lost.

Rhun had been brother, companion, and friend. Hywel had admired him, trusted him implicitly, and the hole in his life left by Rhun's absence was nearly impossible to bear. Certainly it was impossible to fill.

What was occupying his thoughts now was the memory of that last week in Aberystwyth during the music festival when Hywel had boldly proclaimed his desire for Cadwaladr's next misdeed that would require his banishment from Wales forever. Rhun had cautioned that he didn't really want that. *"Hate blinds you to what is before you in favor of what you want to see—or hope to see—or perhaps even need to see,"* he'd said.

Rhun had been right. At the time, they'd feared for their father's life, but Rhun's concern had been that whatever their uncle might unleash would be far worse than having Cadwaladr himself sitting beside their father at Aber's high table. Again, he'd been right. And it had been Rhun who'd been caught up in Cadwaladr's evil. Hywel would give everything he had to go back to that day and make different choices. He could have encompassed his father's death more easily than Rhun's. He'd never admitted that fact out loud, even to Mari. It skated too close to a similar truth that his father felt the same and would have traded Hywel for Rhun any day.

But now, while he never would be glad to have lost his brother, Hywel had grown and changed as a result. He couldn't go back, and although he would give anything for Rhun to be alive again, he didn't want to go back.

As he stood on the wall-walk of his former enemy's castle, he also knew Rhun would not have had a suspicious enough mind to have refused to eat and drink from Cadell's kitchen. He would not have had the knowledge or the men to uncover whatever plot was being played out in Dinefwr's hall. That was Hywel's domain and always had been. Rhun had been the soldier and Hywel the spy. It was long past time Hywel embraced the knowledge that not only did he need to be both, but he wanted to.

8

Gwen

"Go! Go now before they come again!" Gareth moaned and rocked in his sleep.

After the carnage of last night, she, Gareth, and Meilyr had ultimately taken refuge in a closet-like room on the second floor of the guest hall. Gwen glanced to where her father slept on, a hand-span away. Gwen, along with Angharad and Saran, had taken turns nursing the sick through the night, among them her own Dai, but Llelo had finally sent Gwen herself away, declaring he would stay with his brother for the last few hours before dawn. Gwen had gone because Dai still lived, and Saran had been cautiously optimistic that he would continue to do so.

For once Gwen wasn't fearful Gareth would wake Tangwen, since she'd been left at Aberystwyth with her nanny, Abi. But still, Gwen didn't like to see Gareth distressed, and she put a hand on his chest and her lips to his forehead. He tossed and turned for another few heartbeats, but then at her continued gentle whispering, he quieted and opened his eyes. For a moment, they were unseeing, but then they narrowed to focus on Gwen hovering above him. "Did I say something?"

"You were speaking of battle, I think."

Gareth threw an arm across his eyes, breathing deeply in and out. "I'm sorry."

Gwen stroked a lock of hair back from his forehead. Since Rhun's death, he'd worn his hair short, but it had been a month since she'd cut it, and he was developing a curl that kept falling onto his forehead. "You have nothing to be sorry for."

"It is wrong of me to corrupt our bed with war."

"You were sleeping," Gwen said practically, adjusting the blanket that covered him and smoothing it across his chest. "You can't help what you dream, and you *were* just in battle. Will you tell me of it?"

"I will, but not here." Gareth sat up abruptly. His head was still bent, and he wouldn't look at her, but he reached for his boots. "Outside."

Gwen had changed her ruined dress for a fresh one before she'd lain down. But while she'd closed her eyes for a few hours, even exhausted as she was, she'd found it hard to sleep.

Gwalchmai was the only family member who hadn't come to Ceredigion with Prince Hywel. The young bard remained in King Owain's retinue, currently located at his court in the village of Llanfair, across the Menai Strait from Aber. Llanfair was the largest village in Gwynedd. It not only guarded Anglesey at the entrance to the Menai Strait but was also on the other end of the ancient pathway across the Lavan Sands from the mainland.

Traders and travelers had been using the pathway at low tide since before there was a Gwynedd. The king had wanted to spend a few weeks close to his sister, Susanna, who was currently confined to the convent adjacent to the village.

They'd left Gwalchmai behind because, at nearly sixteen, he needed to experience the responsibilities of court bard on his own, without Meilyr looking over his shoulder all the time. Gwalchmai himself had argued for it, saying rightly that manhood came at fourteen in Wales, and if the station was to mean more than words, he had to be given the opportunity to *be* a man, in the same way it was given to the sons of knights (he meant Llelo and Dai, who was still thirteen). If nothing else, Gwen was glad Gwalchmai hadn't been here to get sick too.

Once outside, she took in a deep breath and bent back her head to look up at the blue sky, trying to shake off her exhaustion. There were few enough clouds above her to indicate that a predominantly sunny day might be in the offing, a rare enough occasion in south Wales to warrant celebration.

Gareth reached for her hand. "I want to see Dai."

"He lives, Gareth."

"But many more do not. I'll see him, and then I'll take up the investigation again."

"I'm coming with you."

Gareth gave her a hard look but didn't argue, for which Gwen was grateful. When she had thought last night that Dai was going to die, all she had wanted was to hold him in her arms and weep. But he hadn't died, and while that made her happy, she was also livid at what had been done. If Meicol was the murderer, so be it. He had paid the ultimate price for his treachery. If he was an innocent bystander or had an accomplice, however, she wanted to catch the culprit as much as or more than Gareth did.

And, fortunately, because they were in Wales rather than England, she was going to be allowed to participate. At the very least, questioning suspects and following leads would give her something to do rather than constantly worrying over Dai.

They arrived at the barracks, which, along with the great hall, had been turned into an infirmary. Gareth had spent half the night ferrying the dead down the hill to lie in the church at the local monastery. Gareth had told her before he'd fallen asleep that the bodies were laid in rows in the nave. Some of the family members had protested the haste at their removal from the castle, but it was necessary rather than unseemly. The barracks and hall were needed for the living, so the only other alternative would have been to lay the bodies out in the courtyard of the castle, subjecting them to the elements.

Saran had opened all the windows in the barrack's common room, where she was caring for upwards of two dozen ill people, but even so, the room smelled horribly of urine and vomit. Unapologetically playing favorites, she'd placed Dai on a table that had been pushed against the wall directly under a window facing the courtyard. When Gareth and Gwen arrived, Dai proved to have recovered enough to turn his head and raise a hand.

Gwen's heart swelled with love, and she ran to him, skirting the people lying on the floor. There were fewer of them this morning than there had been last night, but she told herself that was because the missing people were feeling better. If it wasn't true, there was no harm for now in the lie.

"How are you feeling?" She clasped Dai's hand and bent to kiss his forehead, noting as she did so the absence of fever.

"Better. My mouth feels better too." His eyes filled with tears. "I'm sorry, Mam. I didn't think one bite would matter."

Gareth's boots scraped on the floor as he came to a halt beside Gwen. He looked down at his foster son, his hands on his hips. Dai looked up at him, his expression one of utter wretchedness.

But then Gareth's expression gentled, and he also bent forward to brush the hair off Dai's forehead and kiss his foster son. "Just know we're happy you're alive and be glad this mistake is one you can learn from."

Dai closed his eyes, and tears leaked out of the corners and fell down his cheeks. Gareth stepped back so Gwen could sit beside her son and hug him. "Don't cry. Nobody is angry with you."

"They should be." He brushed at the tears with a jerky movement of his hand. "I'm angry with myself."

Gareth grunted. "And that's why we don't need to say anything. You're becoming a man, son. This is a hard lesson, but if you learn temperance and self-regulation from this mistake, it will be worth it."

Gwen just hoped the incident didn't dampen Dai's native enthusiasm, which she loved. Gareth was right, however, that a man-at-arms was useless if he wasn't obedient. He had to trust the wisdom of his superiors. If he couldn't, then he needed to find new superiors, as Gareth had done, or a new line of work.

"Gareth."

They all turned to see Evan standing in the doorway to the barracks, a grim set to his jaw. Gwen's stomach seized. "Who—"

Evan hurried forward, waving his hand to imply that whatever they were thinking was not what was wrong and at the same time rearranging his expression to one of sympathy and understanding. "Don't fear, Gwen. Everyone is well. The prince ... everyone. This is something else."

"Does Cadell live?" Gareth said.

"He does. It's just—" Evan leaned in to speak conspiratorially, "—we have another murder."

Gareth frowned. "Every person in the nave of St. Dyfi's Church was murdered."

Evan shook his head sharply. "Not that kind of murder. This wasn't poison." He drew in a breath. "Some time last night when we were dealing with the poisonings in the hall, Sir Robert was killed in the monastery graveyard."

9

Gareth

If they hadn't been in a sickroom—and the dead man hadn't been an esteemed man of Deheubarth—Gareth might have laughed in morbid relief at being confronted with a much more straightforward death. "Take me to him," he said simply.

Dai struggled to sit up. "You should bring Llelo."

Gareth looked to his eldest son, who had been dozing on a bench against the wall, but who'd perked up at Evan's arrival. An instant later he was on his feet.

Gareth raised his eyebrows at Dai. "You only want me to bring him so he can tell you everything that's happening when he gets back, since you can't go yourself."

Dai didn't even have the grace to look sheepish, or maybe he was too sick. "I don't know what you're talking about." But then he laughed, which did more to ease the tension in Gareth's stomach than anything else he could have done.

"You really must be feeling better." Gwen put her hand to his forehead again.

Then Saran entered the room from a nearby stairwell, reminding Gareth there were more sick people upstairs. Gwen remembered too and asked after Lord William.

"I have a girl watching him." Saran's eyes were tired. "I thought for a few hours last night we were going to lose him, but he pulled through."

"I should take a turn around the keep, give Saran a break." Gwen looked between Evan and Gareth, torn, Gareth could see, between duty and duty.

But Saran shook her head. "I've been in the hall as much as I've been here. I can always use extra hands, but Angharad has been more than helpful and can step in for you. She was sleeping a quarter of an hour ago, but I know she will continue again when she wakes."

Evan cleared his throat. "Tell her I will look in on her when I return?"

"Of course." Saran made a shooing motion with her hand. "Go. We're fine here. In fact, I'm thinking I could use Dai's pallet for someone else."

"We can put Dai in with Father before we go," Gwen said.

Saran shook her head. "I'll do it once I get some broth down him."

Gwen had been perched with one hip on the table, but now she got down and leaned in to kiss Saran's cheek. "Thank you. I am so thankful you're here."

Saran made the shooing motion again, though Gareth could tell she was touched. "Find who did this. Go on."

"Sir Robert was found lying between two tombstones." Evan held the door open for Gareth, Gwen, and Llelo, who didn't need to be told twice that he could come.

Gareth eyed the young man as he strode beside him across the courtyard towards the stables. "This is starting to become a habit I'm not sure I have fully thought out, but I admit you can't learn if you don't come with me."

Llelo's eyes were bright at Gareth's acceptance, and he would hardly be the first son who set his sights on following in his father's footsteps. Besides, the long night had left them short-handed today. Many of the men in Prince Hywel's teulu had stayed up with Gareth, tending the sick and taking over guard positions Cadell's men could no longer fill. Llelo was a man—and not only that, he was a man-at-arms.

Now he considered it, Gareth couldn't think of a single reason why Llelo shouldn't come with them. "You are to stay beside your mam, yes?"

Llelo nodded. "Of course."

As had become more usual than not for Hywel, he hadn't chosen to stay at Dinefwr Castle itself but at St. Dyfi's, the local monastery, located some three-quarters of a mile to the northwest of the castle. This was in part because the monastery provided him and his people with more spacious accommodations, and in part because staying outside the castle walls gave him more freedom of movement. While the bulk of Hywel's army that had attacked the Flemings had been relieved of their duties and sent home to

Ceredigion, the rest—Hywel's teulu primarily—were housed either in the monastery guesthouse or in tents in an adjacent field.

Last night, Hywel had overseen the security of the castle and the transportation of the last of the dead to the church, but had eventually found his bed in the monks' guesthouse. Gareth had left him under the watchful eyes of the Dragons and returned to the castle to be with Gwen and to check on Dai.

"Was that a moan, Evan?" Gwen put out a hand to him after they'd mounted the horses. "You're not sick too, are you?"

"Not at all." He rubbed his side. "A practice injury."

Gwen frowned. "Practicing against whom?"

"Iago," Evan said.

Gareth laughed. "Better you than me, friend."

Evan looked him up and down, a mischievous light in his eye. "Isn't it about time you joined us? You don't want the men to think you're fragile."

Gareth scoffed. "I am fully recovered from the events in Shrewsbury. Conall was too."

"Else I wouldn't have let him go home." Gwen pressed her lips together for a moment. "I do hope he's all right."

"I imagine he's in Dublin, spying on Godfrid," Gareth said—and then at Gwen's startled look, he laughed. "I gave him a letter of introduction. Dublin is subordinate to Leinster right now, so no harm should come to either of them when they meet."

"For now," Evan growled. "You know it's only a matter of time until things fall apart over there."

"Godfrid is focused on overthrowing Ottar, not Diarmait MacMurchada," Gareth said.

Gwen put a hand to her belly, making Gareth think about his promise to Godfrid to stand with him when it came time to claim his birthright. Hopefully, that time could wait until after the new baby was born in the autumn, at which point it would be a bad time of year to brave the Irish Sea anyway. What would be best and most convenient for Gareth was if Godfrid could bide his time for another year.

In short order, they arrived at the monastery and dismounted on the cobbles. The community here was large and prosperous, as befitting its patronage by the King of Deheubarth, much as the community at Llanfair had benefitted from close association with the kings of Gwynedd. Unusually for a monastery in Gareth's experience, the builders had aimed for beauty as well as functionality, and the church and buildings were adorned with stone flourishes on the outside, wooden carvings on the inside, and fancy ironwork, even in the design of the sconces that held the courtyard's torches.

They'd also used different colored stones to create patterns in the walkways, and, in the center of the courtyard, gray river rock was interspersed with red to create a giant cross on the ground. Though beautiful, it had the side effect of making it take twice as long to cross the courtyard as it would have otherwise done, since none of the monks would walk on the cross and made a point of going around.

To Gareth's amusement, Evan had no time for such affectation and dismounted right in the center of the cross. He insisted that Abbot Rhys, had he been with them, would have done the same. While Gareth could admit Abbot Rhys was an eminently practical man, he was also a man of God. Thus, the rest of them milled around the edges, and a moment later two stable boys ran out to take their horses. Evan then led them on foot around the outside of the church, through a gate, and into the cemetery. As in most churches that served both a monastery and a village, lay folk could access the church from the west without having to enter the monastery proper.

They crossed the grass until they reached the body, over which a monk was bent. Gareth blinked back the feeling he'd been here before. For a moment, the monk could have been Abbot Rhys, and they could have been back in St. Asaph. He wasn't, of course, but that wasn't to say the circumstances weren't familiar. Here they were again, in a monastery, facing the body of a man who'd died by another's hand.

Then the monk straightened, and the moment passed. Other than the robe he wore, the hood of which he pushed back as he turned to look at Gareth and Gwen, the monk looked nothing like Rhys except for the age he'd achieved and his station. In his middle fifties, Abbot Mathew was short, slender, and completely bald. Gareth had met him briefly when they'd arrived at Dinefwr, but then Mathew had left them in the hands of the hospitaler, and Gareth hadn't seen the abbot since.

"Deliver me from workers of iniquity and bloody men," Abbot Mathew said by way of a greeting. He'd quoted a psalm, and not one Gareth often—not to say ever—had heard a churchman recite.

Gareth's first impression of the abbot had been that he was scholarly, but also officious and not a man of the world. He'd been prepared to be gracious, but at the same time determined that Abbot Mathew leave them to themselves to take care of the investigation without interference. Now, however, Gareth revised his initial impression. Mathew might not be the soldier and spy Rhys had once been, but the abbot's wry tone had carried the echo of Gareth's friend, so he added the next line. "For lo, they lie in wait for my soul."

Mathew pressed his lips together, his eyes on Gareth's own. "You have studied."

"I was taught to read by a community of nuns, and the psalms were among my most memorable lessons."

"Your prince implied I might benefit from your assistance in this matter." Abbot Mathew's eyes glinted as he studied Gareth. "I confess I am quite out of my depth."

"That is no crime," Gareth said. "There was a time when I would have been too."

Mathew looked down at the body, his expression rueful. "I have thought often of the words of that psalm of late. These are troubled times."

"I suspect Sir Robert would agree with you." Gareth crouched beside the body.

Mathew looked on from above him. “I checked to see if he was dead, but otherwise did not move him.”

Sir Robert lay face down in the grass. He wore the garments of a soldier, including full armor, rather than the festival clothes he’d been wearing in the great hall. He’d changed sometime between leaving the hall and being murdered, which indicated to Gareth that he might not have trusted the person he was meeting in the graveyard, if that in fact was what he’d been doing here. The cause of death seemed plain, even at first glance: the iron-gray hair at the back of his head was matted with blood. He’d been bashed on the back of the head with enough force to break his skull.

He’d never had a chance.

The grass beneath the body was smashed down flat, and though head wounds often bled profusely, there was very little blood on the ground. Either the body had been moved or he’d died nearly instantly, since, of course, once the heart stopped beating, a body no longer bled.

“How did you know not to move him, Father?” Gwen asked the abbot. Without needing Gareth to instruct her, she began to move around the body, looking for anything the murderer might have dropped. In particular, Gareth would like the blunt weapon that had felled him from behind. Llelo copied her, except that he followed a line a few paces farther away from the body, but circling it too.

Gareth glanced up in time to see Mathew direct a sad smile in Gwen’s direction. “I was in Aberystwyth for Prince Hywel’s eisteddfod last summer. The music was wonderful—the murders less so. But in the course of the week, I became acquainted with Prior Rhys from St. Kentigern's monastery in St. Asaph."

As Rhys had been much in Gareth's thoughts since he'd arrived, he nodded his head. "He's abbot now."

Mathew's eyes lit. "I didn't know. You must congratulate him for me when you see him next."

"I'm not so sure he'd say congratulations were in order," Gwen said.

Abbot Mathew gave a single bark of a laugh before clasping his hands before him and sobering once again. "Sir Robert will be much missed. I know the king is much troubled by the poisoning, and he will be even more so now."

"I understand Sir Robert was serving the Earl of Pembroke these days," Gwen said.

"Earl Gilbert asked him to instruct his eldest son, Richard."

Gareth bobbed his chin in acknowledgement. "I met him."

"He is a credit to his sire," Abbot Mathew said, though his voice was curiously neutral.

Gareth glanced up at him, but when Mathew didn't elaborate on his observation, Gareth sat back on his heels. "I was hoping to speak to Robert today of Meicol, the first of the men to fall last night. Robert trained him too."

Llelo spoke for the first time. "If that's the case, it is in my mind that someone didn't want you to speak to him."

Gareth's brow furrowed. "Nobody knew of my intent but Richard, and he would hardly have suggested I speak to Robert if he was only going to murder him later." He shook his head. "Robert had to have known something, however."

"It's hard to imagine otherwise, given that he's dead," Evan said.

Gareth motioned with his head towards the body, so Evan approached, and the two men carefully rolled Robert onto his back.

Evan bent to put his hand to the flattened grass that had been beneath the body. "It's dry."

Abbot Mathew looked on with interest. "What does that mean?"

"It means he died before the grass was wet with dew." Llelo had certainly been paying attention the last few years.

Gareth lifted Robert's arm and gently set it down again. Here at nine hours or so into the new day, the man's body was warm but stiff—so stiff Gareth had difficulty moving the arm at all.

"Can you tell when he died?" Abbot Mathew asked, showing that he too knew something about death, if not murder.

"I saw him in the hall yesterday evening, after Meicol fell," Gareth said. "Was he there afterwards?"

"I did not seem him," Evan said thoughtfully. "Perhaps he left with Lord Maurice's men."

"That would be before the dessert was served." Gwen frowned. "Surely he couldn't be the poisoner and have been ... running away?"

"Remember, it is Sir Robert who is dead." Gareth looked at the abbot. "How is it you are not ill? You were at the feast last night."

"I briefly attended the festivities. Certainly I was pleased to give the opening blessing, but I find revelry after battle not to my taste," he put a hand to his stomach, "and the food at the castle is too rich for me."

"So you didn't eat the pie?" Gwen said.

"I had a bowl of chowder and a goblet of wine. And then I left." His expression grew haggard. "So many dead. So many good people dead."

Gwen put out a hand to the abbot. "I'm sorry for your losses."

"Look at this, Father." Llelo, who'd continue to search the graveyard, held up a thick branch some three feet long.

Gareth motioned that he should bring it to him and, when Llelo obeyed, was sadly unsurprised to find a few strands of hair that matched Sir Robert's and dark blood marring one of the rough ends.

Mathew sighed. "The Lord giveth, and the Lord taketh away."

That was from Job, another passage with which Gareth was distressingly familiar. He had by now patted Robert up and down and come up with two things of interest: one was a slim iron key that had been sewn into the hem of his cloak. A man didn't do that unless he feared losing it—or someone else finding it. Gareth put it in his scrip to show to Cadell and Maurice at their next audience.

The second was a signet ring stamped with the head of a horned goat. Gareth paused as he looked at it and then showed it to Abbot Mathew. "It isn't exactly Walter FitzWizo's mark, but—"

"But it's close." Mathew shook his head. "If you're thinking treachery, think again. I knew the man well. Sir Robert was loyal. He could have acquired this signet in any number of ways, including from his late wife, who was Flemish."

That gave both Gareth and Gwen pause. "His wife was from FitzWizo's colony?" she asked.

Abbot Mathew nodded. "That was many years ago, of course. He could be carrying it in memory of her, or he could have acquired it recently when Wiston was sacked."

"Or it could be a token he bore as proof of his allegiance to whomever he was meeting in this graveyard," Llelo said, "who then killed him."

Gareth stowed the signet away too. "I'm sure you can understand the need for urgency and discretion in this matter."

"Of course." Mathew nodded. "King Cadell asked you to look into these deaths, and I know Abbot Rhys thinks highly of you. Just tell me what I can do."

"Give us a private space to work," Gareth said, thinking of Meicol's body back at the castle, also in its private room, "and free rein to ask questions. We can only pray somebody, somewhere, saw something that will help us."

10

Gwen

"What is happening here, Gareth?" Hoping to let in more light, Gwen opened the shutters in the little room in the monastery they'd been given to examine Robert's body. "Robert was murdered, but not by Meicol, and more and more I'm thinking Meicol was murdered too, rather than a casualty of his own malfeasance. In fact, I have to wonder if Robert isn't somehow at fault for some of this."

"But poison? Treachery? I can't believe it of him." Evan's casual stance, braced as he was against the frame of the door with his arms folded across his chest, in no way belied the seriousness of his words. He was on guard. Admittedly, he may well also not have wanted to come any closer.

Gareth glanced at his friend. "The poisoning was an urgent enough case to solve, but I think Gwen is right. We not only have a poisoner on the loose, but a cold-blooded killer as well, who may or may not be the same person."

"The world has suddenly become far more dangerous," Evan said.

Gareth returned his attention to Robert's wounds. "It was dangerous enough as it was."

Every monastery had different procedures for dealing with the dead. Here, they were in the washing room, adjacent to the actual washroom, to make easy the process of preparing the body for burial. Gareth had stripped Robert of most of his clothing.

"Maybe Meicol snuck a piece of pie early," Llelo said.

"He had the vial in his satchel," Gwen pointed out.

Llelo made a face. "I forgot about that."

"If Meicol was murdered, the vial could have been planted," Evan said. "Meicol would be dead and take the blame for the poisoning."

"If the poisoner knows what's good for him, he'll be long gone, and we'll never find him," Llelo said.

Gwen glanced at her foster son. He was watching Gareth intently—and apparently thinking intently too. So she nodded encouragingly. "It would be good to know if anyone is missing after last night."

Gareth chewed on his lower lip, though his eyes remained on the body. "I'll be sure to check that too with Cadell and Maurice."

"And our own men," Llelo said, "just to be fair."

"Alternatively, murdering Robert and framing Meicol implies that either or both of them knew something about the killer and they were a threat to him," Gwen said.

"That implies the murderer is still here because if he was going to flee, he wouldn't care," Llelo said.

"I'm terrified to say I like the way you think, Llelo." Evan straightened from his position in the doorway. "You realize anyone involved in the investigation is in danger now—particularly Gareth."

Because of that possibility, they'd already decided Gareth alone would be the point man in all dealings with the lords of Deheubarth. Gareth was happy with Gwen's participation, but the less said about it, the better. She'd been the target of bloody men, from Abbot Mathew's quote, far too many times.

Gareth shook his head. "We swore we would be more careful, Gwen."

"Tangwen is far away and safe," she said, "and we can hardly turn our backs now. Who else is still standing and capable of finding the truth?"

She sensed more than heard Gareth's groan. "I should send you away."

Gwen folded her arms across her chest. "Who's to say danger wouldn't come with me to Aberystwyth? Perhaps the murderer would follow me, thinking I'd stumbled onto an answer I don't have. I'm safer with you and the Dragons." She tipped her head to Evan, who squared his shoulders.

"I'll speak to Prince Hywel immediately. You're going to have a guard whether you like it or not." He left.

Gareth rolled his eyes at Gwen. "Now you've done it."

"I've been watching the Dragons for a while now, and they're no different from most of your men, albeit more individually skilled. They are happiest when they're fighting or feasting. Protecting us will give them something to do—and keep them out of Cadell's way."

Gareth frowned. "What do you mean by that?"

"The Dragons got Cadell into Wiston, and then Evan says they were reined in at the last moment, just when the keep was theirs for the taking. Why?"

"We don't know why."

"Exactly. Something is going on here we don't know about. Don't you think we should? How are we to solve these murders when the king himself is withholding crucial information?"

"Perhaps he thinks it isn't pertinent."

Gwen scoffed. "He's the king. That's for him to decide. But Robert was at Wiston. Perhaps his murder is related to whatever they're hiding. And you realize who the king going to blame if we don't discover who did this."

Gareth paused and sent Gwen a piercing look. "Cadell will blame me."

"A man from Gwynedd. How convenient."

Gareth suddenly looked very wary. "I didn't consider that when I agreed to head up the investigation."

Gwen canted her head. "Not to say you could have done anything else. It was up to Hywel and Cadell more than you."

The doorway darkened, and Gareth and Gwen turned to see that it wasn't Evan returning but Abbot Mathew, who had brought a stable boy with him. "May I come in?" Mathew's eyes tracked from Gwen to Gareth to Llelo, still in his corner. Mathew was a priest, so it was no surprise he sensed something amiss, but he didn't speak of it. "Young Pedr has something to tell you."

Gareth raised his eyebrows at Gwen, asking without speaking, which it seemed they were doing with each other more and more often, that she should take charge of this. He didn't want the boy telling his story while standing over Robert's dead body. Pedr's eyes were wide enough as it was. Gwen moved to the doorway, blocking the boy's view and at the same time gesturing that they should return to the shelter of the walkway between the cloister and the washroom.

Once there, Pedr couldn't wait to speak. "I saw Sir Robert last night!" The boy was endearing, with his bright red hair that stuck straight up and a collection of freckles that covered his nose and cheeks. Gwen put him at about twelve years old.

"When was this?" Gwen flicked her eyes to Mathew, who was looking at the boy with a paternal air.

"After compline." Compline was the prayer vigil before the monks retired to bed.

"Should I not ask what you were doing awake at that hour?" Gwen said.

The boy looked sheepish, his eyes going to Mathew, who shook his head gently. "We will discuss your infraction later. Tell Lady Gwen what you told me."

"Sir Robert was leading his horse around the side of the church, heading to the cemetery." Pedr paused. Where before he had been anxious to tell his story, now he was suddenly hesitant.

"It's all right, Pedr," Mathew said. "Just say it."

"I'd startled him, and he took the name of the Lord in vain." Pedr hastily crossed himself. "But then he smiled and said he had a treat for me."

"A treat? What kind of treat?" Gwen's intensity had Pedr leaning away from her, and she took in a breath to calm herself. It was rare enough for someone to come forward with information, rather than her having to pry it from him, she was almost flustered.

"He rummaged in his saddle bag and pulled out a tart wrapped in a cloth." The boy's eyes went to the ground.

Gwen suspected he was feeling guilty about taking it, but it was another infraction for Abbot Mathew. She didn't care about that. "Did you eat it?"

Pedr's head came up. "No! I wouldn't!" Then he looked rueful. "I know that tart, and something the cook puts in it gives me a rash and makes my mouth itch. Besides, Sir Robert had already cursed, and I wasn't supposed to be out of the dormitory, and ... and he'd muffled his horse's hooves with cloth so they wouldn't sound on the cobbles."

Mathew nodded. "I spoke to the gatekeeper. He knew none of this and heard nothing in the night."

"I'm telling the truth!"

Gwen turned back to Pedr. "We believe you. How long after compline was this?"

Pedr's eyes skated to Mathew and back to Gwen again. "Maybe ... three hours?"

That would be midnight, which would be in keeping with the state of Robert's body if he died shortly thereafter. "You were alone the whole time?"

This time his nod lacked conviction. Abbot Mathew sighed. "You were running with that village boy, weren't you?"

Pedr let out a breath, but he didn't look unhappy to discover Mathew already knew—quite the opposite. He was relieved. "He'd just left."

Gareth probably could have related to these boyish hijinks. For Gwen's part, she was trying to make sense of Pedr's story. Not that she didn't believe him. The problem was what he'd described Robert to have done. It was a simple matter to reach the graveyard without going through the church, and it made no sense that he would risk waking the gatekeeper and being seen. But then, perhaps the issue was the horse. If the animal had been kept in the stables, Robert had to go through the monastery to take it away. Why he'd left it there and why he was taking it away at midnight remained a mystery, along with the location of the horse now.

None of those questions were necessary to share with Mathew or Pedr. "I'll leave that to your abbot. Where's the tart now?"

"In the stables. I'll show you." Pedr set off at a run, leading them along the walkway and around the main monastery buildings until they arrived back at the courtyard and the adjacent stables. Once inside, he went straight to a pile of hay, knelt to dig within it, and came up with a small, wrapped package.

Gwen hadn't expected to find the large pie that had been served in the hall, and this was, indeed, hardly larger than her palm. She took it from Pedr, who eased back on his heels, glad to be rid of it.

"After he gave this to you, did he leave by the graveyard gate?" Gwen asked.

Pedr nodded.

"And you didn't see him again?"

"I went straight back to bed."

Mathew put a hand on the boy's shoulder. "Thank you, Pedr. Off you go."

With a buoyant smile, relieved of his burden, Pedr left. Mathew's expression immediately sobered. "Why do you care so much about the tart?"

While Gareth preferred not to share information with anyone who might be a suspect, Gwen didn't include Father Mathew among the possible villains. The whole castle probably knew the truth by now anyway. It was only a matter of time before everyone in the monastery did too. "It was the custard pie that killed all those people last night."

Abbot Mathew's eyes widened. "Surely Sir Robert didn't know the tart was poisoned. He couldn't have meant to kill the boy!" He gazed unseeing at the open doorway through which Pedr had disappeared. "I've known the man our entire lives. He was a warrior. How could he be involved in something so underhanded?"

Gwen tipped her head from side to side, conveying doubt. "His behavior is suspicious, but again, he was the one who ended up dead, and he didn't murder himself."

Mathew looked down at the ground. Fresh hay had recently been laid across the dirt floor. "I'm not sure that's a comfort. What was he doing here so late? Whom did he meet?"

"His murderer." She felt sorry for the abbot, but nobody could ever truly see what was in another's heart. "Can you tell me when Robert left King Cadell's service for Earl Gilbert's?"

Mathew's head swung around to look at her. "Who said he did?"

Gwen blinked. "Richard, Earl Gilbert's son, told Gareth that Robert was *his* swordsmaster now. You confirmed it in the graveyard."

"Oh, that." Mathew waved his hand dismissively. "That was a courtesy from one lord to another. Richard has designs on becoming a great warrior. Last year, his father asked Cadell for the loan of Robert, in preparation for Richard's ascension to knighthood next year."

"When he'll be eighteen."

"Yes. He, Prince Maredudd, and Prince Rhys will be knighted together, even though Rhys is two years younger than the older boys."

"In Wales, boys become men earlier," Gwen said, thinking of Llelo.

Mathew nodded. "Maredudd could have been knighted already. Should have been in my opinion."

"Why hasn't he?"

Mathew gave her a baleful look.

Gwen tipped her head, putting one small piece of the very large puzzle in place. "Cadell doesn't want it for him? He is worried about being outdone?"

"I shouldn't speak of this," Mathew said, but then continued anyway. "Maredudd is a natural leader. What's more, he and Rhys are close companions in temperament and wisdom. All the men know it. They are young now, but Cadell already feels them pushing up behind him."

Gwen was pleased to know more about the intricacies of Cadell's court, because it would help her understand some of the undercurrents. Sir Robert's death touched both the court at Dinefwr and at Pembroke. They needed to find his killer.

Mathew knew it too. "I'm wondering what happened to Sir Robert's horse."

Gwen looked down the row of stalls. "Do we know for certain it isn't here in your stables?"

"Not that I've heard or that I see." Mathew walked down the aisle. When he got to the end, he shook his head regretfully. "Perhaps it returned to the castle or found its way to Robert's manor."

"Robert has a manor?"

"Oh, yes. His father was well rewarded for his service to King Cadell's father. It's just too bad Robert himself never had any children."

"Did he ever marry?"

"When he was a young man, his wife and child died, and he never formed another attachment."

Some would say he had shirked his duty to his name, but Gwen could understand not wanting to risk going through that kind of pain and loss again. She was just happy that her father, after nearly sixteen years of being alone, had found it in his heart to love again. "Who oversaw Robert's possessions when he was away?"

"That would be a member of Cadell's retinue, one Alban. His wife, Caron, is Robert's niece."

11

Gwen

Gwen waited patiently for her husband to finish his examination of Sir Robert's body, by which point the Dragons had arrived to escort them to the manor Robert owned (and Alban oversaw).

"Alban and Caron were among the diners at the castle," Evan said when Gwen told him what she'd learned from Abbot Mathew.

"Did they survive?" Gareth said.

"I have not seen them since last night, but they are not among the dead," Evan said.

Gwen hadn't thought to do a more complete accounting of the survivors, beyond those from Aberystwyth. "Robert's murderer, as well as the person who poisoned the diners last night, would not be among the ill—unless he was very clever and willing to risk his own life for his cause."

Evan nodded. "So we'll add two more to the list, if only because of their connection to Robert."

Gwen shot him a look. "Are you all right with that? These people were your friends."

"It was a long time ago, Gwen."

Gwen didn't press him further, not feeling the need to question him at all, since he was hardly a suspect. Though, as Gareth mounted, he shook his head. "I feel foolish that you think we're in any danger, Evan. The poisoner is clearly not one for open confrontation and neither is Robert's killer. Poison is by nature a coward's weapon, and Robert was struck down from behind."

"Then a show of force may be all we need to dissuade him." Evan grimaced. "Her. Them."

Once on the road, Gwen and Gareth rode side-by-side, with three guards ahead and three behind. Gwen wasn't sorry to be moving. For the moment, no more information could be found at the monastery, though Abbot Mathew said he'd let them know if any of the monks came forward with a further thought.

Gareth kept swiveling his head, surveying their surroundings. They were riding through pastureland with few trees to hide behind, however, and there was nobody in sight but them.

She put out a hand to him. "Are you going to tell me about the dream?"

Gareth laughed under his breath. "I was hoping you'd forgotten."

"Just because I'm pregnant doesn't mean I'm always foggy," she said tartly.

Gareth grunted. "You don't normally ask about battle. Why now?"

"Because whatever happened to you obviously bothers you enough that it's coming out in your sleep."

Gareth sighed, and his eyes took on a faraway look. "We are celebrating a victory over the Flemings, who have been a sore in the side of everyone in Deheubarth for years, but that doesn't mean destroying their settlement didn't come at a price."

"Men died. I know," she said.

Gareth took in another breath. "Once we took Wiston Castle, and Cadell and his allies overcame FitzWizo's army, we turned on their main village, Gwen. Prince Hywel held his own men back, but the rest of the army didn't hesitate. Every house and barn was ransacked, and anyone who resisted was struck down."

Gwen bit her lip, searching for a reply. "I'm sorry," was all she ended up saying. "I love you."

"I know you do, but I can hardly love myself for standing by and letting it happen. How does it make me different from the murderer we're pursuing?"

It was very different, and he knew it, and she said so.

But still Gareth shook his head. "It isn't even as if we killed Walter FitzWizo himself. He escaped, and it's probably only a matter of time before he and his men regroup and try to take back what we took from them. I fear that could be what is happening now."

"You fear the gains will come to nothing?"

"After last night, they may well anyway, without FitzWizo needing to interfere at all." Then Gareth shook himself. "The victory is to be celebrated, and I am glad to be part of an alliance between Ceredigion and Deheubarth. The last thing Hywel needs is hostile army on his border."

"Hywel was quick to forgive Cadell for sending Anselm to St. Asaph and interfering in Gwynedd." Gwen was glad to see her husband put aside his guilt, at least for the moment. If his dreams were troubled again, she'd ask Prince Hywel or Evan to talk to him. Many men only wanted to talk about battle to other men who shared their experience.

"You think so?" Gareth let out a snort. "Forgiveness had nothing to do with it. You'll note we have seen neither hide nor hair of our wayward prior. Believe me, the first thing I did when we arrived in Aberystwyth was inquire at St. Padarn's if Anselm had joined their number. He had not. He is not at St. Dyfi's either."

"Cadell assuredly has sent him off to do mischief somewhere else. Better there than here."

"I can't decide if that's something to hope for or not. It all depends on whom he's making mischief for." Gareth gave her a rueful smile. "If it wasn't Cadell's own household that was poisoned, I would have pegged Anselm for the murderer."

They'd come to a wide place in the road, and Evan urged his horse to come abreast of Gareth and Gwen. "It might be best if you leave the initial questioning of Alban to me."

With that statement, Evan had Gwen and Gareth's full attention. Gwen didn't know if he'd overheard any of her conversation with Gareth, and she hoped he hadn't taken offense at Gareth's description of the battle. After all, it was the Dragons who'd opened the castle for the invading army, which meant he'd killed men too.

"Are you sure about that?" Gwen said. "You already told me how Alban treated you at Wiston."

Evan nodded. "Badly, I know. But then he tried to smooth it over. He is both wary of me and feels superior to me. That could be a good combination for getting the truth out of him."

"Was Meicol among the company that entered the keep?" Gwen asked.

"No." Evan shrugged. "It was an elite force. Meicol was not that trusted."

"Perhaps young Prince Rhys can tell me more," Gwen said.

Evan guffawed. "That boy."

Gwen looked at him, eyebrows raised. "Why do you say it like that? I like him."

"I do too, but his mind doesn't work like a normal man's. He's too smart by half."

Gwen nodded to herself. "And that makes him unpredictable, and whether or not you like him, above all you want the throne of Deheubarth to be predictable." She paused. "Or rather, Prince Hywel does."

"Not only wants it—needs it," Gareth said. "Hywel's rule over Ceredigion is growing more established with every month that passes, but this business with Anselm showed him how two-faced Cadell truly is, and he isn't the only one. Prince Cadwaladr is an arrow just waiting to be loosed. Who knows where it will land? Cadell would have much preferred Cadwaladr, an enemy he knows, in Aberystwyth than Hywel. Thus, the spying."

By now they'd passed through Dinefwr's village in the valley below the castle and reached a side track that followed the course of the River Towy. Both went by the manor house, located approximately three miles from the castle. The valley through which they were riding consisted mostly of stands of trees interspersed with fields and pastureland. This region of south Wales wasn't as flat as Anglesey, but it was flatter than all but the seashore of Gwynedd, and the river wended its way through the whole of it.

"This way." Evan jerked his head, and they followed the well-worn track. The ruts were deep, indicating that Robert—or more likely, Alban, as the steward—was not maintaining it properly. He needed to send a work crew with shovels and stone to fill the ruts and smooth the dips. As it was, when it rained again, as it surely would, any cart that attempted to drive along the road would be instantly mired in mud.

Then, up ahead, a woman screamed, and the whole company urged their horses into a gallop. After fifty yards, they came around a bend and into a grassy clearing that fronted the manor house. A large company of men was already milling around on the circular green, where sheep might occasionally graze. They appeared unconcerned about the screaming. As Gwen reined in, she realized why: it was a woman doing the screaming, and she wasn't hurt or afraid. She was angry, and her ire was directed at Richard de Clare, the heir to the Earldom of Pembroke.

12

Gareth

Gareth's feet were on the ground before anyone else's, despite Gruffydd's protest that there was no point in guarding a man who refused to be cautious.

"The day I'm in danger from a pregnant woman is the day I hang up my sword." Gareth strode forward towards the altercation, which appeared just short of coming to blows—and might have but for the arrival of Gareth's company.

He halted in the circle created by the woman, Caron he presumed, though they hadn't officially met, young Richard, and Alban, Caron's husband.

Hands on his hips, Gareth surveyed the trio and said in the voice he normally reserved for recalcitrant men-at-arms. "What seems to be the problem here?"

Richard lifted his chin. "I simply asked her a question, and she started screaming at me."

As if on command, Richard's denial set Caron off again. "Simply asked a question? You accused my husband of murdering Sir Robert!"

Gareth looked at Alban. "*Did* you murder Sir Robert?"

Alban huffed out a breath. "It's ridiculous even to suggest such a thing. Sir Robert has been nothing but good to us." He put an arm around his wife's shoulders.

Caron, meanwhile, dabbed at her eyes and cheeks with the hem of her apron, wiping away tears. Her anger had turned to sudden grief. "How could you accuse Alban of such a thing? We loved Uncle Robert!"

In Gareth's experience, love and hatred were two sides of a single coin. In addition, training men in war made them very good at killing other men. No man reached Alban's station as second-in-command of the king's teulu, essentially Evan's position in Prince Hywel's company before his transfer to the Dragons, without a skill and familiarity with it. Gareth had it too, but if he ever decided murder was necessary, he wouldn't be bashing a man on the back of his head and leaving his body to be found.

Richard appeared to give up on Caron and turned to Gareth. "Were you able to speak to Sir Robert last night?"

Gareth shook his head regretfully. "By the time I'd finished examining Meicol's body, dessert had been served and people were dying. Sir Robert himself had left the hall before I returned, and was dead soon after—though not of poison, of course."

Richard harrumphed his disappointment and looked back at Alban and Caron. "I don't see the two of you sick. How did you escape?"

Caron was sobbing too hard to speak, but Alban's eyes were clear, and he retorted, "How did you?"

For a moment, Richard looked thunderstruck at the lack of courtesy, but then he relaxed and shrugged his shoulders, perhaps thinking they could get more out of the pair with honey than with vinegar. “I was among the men who carried Meicol from the hall and chose not to return afterwards. I didn’t hear of the poisoning until one of my men reported people were dying.”

Gwen arrived at Gareth’s side and gently rubbed elbows with him, not because she wanted attention but to let him know she was there. She was with child—by all appearances a similar length of time along to Caron—and the sight of Gwen reminded him that no good could come of accusing Caron of murder. The idea was absurd. Alban, however, was a different matter.

Which gave him an idea. “Perhaps my wife could assist you inside, Caron. I’m sure both of you could do with sitting down with a warm cup.”

Alban’s expression turned to one of relief, which was the first instance where Gareth felt some sympathy for him. If Caron was often as hotheaded as this, their marriage might be stormier than most.

Caron, for her part, continued to weep, but more quietly, and she tipped her head towards the door. “Of course. If you would follow me, Gwen.”

That left Alban alone with Gareth and Richard, who was a smart enough young man to realize exactly what Gareth had done. Separating the two of them prevented them from colluding on whatever story they were going to tell, if they, in fact, had something to do with Robert’s death.

Alban didn't look like it, however. As Caron departed, he heaved a sigh, and his expression cleared. "I apologize for my wife's behavior, Lord Richard. Sir Robert's death, on top of what has been a difficult pregnancy, has been hard on her."

"Better them than us, eh?" Richard said.

Alban let out a genuine laugh. "You have the right of it."

It was the opening Gareth had hoped for to catch Alban when his guard was down. "Tell me about Sir Robert."

Alban was ready this time with his defense. "I really didn't kill him."

Gareth made sure his voice was all patience. "I didn't say you did. I spoke with him only in passing and didn't know him at all, but you did. I genuinely want you to tell me about him."

Alban pressed his lips together, and for a moment Gareth wasn't sure Alban believed his assurances, but then he nodded. "He was a fine swordsman, as I'm sure you know." Alban lifted his chin to point at Richard. "So good that King Cadell loaned him to Earl Gilbert." Then his eyes grew thoughtful. "He was genuinely a good man too. Lonely though, since his wife and child died."

"When did that happen?"

"Oh—" Alban waved a hand dismissively, "—twenty years ago or more. Robert devoted himself to his work after that."

"Who inherits his estate? You?"

Alban nodded. "Caron is—was—his niece. That's why he put me in charge of his manor in the first place. It would make the ultimate transition easier."

Gareth rubbed his chin. Alban spoke straightforwardly, and Gareth's initial thought that Alban might have killed his benefactor faded. It would have made no sense to do so when he himself was going to inherit eventually—and already had the benefit of the manor house. Robert was never home, and by the look of the estate—which on second glance was not so much run-down as lived-in—never made demands.

"Where were you last night that you weren't poisoned?"

Alban made a rueful face. "Caron has been ill nearly continually with this child. She ate nothing during the feast, and though I would have stayed, she asked me to take her home right after she spoke to Evan."

Gareth glanced at Evan, who was standing in the middle of the green talking to one of Richard's men, having dispensed with the initial plan to have him speak to Alban and Caron the moment they heard Caron scream. "This was just after Meicol's death?"

Alban's lips twisted. "She didn't know about it when she met Evan in the courtyard. She'd just come from vomiting up the little she did eat. The atmosphere in the hall was not pleasant, not to mention hot and stuffy, so we left before dessert was served."

"Where did you go?"

"Home. Here. If you want proof, you could speak to the midwife. I sent for her, just to be safe. She was here most of the night."

That sounded definitive enough for now. "Thank you for talking with me. I'll let you know if I have further questions."

Alban bowed and entered the house, leaving Gareth with Richard on the porch. Though Richard's Welsh counterpart, Prince Rhys, showed knowledge and an ability to analyze beyond his years, it was clear to Gareth that he was still very much a fifteen-year-old who didn't yet know his place or his limits. Richard, on the other hand, gave every impression of being much older than his seventeen years. He had a shadow in his eyes that belonged to a man who'd seen too much and was no longer surprised by evil. It could be a product of his recent narrow escape from Chepstow Castle with his father or the battle against Walter FitzWizo, but Gareth thought it went deeper than that.

While Rhys had lost both parents at a young age, which couldn't have been easy—he and Gareth shared that fate—Richard was the son of a hard-driving father and a mother who'd once been the mistress of King Henry I of England. That couldn't have been an easy household to grow up in either. Richard's skin was so thick, Gareth could almost see the extra layer surrounding him.

So he took a chance. "You're not a hothead, my lord. Why did you get into a shouting match with Caron?"

Richard laughed as genuinely as Alban had done earlier. "I was never angry, though I pretended to be. I wanted to catch them out in their wrongdoing."

Gareth's eyes narrowed. "You were looking to do my job."

Richard's expression turned regretful. "I was simply looking to help the investigation along because I could."

"How did you know Sir Robert was dead?"

Now Richard's eyes grew sad, and he looked down at his feet for a moment. "To tell you the truth, I didn't. I came here looking for Robert. After last night, my men are wary of staying here even another day and are ready to depart. Robert was not with us, however, though I didn't know why at the time, and nobody had seen him. It was Alban who told me he was dead."

That gave Gareth a moment's pause. "How did he know? I have just come directly from the monastery myself."

"He said a messenger came to tell him. He'd just left when I arrived." Richard grimaced. "I wanted to accuse them before they had time to prepare a story."

"If Alban murdered Robert, he surely would have already prepared a story," Gareth pointed out.

Richard sighed. "In retrospect, I can see how that might be true. I was too upset at the time to consider anything beyond the shock of Robert's murder."

Gareth put a hand on his shoulder and shook him a little, conveying sympathy. He hadn't known Robert himself, but he'd been a man of stature—and one who appeared to inspire loyalty, even in a Norman lord. In Gareth's experience, Norman lords—especially one as young as Richard—who could admit they didn't know everything were few and far between.

"No harm done, as far as I know." But then Gareth frowned. Something about Richard's story didn't make sense. "Why didn't you send one of your men to collect him? Surely that would have been more usual."

Richard snorted under his breath. "Yes, of course it would, but I also wanted to speak to Robert of Meicol and urge him to speak to you if he hadn't already."

Understanding dawned. "You wanted to be with him when he talked to me."

Richard was completely unembarrassed. "I did, yes. As I told you last night, I have heard many stories about what has gone on at Dinefwr over the years and few of them are good." He gestured to the manor's front door, which Alban had closed behind him. "Take these two, for example. I accused Caron and Alban of murdering Robert because they have the most to gain from his death. Robert knew it, and he was not happy about it."

"Wait. Wait," Gareth said. "How is that? Alban inherits. He just said so."

"I heard him." Richard glared at the closed door, as if he could see right through it to Alban and Caron if he looked hard enough. "But that's not the whole story. Yesterday Robert told me he was thinking about leaving the estate to the monastery. I don't know if he'd yet mentioned it to Caron and Alban, but he was going to speak to the abbot about the possibility before we left Dinefwr. I'm thinking he was killed before he could."

Gareth let out a long breath. "A better motive for murder could not be found."

Richard clasped both hands on the top of his head and looked up at the sky. It was blue, for the most part, with a few clouds scattered across it. Another lovely June day. "Could Robert have been the poisoner's intended target, and when Robert left the castle before the dessert, he resorted to bludgeoning him?"

"It's possible," Gareth said slowly, "though a woefully imprecise method of murder."

"The poisoner didn't appear to care how many died or who they were, did he?"

"No. It was very hit or miss," Gareth said.

"More miss than hit, if Robert was the target." Richard dropped his arms. "Only two of my men fell ill, and none died. Cadell is going to think I did this."

"Or the Fitzgeralds," Gareth said. "Or us. It is he and his people who suffered the most, the implication being that Cadell was the target, not Robert."

"I'm sure you're right." Richard's eyes met Gareth's. "Find the poisoner, Sir Gareth, before he tries again." He turned to the door and reached for the latch, by all appearances preparing to enter Alban's house. "Leave the issue of Sir Robert's death to me."

13

Gwen

Gareth had very skillfully separated Caron and Alban, so Gwen went along with his plainly evident plan and escorted Caron to the back of the manor where the kitchen lay. On the way, they passed through the central hall, which was as beautiful a room as she'd ever seen in any dwelling, including the massive great hall at Newcastle-under-Lyme, which was the most ornate castle she had ever been to.

Whoever had ordered the construction of this room—whether Sir Robert himself or an ancestor—the wood had been lovingly fashioned, from the polished floor to the large table at one end of the hall. The mantle, the beams, and the chair legs themselves, were all carved in the shape of animals, to go with the giant mounted antlers that took up pride of place on the far wall. She counted sixteen tines before they were through the hall and out the back, heading towards the kitchen along an attached walkway.

It was a beautiful day, so the door to the kitchen was open, letting in the fresh spring air. Inside, the cook was working at a mound of bread dough while directing two undercooks in their duties.

Unlike at the castle, the manor's cook was a woman, and she took one look at Caron and became instantly solicitous. "My lady! You shouldn't be up and about after the night you had!'

That was the best opening Gwen could have imagined. "What happened last night?" She took Caron's elbow and helped her to a bench against the wall.

"Ach!" The cook waved a hand. "Didn't you hear the dreadful news from the castle?"

"You mean the poisoning?" Gwen nodded. "Was Caron poisoned too?"

"She might as well have been," the cook said tartly. "We had the midwife here from before midnight until dawn, looking after her. She couldn't keep anything down."

Caron rolled her eyes. "I never can keep anything down, Heledd. You know that."

"It's been getting better." Heledd put her hands on her hips. "What can I get you now?"

"Just some mead, if you will." Caron canted her head to Gwen. "She's with child too, so we'll both need some."

Heledd bustled off, saying something about women not knowing how to take care of themselves, and Caron patted the bench beside her. "Sit. You must be exhausted."

Gwen found that she was, in fact, exhausted. She leaned her head back against the wall and closed her eyes for a moment—almost dozing off before she remembered what she was here for.

She opened her eyes and looked at Caron, who looked away hastily, since she'd been staring at Gwen.

Caron was a good ten years older than Gwen, and her face showed it, with crow's feet at the corners of her eyes and frown lines around her mouth. On Gareth, the crow's feet only made him look more handsome. Women were supposed to look perpetually young, and Gwen reminded herself not to judge because, God willing, that fate would one day be hers.

"When did you leave the castle?"

Caron rolled her eyes again. It appeared to be something she did to express her displeasure. "That again? We left before the dessert—and yes, one of our men told us what happened after it was served. Once the midwife arrived, Alban went back to help."

Gwen endeavored not to blink because as far as she knew, Alban had never arrived at the castle. But then, it had been chaos, and her focus had been on Dai. "When was this?"

Caron shrugged. "Before midnight. I was too ill myself to care."

Heledd returned with the two cups of mead, and Gwen sipped hers gratefully. She felt less nauseous herself if she ate or drank something every few hours throughout the day, rather than saving her appetite, such as it was, for two or three individual meals. The mead was smooth and sweet, and Gwen was tempted to close her eyes again over it. "When did Alban return?"

Caron shrugged, so Gwen looked at Heledd. "Was the master gone long last night?"

"Not long at all. In fact, I barely knew he'd left before he was back." Heledd looked fondly at Caron, who now had her eyes closed herself. "We've been having a difficult time of it here."

"So I've heard."

Heavy boots scraped on the threshold, and Alban poked his head around the doorframe. "How are you doing?"

Gwen smiled brightly. "Better, thank you."

Alban glanced at his wife before nodding at Heledd. "Send one of the boys to fetch me if she needs me." He made a move as if to go, but before he could Gwen stood.

"Just a moment, Alban."

He turned back, his expression bland.

"Caron said that you went back to the castle last night after the midwife came here. How long were you there?"

"Oh." He waved a hand dismissively. "I started to go, but my horse's leg was hot, so I decided I'd better tend to it instead."

"Did—" She took a step forward. "Did anyone see you?"

Alban frowned back at her. "Are you doubting my word?"

She kept her chin up, refusing to be intimidated. "We just want to clarify the timeline."

"Undoubtedly one of the stable boys can attest to my presence, though I let them sleep. I'll send one to you."

She bobbed a nod. "Thank you."

Alban grunted ungraciously and stalked back into the house, leaving Gwen even more distrusting than she'd been before. Alban might be handsome, though she didn't favor blonds herself, but he wasn't happy. She couldn't see him as the poisoner, and nothing about his life with Caron seemed to indicate anything so radical as murder. But it was plain to Gwen that all was not entirely well at Alban's manor.

14

Evan

"My lord! Sir Robert's death is not something for you to investigate alone." Gareth's voice was raised enough to carry to the far side of the clearing in front of the manor house.

Evan had been lounging in a circle on the grass with Llelo and the other Dragons, but he got instantly to his feet and ran towards the front door, following Gareth, who had entered after Richard. By the time Evan reached the threshold, Gareth had caught the young lord's arm, and the two men were glaring at each other.

Alban didn't live quite like a prince, but Robert's hall was well built. Before Evan had settled in the grass, the Dragons had done a circuit of the holding. The manor's interior consisted of a large main room with a second floor loft, a kitchen off the back, and a master chamber and adjacent room in a ground floor wing to retreat to off the hall. It was smaller than a typical royal llys, but not by much. Admittedly, it was built entirely in wood, without even a palisade, so it had never been intended as a defensible holding. It was to the castle of Dinefwr that the people of this region would retreat if the area came under attack.

Perhaps if he'd lived here, Robert would have paid a few men-at-arms to serve him, but Alban didn't have the wherewithal for that. His duty was steward, not chieftain. Still, Robert was obviously an important man, upon whose lands a hundred people depended.

By the time Evan came halfway across the floor of the hall, Gwen had arrived from the opposite side where the kitchen lay. Richard had halted at Gareth's insistence, but he was clearly struggling to control his temper. His anger may have been feigned earlier, but now his color was high, and he was glaring at Gareth.

But Gareth didn't let go of Richard's arm, and Evan arrived in time to hear Gareth whisper urgently, "Robert was on loan to you. Cadell is his liege lord—and Alban's. This is messy enough without you going in there with your arrow nocked when you don't know the full story."

Gwen hurried closer. "I know you are angry about Robert's death, but you don't want to murder Alban yourself in cold blood only to find he didn't do it!"

Richard didn't quite jerk away, but from his expression he really wanted Gareth to let go of his arm. Evan stepped closer too, mirroring Gwen on Richard's other side. "I have known Alban nearly the whole of my life, and unlike me, he has lived in Deheubarth his entire life. His family is here. His life is here. If he killed Robert, it was because he felt that life threatened. He isn't going to run."

Richard's anger dissipated the more Evan talked, and by the time he stopped speaking, Richard's eyes had turned thoughtful. "I never thought about murder that way before. The only murders in my father's domain I know about have been crimes of passion, perpetrated out of anger and in the spur of the moment."

As Gareth finally released the young lord's arm, Gwen nodded. "Robert's death, coupled with the poisoning up at the castle, is different. Someone has a plan, and we don't want to go trampling all over the evidence when we don't even know yet what that evidence might be. You must see that."

It was in moments like these that Evan understood why Gareth continued to allow Gwen to participate in his investigations. Sometimes she could do and say things a man could not. Richard would never harm a woman, so he listened to her reasoning, whereas Evan and Gareth might have had to wrestle him to the ground. Nothing at all good could have come from that.

Fortunately, Alban had delayed his arrival in the hall until now. Evan had assumed he would seek out Caron when he'd left the porch, but he'd come from his private apartments, prompting Evan to look at him with new respect. Alban could have ventured into the kitchen to see what story Caron had put forth. Instead, he'd ignored the women, as if he couldn't care less what tale his wife told Gwen.

Gareth gestured Alban closer. "Lord Richard tells me that Robert intended to disinherit you and Caron."

Alban blinked, either as surprised as Evan to hear this news or shocked Gareth would mention it. Before he could answer, however, a wail came from the loft, and a middle-aged woman appeared with a crying child of two on her hip and holding the hand of a second child, a girl of six or seven with long dark hair and luminous blue eyes. Alban looked up at them and motioned that the woman should bring the children down. "Caron's in the kitchen. Where are Bedwyn and Rhodri?"

"Mucking out the stables, just like you asked." The woman spoke with a thick south Wales accent. It was Evan's guess that Bedwyn and Rhodri were Alban's two middle sons. The eldest two were already squires in the Dinefwr garrison. Alban would not be of a high enough station for his sons to be fostered out to another lord, as had been initially done with Llelo and Dai. Gareth's boys were back among Hywel's teulu because of Hywel's needs, not because they hadn't deserved to stay with Cynan.

Gareth had asked his question specifically to catch Alban off guard, but the delay had given Alban time to think, and he chose acknowledgement, which on the whole was a wise decision. "I'm not going to pretend I wasn't disappointed to hear Sir Robert's plan."

"So you knew," Gareth said, not as a question. "When did he tell you?"

"Yesterday."

"Were you disappointed ... or angry?" Richard said.

Alban scoffed. "Of course, I was angry, but I didn't kill him! Why would I? He had agreed to give me another chance, at least through Christmas."

That jibed with the fact that his sons were cleaning the stables.

Richard's eyes narrowed. "That isn't what he told me."

"I obviously talked to him after you did."

"When was this?" Gareth asked.

"Last night at the feast before everything fell apart. He told me he'd discussed the inheritance with the abbot, who urged him to give me another chance."

Evan glanced at Gareth, who was frowning. As far as Evan knew, the abbot hadn't said anything to Gareth—but then, he may have felt that to do so would have been a violation of confidence, even after Robert's death.

"Ask Abbot Mathew," Alban urged. "You'll see what I say is true."

"I will," Gareth said.

Then Alban's chin jutted out. "It's one of those Normans you should be looking to for answers. Robert lived among them recently. Obviously he fell in with unsavory folk down south."

Good Norman that he was, Richard looked affronted. Alban had spoken in Welsh, but Richard's family had lived in Wales long enough for him to speak Welsh as easily as French.

Evan wanted to laugh, but he swallowed it down. "Few men have lived as upstanding a life as Robert. It's a hard thing to blame him for his own murder."

Alban looked like he was struggling not to make a sullen retort and ended up saying somewhat lamely. "Well, then it was Barri who did it. He killed Meicol after all. He was sent to Lord Maurice twenty years ago because of what he did to Meicol, and I know Robert was one of those who argued for a harsher punishment than he received."

"Barri didn't kill Meicol, and the rest was a long time ago, Alban," Evan said.

Alban's chin stuck out. "Barri had inquired recently about returning to King Cadell's service, but Robert intervened and counseled against it. You can ask the king what kind of soldier Barri was."

Evan had already spoken to Barri himself, of course, as well as John, Maurice's captain, and Alban's assessment wasn't far off from what he'd already concluded.

"We will question everyone," Gareth said soothingly.

"Are you really suggesting Barri killed Meicol over a twenty-year-old grudge?" Gwen asked.

Alban shrugged. "Meicol didn't kill himself."

"It is my understanding that Meicol served unwaveringly in Dinefwr's garrison since the accident," Evan said.

"Is that what you heard? He was a poor soldier. He knew it too. Just the other day he told me he'd decided to quit. He was going to make a living at his craft instead." Alban scoffed again. "He used to be good, I'll grant you that, but his hands had started to shake, and there were days he could barely hold a knife. Too much drink, to my mind."

Alban's listeners all raised their eyebrows. "Craft?" Gareth said.

Alban swept a hand around the room. "Meicol did the carvings in here, and when you visit his house you'll see how much more he once could do."

"So Meicol had a house." Gareth met Evan's eyes, and his expression was annoyed and sardonic at the same time. "I didn't know."

"That would explain why he had so few possessions at the castle," Gwen said.

Evan gave a low laugh. "I'd just assumed he had few possessions." It was an odd feeling for Evan to be unfamiliar with the situation at Dinefwr. He felt like he should know what was going on, but twenty years removed from living here, he didn't even know the right questions to ask.

Alban was unaware of these undercurrents and simply gestured west, beyond the walls of the manor. "His house lies a mile back closer to the castle. He rents it from Old Nan."

"The blind woman?" Gwen said.

"That's right." Alban nodded vigorously. "The answers you're seeking lie with Meicol and Barri, not with me."

15

Gwen

"I should have kept a better eye on Dai," Llelo said.

Gwen shook her head. "It's hardly your fault he ended up sick. He's responsible for his own choices."

"He likes secrets, does Dai." Llelo looked down at his hands, clenched as they were around his horse's reins. "The more I see the work you and Father do, the more I realize what you're really doing is uncovering other people's secrets."

Gwen had a feeling he'd been wanting to have this conversation with her for a while. It was only a mile or so to Meicol's house, however, and she guessed either he hadn't been able to wait any longer, or he'd wanted their time to talk to be constrained by the short distance they had to ride.

"While you're right in principle, Llelo, Dai sneaking the pie hardly rises to the level of what's been done here, but it's true that once you start keeping secrets, it's hard to stop. They become a habit." She sighed to see Llelo's stricken face. "They're also destructive, not only just because you've done something you feel must be kept secret. Secrets eat you up inside and put up barriers between you and the people you love and from whom you're hiding."

"Sometimes I think Dai keeps secrets because it gives him something that is his and his alone. Nobody can take them from him."

"Perhaps he's learned his lesson this time," Gwen said.

Llelo shook his head ruefully. "I say that every time."

At a signal from Gareth, they halted in front of a steading that looked to Gwen as if it at one time had been prosperous, but now vines trailed up the walls of both the main house and a second building in the rear of the property, and their roofs would need to be patched before the next serious week of rain. The stable was near to falling down as well.

Llelo was seeing it with different eyes, however, and said, "If Meicol had to end up somewhere other than the castle, this is a pretty spot."

Gwen smiled at her son. Despite all he'd been through in his short life, she was glad he could still appreciate a bit of beauty. And he wasn't wrong. Dappled sunshine shone through trees on a grassy meadow full of wildflowers. It was peaceful here, with birds singing, and the sound of the river running close by through the trees that lined the bank.

Perhaps in a winter rainstorm it would be a somewhat less desirable location, given the danger of flooding, but the houses looked as if they'd been standing for half a century, and even in their present condition, might continue to do so for a good while longer.

A well-worn path led from the track they'd come down to a walled garden on the far eastern side of the property. After dismounting, Gwen followed the path. Llelo's long legs caught up in a few strides. "I'd always heard it said that poison is a woman's weapon."

"Not in our experience."

Llelo put a hand on her arm, stopping her before they reached the garden door. "Really? What don't I know?"

Gwen studied him, a hair's-breadth from telling him King Cadell had poisoned one of his spies at the eisteddfod in Aberystwyth last summer. Llelo didn't know about it because he'd been in Gwynedd at that time.

"Ask me again once we're home." She shook her head. "So many men know how to use a blade, and they're bigger and stronger than women, so it's natural to think a woman might resort to poison. But as a weapon, it works just as well for men when they want to be stealthy about it, and when they have time to plan."

The Dragons and Gareth spread out to secure the perimeter of the steading. Not that they expected the culprit to appear out of the woods unannounced, but knowing the terrain was the first step towards not being caught by surprise. Gareth had managed to persuade Richard to send most of his men back to the monastery. Acknowledging that taking an armed company through the countryside might not be the best way to catch a murderer, Richard himself had continued among the Dragons with only two retainers as support, rather than the twenty he'd brought to Alban's house.

The door into the garden had been left open, and, as Gwen took a step inside, the feeling of peacefulness Llelo had felt when they'd first arrived expanded. The garden appeared to be an island of order and tranquility in an otherwise unkempt property. In fact, its beauty and diversity rivaled any garden Gwen had ever seen, whether at a monastery or castle, no matter how rich.

Flowers rioted in the corners and row after row of carefully tended vegetables covered an area forty feet long and more than half that wide. Trees had been cut down around the wall to provide maximum sun exposure. In particular, the northernmost wall, which inside the garden was south-facing, was in full sunlight so the least sturdy plants and tender herbs planted there could stay warm and grow. A small hut was built against the southern wall, where very little sun shone, and the door had been left open to the day's warm air.

It made her a bit unhappy that immediately after appreciating the peacefulness of the location, her next thought was that the poison could have come from here. If so, the hut should show evidence of its making, and she went straight towards it, skirting the many neatly tended beds. The inside of the hut, however, proved to be as neat as the garden, with rows of jars and vials, some of which were nearly identical to the one found in Meicol's bag, though all of the ones before her were empty. While this appeared to be a perfect spot for the poison to have been made, the worktable had been wiped down, and no herbs hung from the ceiling. There was nothing about the to indicate it had been used recently.

Relieved in a way, Gwen returned to the door and closed her eyes, breathing in the scents of mint and apple blossom, mixing with lavender and rose. She opened her eyes again at the tapping of a cane on the flagstone walkway. Old Nan was coming towards her, so Gwen went to intercept her so she wouldn't have to come so far.

Old Nan's smile was beatific. Though her eyes were open, she was looking at a spot a foot to Gwen's right. "So the young lady from Gwynedd has come to see my garden. Gwen, isn't it?"

"How could you possibly know it was me?" Gwen moved nearer, finding herself staring impolitely, though of course as Old Nan couldn't see her, it was the one time it couldn't matter.

Now that Gwen was getting a closer look in broad daylight, Old Nan wasn't as old as all that—and certainly not the ancient crone her name implied. Though her hair was fully gray, with only a few strands of brown remaining, her forehead was relatively unlined, and her teeth were perfect. Her hands showed signs of age—no matter how many creams a woman used, the skin on her hands and neck always gave her age away—but Gwen still wouldn't have put Nan as more than a few years past forty.

Old Nan put her free hand to her ear. "I heard you come in." She turned her head slightly. "I'm glad you find my home peaceful, young man."

Llelo's face colored, but he bowed, even though Old Nan couldn't see it. "Your garden is beautiful too."

By the same instinct that had caused Llelo to bow, Gwen put up a hand, though she immediately brought it down again. "I am here with my husband at the request of King Cadell."

"Who?"

No response could have been more puzzling. "King Cadell? The King of Deheubarth?"

"Oh. Him." The woman jerked her head, her eyes even less focused than before. "The second son." She grunted and turned away, tapping back to a stool set against the south facing wall by a large patch of newly turned earth prepared for planting. She sat, closing her eyes and leaning back against the wall, allowing the sun to shine fully on her face. "I miss King Gruffydd. Now there was a man."

King Gruffydd had died ten years ago, so Gwen tried to revise her estimate of the woman's age, but she still found herself thinking the woman was far too young for senility. Perhaps the blindness was due less to age than a blow to her head, which had also affected her memory.

By now, Gareth had arrived at Gwen's side. "Madam, we're wondering if you would speak to us of a man named Meicol. We understand he lived here." He'd come into the garden holding the sketch he'd drawn of the dead man, but at the sight of Old Nan, he folded it carefully and put it away in his coat.

Old Nan's face fell, and she spoke through sudden tears. "He was a wonderful boy. So helpful around here." She wiped at her cheeks with the back of one hand. "He really is gone? The messenger didn't lie?"

Gwen moved to her and took her hand. "I'm sorry. He is."

Old Nan shook her head. "I was hoping when I woke this morning that I'd dreamt it. King Gruffydd is still alive to me sometimes. Why not Meicol?"

"I'm sorry for your loss."

"I will miss him."

Gwen looked helplessly at Gareth, and then brought the old woman into her arms and let her sob on her shoulder. Old Nan gripped Gwen hard, and Gwen could feel the muscles in her arms and back, evidence of her work in the garden.

Finally her sobs began to wind down. "He wasn't the only one who died last night, was he?"

"No," Gwen said. "I am not from here, so I don't know all the names."

"The king lives?"

"He does."

Old Nan nodded to herself.

Llelo had started to move along the garden paths, peering at one plant or another. "Did Meicol do all this?"

Old Nan managed a small smile. "Much of it. I also have a neighbor boy who does much of the heavy work, but I tend the flowers, of course. You don't have to see well to know what they need."

"I will take you at your word," Gareth said. "Which house was Meicol's?"

"The one in the back."

"For how long was he here?" Gwen said.

"A few years. Back then, I could see more than I do now." Nan gave a low laugh. "I could move better than I do now."

"Do you mind if we take a look around?" Gwen said.

"Of course not, though I don't know why you'd want to, unless—" For the first time, the woman's expression grew concerned. "Why are you here specifically about Meicol? Many died last night, you said."

"He was the first." Gwen squeezed Old Nan's hand, and finally the woman directed her gaze into Gwen's face.

"You are lovely, my dear." She reached up and traced Gwen's cheek with her hand. "I can't see much, but I can see enough to know that."

"You know flowers, Nan," Gareth said. "Do you know anything that might help us find who did this?"

Old Nan blinked. "Did this? What do you mean?"

Gwen bent further so she could look into Old Nan's eyes. "Didn't you hear how they died?"

Old Nan frowned. "Tainted meat, wasn't it? Or milk?" Her eyes narrowed. "I never liked Grygg's chowder."

Grygg was the name of the head cook, now gravely ill himself. Gwen glanced at Gareth, uncertain as to whether or not they should tell Old Nan the truth. Gareth shrugged, and he was probably right that it could hardly matter, since the rest of the residents of Deheubarth either knew the truth or would by the end of the day. "It was poison, Old Nan."

The woman reared back. "You're sure?"

Gwen nodded, and then said, "Yes," as an afterthought. She kept forgetting Old Nan was blind. "It was in the pie, which is why nobody fell ill until late in the meal."

Old Nan nodded. "I left right after I spoke with you." She shook her head. "It was too stuffy in the hall, and the noise was overwhelming. I started walking down the hill, and then Alban and Caron came along and took me the rest of the way. Do you know what the poison was?"

"No," Gwen said. "Something that worked quickly."

"Monkshood?" Old Nan said.

"Perhaps."

Gwen paused, studying the older woman. "You know your herbs."

"Naturally." Old Nan gestured to her garden, implying it should have been obvious. "I know Grygg's pie. He puts currants in it, which would have masked the taste and color of any poison." She frowned as she looked at the ground, and Gwen waited, wondering if she was going to say more. Old Nan's thoughts had matched theirs, and she hoped Nan might have more insight. After a moment, however, Old Nan seemed to realize that Gwen and Gareth were still watching her, and she waved a hand. "Go on into the house. Do what you must. Meicol is past caring."

16

Gareth

Though he'd been about to go anyway, since Old Nan's last words had been a clear dismissal—as well as permission—Gareth turned at the sound of wheels rolling over dirt and stone. A woman pulling a handcart appeared in the pathway below the garden. She was completely focused on her feet and pulled the cart towards Meicol's house without looking up or appearing to notice Gareth in the garden doorway a hundred feet away.

The Dragons had staked out positions around the perimeter of the property, and they watched her with interest, but without moving to intercept her. Since Gareth had convinced Richard to leave the questioning of Old Nan to him and Gwen, he and his men had gone to water their horses at the river.

Then, still without looking up, the woman left the cart a step from the threshold and entered Meicol's house without knocking.

Old Nan frowned and spoke from her spot against the wall. "Was that a cart?"

Gareth turned to her. “Yes. A woman was pulling it. Do you know her?”

“My guess is it’s Meleri. She is Meicol’s friend,” Nan said, her expression sour. “Was.”

“You don’t like her?”

Old Nan shrugged. “There’s nothing to like or not like. She’s simple.”

Gareth turned back in time to see Meleri leave Meicol’s house and finally see the soldiers waiting for her. Even from this distance, he could see her shrink back against the house, cowering in fear. From beside Gareth, Gwen saw it too, and she immediately set off across the grassy expanse that made up the clearing in front of Nan’s house, heading towards the woman.

Meanwhile, Gareth waved off his men. All soldiers had long experience with waiting, and nobody was sorry to have a moment to relax in the sun. Richard was just returning from the river, and his men stretched out on their backs on the grass too, their heads pillowed in a cloak or coat they didn’t need on such a fine day. Gareth would have liked to take a nap himself.

“It’s all right,” Gwen said as she approached the woman.

Gareth came closer as well, making less for the woman than for her cart, which she’d left by the front door, and when he reached it, he pulled back the hemp fabric covering the contents. Meleri possessed a pot and a pan, a fire starter kit, a blanket, a cloak and ... a bound stack of paper that, as he flipped through it, proved to be a book of sketches.

As he looked through it, Meleri stabbed out with her hand. "That's mine! It's wrong to take other people's things or reveal their secrets." The words came out strangely, as if she was quoting what someone else had said to her—and perhaps she was because Meleri's eyes were wide and guileless.

"I won't hurt it." Gareth showed her the way he was handling the pages gently.

Upon closer inspection, Meleri was sun-browned but not scrawny or underfed, and her face was clean. Her brown curly hair was untamed by any scarf or wimple and contained a substantial number of gray strands, but it was brushed and appeared to have been washed recently. She had white, straight teeth as well. Gareth himself had been taught to care for his teeth by the uncle who raised him, and it was the subject of a lecture he gave his men once a year—or whenever one of them fell victim to an abscess. Now, Gareth sucked on his teeth, regretting that, with the urgencies of the day, he'd neglected to partake of the vinegar and mint mouthwash he endeavored to use every morning.

He had met people like Meleri over the years. Their bodies grew but their minds did not. Often, however, they had a single gift. Some could do sums; others could play an instrument with exquisite beauty. Meleri, it seemed, could draw.

With gentle hands, Gwen took the book from him and indicated with a tip of her head that he should move a few paces away. "It's all right, Meleri. We aren't here to hurt you or take your things."

Then Gwen's eyes went to the open page in front of her, and what she saw gave her as much pause as it had given Gareth. This particular sketch was of Old Nan. Gareth worked mostly in charcoal, conveying in a few strokes the likeness of a person. What Meleri had drawn, if this was indeed her doing, was a more complete picture, employing color and an instrument other than a simple piece of charcoal to show Nan seated on a bench underneath a trellis of red roses.

"Did you draw this?" Gwen turned the book to show Meleri. "It's beautiful."

Meleri smiled beatifically, apparently forgiving them their trespass.

Gwen handed the book back to Gareth and spoke to Meleri as if she were a small child. "Why did you come here today?"

"I was looking for Meicol."

"When did you last see him?"

"I don't know."

"Was it before or after the battle against the Flemings?"

Meleri's brow furrowed. Gareth had seen such an expression on Tangwen's face many times as she thought hard. "After."

"Come sit here." Gwen moved Meleri out of the direct line of sight of the men on the green, going with her instead to a bench set against the side of Meicol's house. Meleri was clearly was uncomfortable in the presence of so many people, and they didn't want her to freeze up completely.

"Where is he?" Meleri asked once she was seated.

Gwen put a gentle had on her arm. "He's dead, Meleri."

Meleri blinked her eyes rapidly. "He isn't coming back?"

Now Gwen put an arm around her shoulders. "We came here in hopes of finding some answers to what happened to him. You are the first person to come to his house since he died. Can you tell us anything about who might have wanted to hurt him?"

But Meleri wasn't listening anymore. She had bent forward, and was rocking back and forth and weeping. Then Evan appeared at Gareth's back. "I can tell you right now Meleri is no killer."

"You know her?"

"Of course I know her." Evan's voice was a harsh whisper. "She grew up here, just like the rest of us. She's Alban's cousin." Evan looked past Gareth to where Meleri sat. "If she was friends with Meicol, that was kind of him."

"That he'd befriend her surprises you?" Gareth said.

"As you know, I didn't like Meicol. Nobody did."

"Except, apparently, Old Nan and Meleri."

Evan gestured helplessly. "You see her. She's always been like this. Trusting."

"Would you like to talk to her?"

"I suppose I could. Perhaps she'll remember me." Evan found an overturned bucket near the woodpile and brought it over so he could sit on it in front of Meleri, though making sure not to get too close in case his proximity frightened her.

Gwen, meanwhile, went to her saddle bag and took out a small loaf of bread wrapped in a cloth and a hunk of cheese half the size of her fist. She came back to where Meleri was sitting and placed them in Meleri's lap. "Eat."

Meleri looked at the food for a heartbeat, and then her eyes went to Gareth's face. The eagerness in her expression had his stomach clenching. She was asking his permission. He felt like he'd kicked the puppy they'd acquired to entertain Tangwen at Aberystwyth while they were away. "Go on."

Meleri set to the food with a will that Gareth had seen in few people outside one of his sons after they hadn't eaten all day—or Rhodri, perhaps, one of the men in Hywel's teulu, who still ate like a man twenty years younger. He wasn't pleased to see the weeping rash on Meleri's hands either, and he made a note to himself to speak to Saran about it. Some people got rashes in the spring when new flowers bloomed, and he'd always been thankful he wasn't one of them.

Evan lifted a hand to gain Meleri's attention. "Do you remember me?"

Meleri stopped in mid bite to look at him. "Evan." She continued chewing.

"That's right. I haven't seen you for many years."

In Gareth's experience, few thirty-five-year-old men bore much resemblance to their eighteen-year-old selves, while many women were fully mature by that age. Meleri, however, had recognized Evan easily.

Meleri swallowed. "You went away. Everybody went away."

"I'm sorry." Evan glanced at Gareth, who made a motion with his hand that he should continue. "Did you know someone beat Meicol before he died?"

Meleri frowned. "Someone hit him?"

"A few days ago," Evan said. "Do you know who that could have been?"

Meleri shook her head, looking genuinely confused.

Gwen handed Evan the book of drawings, open to a page showing Meicol preparing to mount a horse. "Did you draw this?" He turned the book to show her.

Meleri nodded, and then Evan flipped through the book to another sketch. "It seems you've seen Barri recently too. This could have been drawn yesterday."

Meleri spoke around a full mouth. "I saw Barri arguing with Alban in the lane."

"Do you know what they were fighting about?"

Meleri shrugged.

Evan kept his patience, presumably used to how she communicated. "How did you even know they were arguing?"

"Because they held their shoulders like he is—" she pointed to Gareth, "—and they were right in each other's faces."

"Did they see you?"

"No. I was in the woods."

"And then what happened?"

Meleri shrugged again. "I went back to my room."

"At Alban's manor?" Evan asked.

Meleri nodded.

"Is there anything else you can tell us about Meicol?" Gwen said.

"It's wrong to take other people's things or reveal their secrets." It was exactly what Meleri had said before.

Gwen asked gently. "Who told you that?"

"Everybody says it."

"Caron?"

Meleri shrugged.

Evan handed Meleri her sketchbook and stood. "Can I have someone take you home?"

Meleri shook her head. "No. I know the way."

17

Gareth

The door to Meicol's house squeaked open. Gareth was reminded of entering Wena's hut with Llelo, back when the boy was sure it was haunted. Llelo was right behind him this time too, but he didn't jump. Instead, his eyes were alight, and he grinned. "Same tune, different castle, as Grampa Meilyr likes to say," clearly remembering that day too.

"What are we talking about?" Richard de Clare was right behind them. He had thankfully left the questioning of Old Nan and Meleri to Gareth and Gwen, but he refused to be left out of anything else.

Llelo glanced over his shoulder. "I was referring to another investigation my father and I were involved in, my lord."

Richard's eyes narrowed. "How many have there been?"

Gareth laughed under his breath. "Too many."

The house consisted of a single room, twenty feet on a side, which was more than adequate for a single man. A large bed took up the center of the room—and it was quite a bed. It was worthy, in fact, of a lord, with ornately carved posts and headboard. The floor was wooden and as highly polished as that of Sir Robert's manor.

In addition to the ornately carved bed, a long table lay against a side wall. Around it sat three chairs, each as elaborate as the bed, and a match to the chairs back at Sir Robert's manor. Meicol appeared to have had a whimsical side that had not been apparent until now, in that the animal models he'd used for these were less traditional: a duck, a mouse, a rabbit. The table itself was covered with whittled carvings, ranging in size from an inch-high frog to a two-foot magnificent hart.

"Meicol loved wood, didn't he?" Llelo said.

"And had an artistry fit for a king." Richard trailed his hand around the doorframe, which had been carved to look like an ivy trellis. "Why was he a lowly man-at-arms with this kind of skill?"

"According to everyone I've spoken to, he was a drunkard and could no longer hold a steady knife," Gareth said.

"It's quite a contrast to the outside of the building, isn't it?" Gwen entered with Evan. She left the door open, but the light coming through wasn't enough to allow them to see well, so she lit a lantern that had been left on a the table and raised it high.

Evan rubbed his chin. "From the outside, it resembles the barn that guards the entrance to—" he stopped abruptly with a baleful glance at Richard.

Gareth didn't need him to finish his sentence to know to what he was referring: the barn that guarded the entrance to the tunnel into Aber Castle.

"You're right, Evan." He glanced at his friend. "Perhaps too much?"

Evan grinned. "We're looking for secrets, aren't we?" He rubbed his hands together. "It would be my pleasure." He began to circle the room.

Gwen followed close on his heels, still with the lantern. But though Evan knocked on the walls and stamped his feet on the floor, there didn't seem anything out of place or unusual—beyond the obvious oddity of the presence of so many carvings.

As Richard had done a moment ago with the doorframe, Gwen stroked her hand along the length of one of the hart's antlers. "I'll raise my voice to the question too. Why would he hide all this away?"

"I see you've found his secret." Old Nan's voice came from the doorway. "Meicol was a dear boy, and he loved animals. He loved wood too. Everything here he made himself."

"We have seen that," Gareth said. "Sir Robert seemed to be one of the few to benefit from his skill."

Old Nan tapped her way unerringly to the table. She put out a hand, gently moving it until she hit upon one of the carvings, this one a hedgehog. She picked it up and lovingly petted it. "He occasionally worked for others, but—" she shrugged, "—he was deemed unreliable."

"Did he have any kin, any family who might cherish what he left behind?" Gwen said.

Old Nan was shaking her head before Gwen finished speaking. "No." And then she amended, "Not that he ever said."

Always kind, Gwen put a hand on Nan's arm. "Again, I am very sorry for the loss of your friend."

"I suppose these all belong to King Cadell now, as his liege lord," Gareth said.

"I suppose." Nan canted her head. "Perhaps you could ask him if I could keep one or two?"

Gareth bowed, even knowing she couldn't see him. "Of course."

She nodded and departed, followed by Richard, though not before he made a disgusted grunt that there was nothing else to find. A moment later, however, he poked his head back inside. "Sir Gareth, I think you should get out here."

Gareth went to the door to find a company of a dozen horsemen approaching, led by Barri, having come down the track from the main road. Meleri had dragged her cart towards the garden and, to Gareth's surprise, Old Nan gestured her inside. Meleri gave an anxious glance back, but none of the newcomers had any thought for her.

Instead, Barri dismounted, the only one of his men to do so. The Dragons and Richard's two men were all on foot, but they formed a defensive arc in front of Meicol's house. Their hands were on their swords, and Cadoc, the archer, had gone so far as to pull his bow from its rest on his back, though he hadn't yet drawn an arrow from his quiver.

Barri put out his hands in an appeasing manner. "We're all friends here, aren't we?" Then at the sight of Gareth, who moved between two of the Dragons, his expression turned to one of relief. "I'm not here to cause trouble. I promise!"

"What are you here for, Barri?" Richard said, as was his right as the highest-ranking person present.

"To speak to Sir Gareth, of course," Barri said. "My lord, Maurice, wanted an update on the investigation, and he sent me to bring Sir Gareth back to the castle to discuss it."

Gareth studied Barri, just short of narrowing his eyes at him. Cadoc, however, was far less accommodating. "Where's your captain?"

"John remains with Lord Maurice, as is his duty," Barri said. "Since I know the area, my lord thought he'd save time over sending someone who might get lost."

Gareth glanced to the west where Dinefwr castle was clearly visible on its mountain. He was inclined to agree with Cadoc that Barri had an ulterior motive for coming here. He wasn't even second-in-command of Maurice's company—though it was true he knew the area, having grown up here. Gareth would be interested to know whose idea it was to send a company at all, rather than wait for Gareth to return with news of the investigation in his own time.

Then, to add to the oddness of the situation, another company of men rode into the clearing, this one led by Prince Rhys, who dismounted and walked forward to stand a few feet from Barri, beside him but not with him. His eyes swept suspiciously over Barri's company before he directed his attention to Gareth.

"My brother asks that you return to Dinefwr. He has learned that Sir Robert has been murdered and is concerned that you have not spoken to him of your findings." Distrust radiated from him, and Gareth had no notion as to its source. Rhys had treated Gareth with nothing but respect up until now, but his eyes were hooded, and there was no friendliness in him.

"I would have sought him out sooner," Gareth said, "but I believed him too ill to hear me."

"He is better now," Rhys said shortly.

Gareth had been ready to leave to return to the castle anyway, but he didn't tell Rhys that. It was important to know just how far Rhys would go to ensure that Gareth did his bidding. "I have just a few more things—"

Rhys cut him off, answering Gareth's question. "My brother would speak to you now." And at his sharp words, the hands of every one of Rhys's twenty men went to the hilts of their swords, though they didn't draw them.

"This is mad," Evan said from Gareth's right shoulder.

"But informative," Gareth said in an undertone. He studied the young prince, realizing that he himself was entirely unconcerned about this new development. Gareth had been accused of wrongdoing by far more threatening men than this boy—or Cadell, for that matter. And this time, he wasn't here on his own. He had the Dragons at his back, as well as young Richard. Nobody was throwing him in a cell today. "What changed? Why am I now so distrusted?"

Rhys lifted his chin. "My brother has done an accounting and found that only one man from Gwynedd fell ill last night."

"I know," Gareth said. "You are speaking of my son."

Rhys pressed his lips together for a moment, and Gareth realized he hadn't known it was Dai.

So Gareth added, "Do you really think I would sacrifice my own son in a less-than-sure attempt to murder King Cadell?"

Rhys took in a breath through his nose. "No, but Prince Hywel might."

"You should be ashamed of yourself—and King Cadell too." Gwen stepped between Cadoc and Steffan. "It was Cadell who asked Gareth to investigate Meicol's death. Gareth didn't even want to do it. We are not responsible for this tragedy, and it is wrong of you or your brother to suggest it. What could you possibly be thinking?"

Gareth put out a hand to her. "It is easier to blame a stranger, Gwen, than look close to home."

Gwen turned on him, and she was as angry as he'd ever seen her. "What did they do—convince themselves that *we* killed Meicol and planted that vial of poison on him after he was dead?"

Rhys's eyes widened, telling Gareth that was exactly what his brother supposed.

Gwen laughed without humor and turned back to Rhys, who was suddenly looking a little nervous. Gwen pointed at Gareth. "He is the most honorable man you will ever meet, and if you don't know that, even on short acquaintance, then you don't deserve to call yourself a prince!"

She stomped forward, and for a moment Rhys recoiled, perhaps fearing she might actually hit him. Instead she passed him and went to her horse. Llelo was right behind her, and he boosted her up before mounting his own horse.

From the saddle, Gwen glared at the thirty men gaping at her. "What are you waiting for? Come on. The sooner we dispense with this ridiculous accusation, the better!"

Gareth decided the time had come to intervene. Gwen had done an excellent job of playing the angry investigator—even though she hadn't been playing. Now it was his turn to soften her blows. He stepped nearer to the young prince. "You're smarter than this, Rhys. Don't let anyone else do your thinking for you."

"You might as well accuse me." Richard had been holding back, but now he approached too. "Few of my men are ill." He gestured to Barri. "And only a handful of the Fitzgeralds as well. Why is Cadell's ire not directed at us?"

Gareth lowered his voice even further. "I do not have anything close to the answers yet, but there is more here than it appears. Under the circumstances, I think it far more likely that your brother has a traitor in his midst, one who serves King Stephen, perhaps?"

Rhys looked away, not ready to concede anything. Meanwhile, Evan nudged Gareth in the back and spoke in a low voice only Gareth could hear. "You don't have to do this. Rhys has put us on notice that Dinefwr is now enemy territory."

Gareth turned to look at his friend. It was frustrating how since Meicol died they'd barely finished one aspect of the investigation before they were confronted with another. Still, Rhys was right that King Cadell deserved an accounting. "You're not wrong, Evan. And yet, I have to wonder what this is really all about."

"What do you mean?"

"Any soldier knows that a man reveals himself most when he is under duress." He pointed with his chin to the men who had come for them. Between Barri and Rhys, they'd brought several dozen. "All this to corral me? Why?"

Evan's eyes narrowed, and he made a *huh* sound at the back of his throat. "Because you're getting too close to something they'd rather you didn't know about—just like we did at Wiston's keep?

"All this does is make me want to know about it more."

18

Hywel

As Cadell paced around his hall, irritated and muttering to himself, Hywel studied him with an inward amusement he made sure didn't manifest on his face. Hywel had enough experience with Cadell by now to know he was too ruthless by half. He didn't like any of these kings of Deheubarth. And—contrary to what one might assume—he'd discovered that the longer he spent in their company, the easier it was to hide his distrust.

Since his revelation on the wall-walk, he'd found himself slipping more and more into to his old role of spy—a role he'd relished for ten years before Rhun's death. It was as if he was living a double life, and there were two of him occupying the same space: the spy and the edling. It reminded him of something Gwen had said to him about how he didn't need to *be* Rhun, or replace him. He would be his own kind of edling, and he was astonished to find himself, for the first time since he'd lost his brother, comfortable in his own skin.

Hywel thought one reason Cadell had given the job of investigating these deaths to Gareth was out of a kind of bravado, as a way to show he was so confident in his men and his rule that he could allow a stranger to probe into a dark moment. But it was a dangerous game he was playing, and it was almost as if the more Gareth headed down the path his inquiries led him on, the more Cadell lobbed boulders onto it to bar his way and deter him from digging up whatever else he wanted to know.

And yet, even with the poisonings and murder, Hywel wasn't yet at the point that he was regretting his alliance with Cadell, though he was well on the way to doubting it. Truth be told, he'd had doubts from the start. Four years ago when his uncle Cadwaladr had conspired with Cadell to have Cadell's brother, Anarawd, murdered, Hywel had given free rein to his aversion to an alliance between Gwynedd and Deheubarth. That aversion had stuck with him through Cadell's crowning and had grown with every hour he'd spent with the new King of Deheubarth.

Cadell was a man who did what was expedient. He'd allied with Cadwaladr because it benefited him. He'd eliminated that merchant at Hywel's eisteddfod because he'd become a liability, and he had sent his spy, Anselm, north to meddle in Gwynedd's affairs because the information was worth having, even if Anselm was caught. Which he had been. Cadell had also laid down a challenge, and the last thing he should expect was for either Gareth or Hywel to back away from it.

To be fair, Hywel had made a similar compromise in allying with Cadell to take down Walter the Fleming because it had seemed like a good idea at the time. But when Evan had told Hywel what had happened during the attack on Wiston Castle, the suspicion he was being played for a fool had shouldered its way to the fore. Before Hywel had committed them all to the fight, Gareth had pressed Hywel to consider *why* Cadell had invited him to this endeavor in the first place. Every reason they could think of pointed to a nefarious ulterior motive.

And Hywel had agreed to it anyway.

What kept him here now wasn't a sense of obligation to Cadell. Nor was it because he'd agreed to loan him Gareth to head up the investigation and wouldn't want to abort the task with it undone. It certainly wasn't because he feared the consequences of leaving. Hywel would have been pleased to thumb his nose at Cadell if the circumstances had been right. No ... it was, quite frankly, *curiosity*. Hywel liked to know what was going on, and he was happy to loan out Gareth so he would.

The whole scenario, in fact, had sent him thinking along lines where distrust and suspicion were his paramount emotions. It had been Sir Robert who'd led that charge up the motte, overtaking Hywel's Dragons and preventing them from entering the keep, and now Sir Robert was dead. Hywel didn't know what the two events had to do with one another, but he was long past starting to wonder how much more there was that he and Gareth were not being told.

Maurice sat tipped back in a chair near the hearth, his hands clasped behind his head. He seemed awfully comfortable for a man who'd more often been enemy than ally to his cousin. Or he was as good as Hywel at feigning allegiance. Then Maurice's head turned to see Hywel watching him, and he surprised Hywel by winking. Hywel coughed a laugh, knowing that whatever his thoughts were about this Norman lord, they might well be very far from the truth.

Then the door behind Hywel opened, and he turned to see Gareth, Gwen, and Hywel's Dragons coming through it. Hywel's eyes narrowed to see how much they looked like prisoners rather than allies, but Gareth signaled to him in their personal sign language that all was well—for now.

The front legs of Maurice's chair hit the floor, and he stood to greet them, but Cadell was not nearly so friendly.

"You!" He focused on Gareth as he walked towards him. He'd been striding around the hall just fine for the last quarter of an hour, but he hadn't gone five steps before his hand went to his stomach, and he wobbled.

Putting animosity aside, Hywel leapt forward and grabbed the king by the shoulders, setting him down heavily on a nearby bench before he toppled over onto the floor. "You shouldn't even be out of bed."

"Brother!" Likewise, Prince Rhys sprang from Gareth's side, but when he saw Hywel had caught Cadell, he grabbed a pitcher of mead from the sideboard and poured the drink into a cup.

"I'm well enough. Recovering anyway." Cadell made a motion as if to brush Hywel's concerns away, but then Rhys arrived with the cup, which Cadell accepted. He cleared his throat, his voice stronger, and directed his attention again to Gareth. "Tell me what you've discovered."

Gareth's lips twisted. "Am I not under arrest?"

"Of course not," Cadell barked. "Why would you think so?"

Gareth looked first to Rhys and then to Barri. Neither man met his eyes. Hywel wanted to know what had happened that had his captain struggling to control his temper, but instead he just nodded his head at Gareth.

Gareth gave him a wry smile and then complied: "The facts are simple on the surface. Your man, Meicol, died on this very floor of what we believe to be poison. In the course of searching his satchel, we found a suspicious vial, at the time unopened. Unfortunately, it was not the only vial, as it seems poison was introduced into the ingredients of the pie, probably through the currants, sickening many people in the hall, some to death."

"And you're sure the same poison was used in the hall as killed Meicol?" Cadell asked.

"Nausea and vomiting are unspecific symptoms, but this poison blisters the mouth, a side effect both Meicol and those in the hall experienced."

"What does the healer say?"

"He's never seen anything like it," Gareth said. "Saran cannot at this time name it either."

Hywel refrained from asking Cadell what poison he'd put into the wine bottle that had killed the merchant in Aberystwyth. Now was not the time to confront Cadell with it.

Cadell grunted, but his discontent was directed at the circumstances, not at Gareth, who went on. "Meanwhile, Sir Robert was murdered near midnight in the graveyard at St. Dyfi's. He was struck on the back of the head, indicating that he never saw death coming. Either that or he'd met his killer in the graveyard and trusted him enough to turn away."

"Is one conclusion that Meicol poisoned everyone in the hall, but mishandled the poison so he died himself?" Maurice said.

"We don't know, my lord," Gareth said. "A moment ago, Prince Rhys accused me of planting the vial on Meicol. Obviously, we did not do that, but you could as easily conjecture that Meicol stole the vial from whoever did poison the hall, in an attempt to stop him from poisoning anyone else—not realizing it was already too late."

"You would think, if that were the case," Maurice said, "he would have said something to the king—or at least to his captain."

Gareth lifted one shoulder. "The vial was sealed. That is all I can say."

Hywel stepped forward. "As you can see, my lords, we have theories, but no hard evidence." He looked at Gareth. "Meicol was also beaten a few days before he died."

Gareth nodded. "We also can't find Sir Robert's horse, which he was seen leading out of the church stables in the midnight hour. I have been to Sir Robert's manor and Meicol's dwelling." He fixed his eyes on Cadell. "It is your man, Alban, of course, who has the most to gain from Robert's death, but so far, I have found nothing to implicate him other than motive. There was also nothing at Meicol's house to indicate he had knowledge of herbs or concocted potions."

"He was a woodworker. And a good one," Gwen said, speaking for the first time.

"I concur with Sir Gareth, as I was present throughout his investigation this afternoon." Richard de Clare had been hanging back while his elders talked, but he came forward now, and his attitude was not conciliatory. "It was a mistake to summon him back to the castle before he was ready to return."

Neither Maurice nor Cadell responded to Richard's admonition, but Barri, who to Hywel's mind should have been far more reticent, snorted his disbelief. "I'd be happy to point the finger at Meicol if it would get this over with more quickly, but I have to say, he was never a great thinker. A plot of this complexity would have been far beyond him. Though—" he tipped his head, "—bringing a man down from behind would have been within range of his abilities."

Cadell sighed. "I would have to agree, though, of course, the man was already dead before Robert was killed." The king closed his eyes and leaned his head back against the wall. Cadell really couldn't be feeling well and shouldn't have been out of bed after his close call with death last night. Hywel couldn't suppress a tinge of admiration for him for persevering. "To be fair, it's a hard thing to blame a man for his own murder."

Maurice waved a hand airily. "I'm sorry I summoned you, Sir Gareth. Keep at it, if you will."

Cadell grunted his assent. "I'm for bed." He allowed Rhys to help him up, and then, with another man-at-arms on his other side, limped away.

While Richard moved to speak to Maurice, Hywel motioned with his head that Gwynedd should take the conversation outside. Darkness was coming on, and with Cadell off to bed, Hywel wouldn't be expected back inside again tonight. Once in the courtyard, to the right of the main steps where he was sure they could not be overheard, he turned to Gareth. "Is that really all you have?"

"Of course not." Gareth gave Hywel a more complete summary of finding Richard at Robert's manor, Alban and Caron's testimony, and their conversation with Old Nan. Then he looked away for a moment, frowning.

"What is it?" Hywel said.

"Evan looked at Meicol's house and thought of the barn at Aber," he said, "but that observation could equally apply to Alban's manor. It was somewhat neglected on the outside, but spotless on the inside."

Hywel nodded. "Which could mean Alban isn't lazy so much as hiding something."

"It could just be the difference between Caron's proclivities and Alban's," Gwen pointed out. "As the lady of the manor, the inside is her charge."

Llelo poked his nose into their little circle. "If I may, my lord, you'll notice too that at neither place did we really have free rein to look at everything. Richard was at the manor, and Barri and Rhys interrupted us at Meicol's house." Hywel was pleased with how Llelo had grown into an upstanding young man, so much like Gareth in so many ways that Hywel usually forgot Gareth was not his natural sire.

Gareth agreed. "I think it's worth going back to find out what we missed." This was the grind of solving a murder. It was one thing to find a body. It was quite another to meticulously put the pieces together to discover a murderer. And in this instance, they might even have two. Hywel couldn't believe the deaths of Sir Robert, Meicol, and the poisoning of the residents of the castle weren't all intimately related.

So he grinned. "Good thing we're staying down at the monastery. You can go back to Alban's manor first thing tomorrow—and how about this time we don't tell anyone else what you're doing."

19

Angharad

Angharad sat in the kitchen nook, sharing a cask of sweet mead with Evan—one that he'd brought from Gwynedd's own stores. She didn't see how it could be anything but difficult for the residents of Dinefwr, her among them, to eat food prepared here again. They were having to, however, and her uncle had already installed a serf to taste anything and everything that came out of the kitchen. It was standard practice for lords and kings in England, but never in Wales, where hospitality was sacrosanct.

She glanced at Evan, wondering if he was thinking the same thoughts and if he resented sitting with her instead of going off this morning with Gareth and the other Dragons. Hywel too had come to the castle, however, and Evan had said simply that someone had to come with him, and it might as well be him.

The plan of the day was to make better headway questioning the residents of the castle than they'd had time for yesterday. To that end, Evan had enlisted Angharad to help, something she was only too happy to do—and even more happy to do with Evan. He had reached that age when, in Angharad's opinion, men grew into their own. He was sure of himself but without a need to boast about his accomplishments. He was a knight and second-in-command of the Dragons. It was obvious Prince Hywel trusted him.

The only problem was that she was having trouble not getting lost whenever she met his gaze. Those green eyes of his drew her in, and it always took a moment or two longer than it should for her to remember herself and look away.

Before sitting in the kitchen, Evan had given Angharad a summary of where they were with the investigation so far. It made her think not only was she trusted too, but that she knew as much as or maybe even more than her uncle. Still, while Angharad hadn't participated in any investigations before, other than peripherally in Aberystwyth, she had the idea Evan hadn't quite told her everything. It occurred to her Evan and Hywel were here to distract her uncle from the fact that Gareth wasn't.

So she took a guess. "Gareth isn't really just questioning the monks this morning, is he?"

Evan turned to look at her, and she felt again that he, unlike most men, was really seeing *her*. Most men dismissed her as a pretty face. Her uncle certainly couldn't have cared less about her now that Rhun was dead and he couldn't marry her off to a prince. The sons of the King of Powys were still too young for marriage, at least to her, and the older she grew, the less likely it was that an advantageous marriage could be arranged.

Before Evan could answer, however, the undercook sat heavily across from them. He sighed deeply and rested his head in one hand, elbow on the table. "I can't believe the poisoned food came from *this* kitchen!"

His name was Sior, and he was a thickset man in his early thirties with red curly hair cut close to his head, the better to keep it out of his eyes and the food. He had what Angharad perceived to be a prematurely bulbous nose from excessive drinking, so she wasn't quite as disbelieving about the unlikelihood of his food being poisoned as he. He'd been drinking too much yesterday, as he did every day, and couldn't have been as observant as if he'd been sober. His eyes were bloodshot too, but that could have easily been from weeping and lack of sleep.

"What can you tell us about what happened last night?" Evan said, starting off with a question that was in no way meant to be accusatory.

The cook took it badly anyway. "I don't know. I didn't see anyone or anything suspicious. My own wife is ill. Don't you think I'd tell you if I knew anything?"

Gareth had done an initial questioning of the kitchen staff last night, but many had been ill, and nobody had recalled anyone they didn't know entering the kitchen. It was time to ask about people they did know, which Angharad knew without being told would be more difficult. Gwen and Prince Hywel were interviewing other servants who were still alive, and the four of them would compare answers when they were done. This was the last servant Evan and Angharad had to question, and he was the only cook still on his feet. The castle's servants had lost more than half their number, casualties in a war they hadn't known they were fighting.

Evan pushed a cup of mead closer to Sior, who looked at it balefully before reaching for it and taking a sip.

"You were here all day?" Angharad said.

"You know I was, my lady. All day. All night."

"And the cook made the pie personally?"

"Yes! Yes! I had nothing to do with it. I never do. He won't let me touch it."

Angharad put her hand gently over Sior's. "We are not accusing you of any wrongdoing. You are only confirming what Grygg said." She gestured to herself and Evan. "We too did not eat the pie and did not fall ill. We aren't accusing Grygg either, since he would hardly have poisoned himself."

Evan nudged Angharad with his elbow and gave her a meaningful look. She looked at him, puzzled, and then he leaned in to whisper in her ear, "That might not be true."

She gaped at him for a moment, but then narrowed her eyes at the implications of what he'd said. She didn't believe it.

Her expression must have said as much, because Evan cleared his throat and returned his focus to Sior. "Can you name three people who were not servants who passed through the kitchen yesterday?"

The undercook put a fist to his lips as he thought. "Lady Angharad, here, looking for mead for your uncle; Caron and Alban, escorting Old Nan—" he leaned in and whispered conspiratorially, "—she likes her wine, does Old Nan. She sat a while right here, chatting with Grygg while Caron and Alban went off; Saran and the healer, arguing about a remedy; and Prince Rhys, sneaking cheese and bread, like he does every day." He shook his head. "There were a dozen others, plus all the extra help we brought in from the village." He looked down at his cup. "Most of them are dead or ill."

But out of the people he'd named, none were ill, herself included. Angharad folded her hands in her lap and opted for flattery. "You know Caron and Alban perhaps better than I. Can you tell me about them?"

Sior sneered. "Alban." Then he looked hastily down at his cup, realizing how much he'd given away with that one word. The mead had loosened his tongue, and his resistance was down anyway thanks to his illness.

Angharad tried to keep her expression serene. "Why don't you like him?"

Sior's jaw clenched, and he didn't look up. "You didn't hear it from me."

"Tell us," Evan said.

"We aren't accusing Alban of anything," Angharad said soothingly. "We're just trying to understand what might have happened. I wasn't raised at Dinefwr, and though I've lived here for two years, I don't know the history."

"Have you heard already that the child Caron is carrying isn't Alban's?"

Angharad blinked. This was not a topic than would normally be discussed in front of her, an unmarried woman. Sior really must be drunk. Even Evan, who carried an air of unflappability about him and an immunity to the mischief people got up to, looked surprised. She found herself stuttering, "I had not heard that. Whose is it if not Alban's?"

"Sir Robert's."

"His own niece?" Evan eased back against the wall behind them, as disappointed as she. With Sir Robert dead, such an accusation would be impossible to prove or disprove—though it did give Alban yet another motive for murder.

"They were no blood relation. She was the daughter of his wife's brother." Sior made a dismissive gesture with one hand. "It has to be him. Rumor has it he's had a woman on the side for years, but he would never produce her. She has to be married."

Angharad had heard no rumor of a woman for Sir Robert either. "That doesn't mean his lover is Caron. You must have more evidence than that."

"Everyone knows Caron has been unhappy with her life with Alban. He has not advanced in a way either of them wanted."

Angharad nodded. "That I do know. He expected to be captain of the king's guard by now."

Sior wrinkled his nose. "This Cadfan is an outsider, not one raised or trained at Dinefwr, but it was he who was chosen as captain last year."

"He is very ill today," Evan said.

Sior's eyes widened. "All the more reason to think Alban did this! In one day he gets the manor free and clear and eliminates his rival!"

Evan rubbed his chin. "We are exploring every option."

That was a vague answer if Angharad ever heard one, and she admired Evan's ability to speak the line with a straight face. "You really don't like Alban, do you, Sior? Why? What's he to you?"

Sior grumbled under his breath, but then he said, "I was undercook at the manor since I was a boy until Alban fired me. He said I stole food from him. I didn't!" He was suddenly all outrage.

"When was this?" Evan asked.

"A few years ago." Sior pointed with his chin to Angharad. "Before your time but after Alban came back from the war in England. It changed him, made him short of temper and secretive."

"War can do that to a man." Evan spoke straightforwardly, but Angharad could tell there was a tale there. Someday, she hoped to hear it. "How many men of Dinefwr went to Oxford?"

"A small army, led by Cadell. Anarawd was king at the time, and they marched off in alliance with the Fitzgeralds, in service of King Stephen, who was besieging the castle."

Both Angharad and Evan nodded. It was the same string of allegiances that had been broken this spring: Cadell was cousin to Maurice and William, who served the Earl of Pembroke, who had been loyal to Stephen. Angharad didn't know what Anarawd had hoped to get out of giving men to Earl Gilbert to fight in England, but land and loyalty were the coin of noblemen. The kings of Deheubarth had always been expert in calculating their worth. A year earlier, Cadwaladr of Gwynedd had made a different calculation and had joined Empress Maud, following Earl Ranulf of Chester and his father-in-law, Robert of Gloucester, to besiege Lincoln Castle.

Evan leaned in. “If you have any other thoughts as to who could have done this, please come find me or Sir Gareth.”

The undercook nodded. “Yes, my lord.”

“Thank you for speaking with us.” Angharad said—though, as they left the kitchen, she added for Evan’s ears, “I don’t know if I believed a word he said.”

“Lies can be as informative as truths,” Evan said.

“So you don’t think Sir Robert is the father of Caron’s child either?”

“That wouldn’t be the Sir Robert I knew. People can live secret lives nobody else knows about, but this would be quite a secret.”

Angharad nodded. They were outside now, and the sun was warm on her shoulders. “I think we all live a secret life in the quiet of our beds at night.”

Evan smiled as he looked down at her. “Even you?”

“Why not me?” Angharad lifted her chin, spying Hywel and Gwen coming towards them with quick steps, likely anxious to know if they’d discovered anything. “What I am more willing to believe is the existence of a woman, even if that woman isn’t Caron.”

"I agree." Evan continued to look at her, though she had looked away, knowing she had revealed herself to him in a way she'd done with few others in her life.

Instead she said, "Of all the things he could have told us, if we are to know the truth about Robert's death, that's the thread we need to pull."

20

Gwen

Normally, Hywel encouraged Gareth and Gwen to focus on the evidence and let the *why* of a murder take care of itself, but today Gwen found herself wanting a motive, if only to narrow down the pool of candidates. It couldn't really be *anyone* who had the means and desire to poison an entire castle full of people. That's why they'd started another round of questioning, even to the point of enlisting Angharad and Evan to help. Gareth had thought the pair had done a good job together questioning Barri, and there were just too many people in the castle for her and Hywel to question alone.

She was glad too that Hywel seemed to have encompassed the fact that Angharad was enjoying Evan's company, despite having once been betrothed to Rhun, and was speaking to her like a friend.

"Let's start with Alban," Hywel said to Angharad and Evan. "What have you learned?"

Evan made a motion with his head. "Angharad and I learned little more than before. As you know, the consensus twenty years ago was that Alban was the best of us, and he's obviously done well for himself—up to a point."

"If you'll note, it is Alban's marriage to Caron, rather than his own efforts, that has brought him the most gain," Angharad said.

Evan nodded. "Sior resents Alban for letting him go as cook, and he straight out accused Alban of poisoning everyone in the castle."

Hywel rubbed his chin. "From what you've said, Evan, Alban is one of those men to whom everything came easy. Sometimes that's not good for a man. He comes to think if something doesn't come easy the first time he tries it, it's impossible."

"I suppose that was the case when he was younger, when I knew him. He was the best swordsman, the strongest wrestler, and the fastest runner. I think you're right, my lord." Here Evan paused as he thought, his eye on Angharad, and his next words seemed more for her than for Hywel. "Thinking about it now, that might have been better for me than for him. I had to work hard to be half as good, so I learned to work."

"He did get the girl," Angharad said.

"Caron." Gwen nodded, her attention on Evan. "You loved her once?"

Evan met her eyes without embarrassment or regret. "We all did."

"Meicol too?"

"Meicol, Barri—even Cadell. Caron was beautiful."

"My uncle was interested in Caron, and yet she still chose Alban?" Angharad said.

Evan smiled ruefully. "Cadell flirted with her. That is all. Beauty or not, the old King Gruffydd would never have allowed his son, even his younger one, to marry a girl who wasn't noble. Marriages are about alliances—or at least they are in Deheubarth."

Angharad narrowed her eyes at Evan, and Gwen didn't have to be an investigator to know she and Evan were having a conversation within a conversation. Unfortunately, Evan had a point, and Gwen wondered now if Hywel would have been allowed to marry Mari if he'd already been the edling. Mari had brought no land or status to the throne of Gwynedd. She did bring love, which King Owain claimed to care about.

"He also told us Sir Robert was the father of Caron's child," Evan said.

Gwen couldn't hide her surprise. "Surely not. Besides, Robert has been in Pembroke for the last year."

"I'm not sure that evidence is important to Sior," Angharad said.

"Caron is Sir Robert's niece and heir," Hywel said. "That isn't nothing."

"Now she is, but Robert had a wife and child once. For a long while after his family died, there was every expectation Robert would marry again." Evan glanced at Gwen. "What you don't know is that even though Caron was much like Enid in character, she was always conscious of her own value."

Enid had been a girl whose murder Gareth and Gwen had investigated several years ago.

"She had her eye on the grand prize, you mean," Hywel said. "She didn't lie with just anyone."

"She didn't lie with *anyone*, which made her all the more desirable." Evan pursed his lips. "Come to think on it, she was more like a lesser version of Queen Cristina than Enid."

"Did you ever hope she could be yours?" Hywel asked.

Instead of taking offense, which he could have, or being worried about what Angharad thought—were she genuinely interested in him—Evan laughed, which was the best thing he could have done. "Me? Scrawny child that I was? You didn't know me then." He grinned. "I was not the handsome soldier you see before you today. I got my growth late."

"What about Barri?" Gwen asked.

"Barri never had a chance with her either."

"Mam!" Dai loped up to them with Saran not far behind. The boy was looking far more bright-eyed than he in any way deserved to look after the time he'd given them. Even with a good night's sleep, Gwen herself felt haggard and drawn. Dai stopped in front of Hywel and bowed his head. "My lord."

"How are you?" Gwen wrapped her arms around her son, clutching him tightly to her. "I see and feel that you are better!" As she stepped back, she was brushing tears from the corners of her eyes.

"So much better that he's arguing with me about whether or not he can get up." Saran said, coming to a halt too. "You can see I lost."

Gwen smiled through her tears. "You should have sat on him."

"I did try." Saran took in a breath. "Cadfan, Cadell's captain, asked specifically to speak to Evan. He says he has a confession to make."

That had all of them hustling to the barracks, where they found Cadfan sitting up in bed in a room of his own on the second floor, either due to his high station, or worse, because Saran hadn't thought he was going to live. He was still living, however, though he was very pale, and he kept one hand resting on his stomach—soothingly, Gwen thought.

Since it was Evan to whom Cadfan most wanted to speak, Evan went straight to the end of the bed. Gwen hovered for a moment in the doorway before choosing to sit near Cadfan's feet. Hywel and Angharad made themselves inconspicuous against the wall. Dai kept to the doorway, slipping easily back into his duty as guard and making sure without anyone needing to ask him that they wouldn't be disturbed.

Cadfan met Evan's eyes. "I may not have much longer to live—"

"Shush. That's not true—" Angharad started forward.

Cadfan lifted his hand, asking her to stop. "I wanted to speak to you of Meicol, the man who died. It may be my fault he's dead." Cadfan began to cough, and Angharad reached for the cup on the table beside the bed and helped him to drink from it.

When he'd regained control of himself, Cadfan said to Evan. "When Sir Gareth examined Meicol, did he find bruises on his belly?"

"He did."

"I put them there." And before any of them could ask the obvious question *why*? Cadfan continued, "I have always found Meicol to be a sly one. Untrustworthy. Poking his nose where it doesn't belong. A few days ago, I caught him sneaking away from Alban's manor, and then in the evening, he was eavesdropping on a conversation between Alban and Sir Robert."

"And for that you beat him?" Gwen was incredulous, but she tried to keep most of her disapproval out of her voice.

"Of course not. It was simply the last straw in a long series of offenses, the worst of which was that he'd bedded Caron. Taking another man's wife—especially one who serves the same lord as you—is an unforgivable offense."

"*Meicol* bedded Caron?" Evan narrowed his eyes. "Why would you possibly think so?"

Cadfan shrugged. "Everybody knows it."

"Did Alban?" Gwen shot Evan a disbelieving look. The undercook had just told him and Angharad that Sir Robert was the father of this child. She didn't know that she'd ever encountered a stranger sequence of accusations. Paternity aside, what seemed obvious to Gwen was that Alban and Caron's marriage was less than happy.

"I would assume so," Cadfan said, "though it isn't as if I asked him."

"Has Caron admitted to the affair?" Evan said.

"I would never ask her either. What do you take me for?"

"Then how do you know?" Evan said.

"As I said, Meicol was a sneaky one. When I caught him leaving Alban's manor the other day, it wasn't the first time."

"Before you beat Meicol, you must have confronted him with your suspicions," Evan said. "What was his response?"

"He denied even speaking to Caron, and he said he was visiting Alban's dim cousin, Meleri."

"As he would," Dai said from behind them, though in an undertone, clearly not intending to be part of the conversation.

Still, Cadfan nodded. "As any man would."

Gwen eyed the ill man, who now closed his eyes and leaned his head back against the wall behind him. He really didn't look well. "You'll be glad to know Gareth does not believe the beating you gave him is what killed Meicol. All signs point to poisoning, the same as you, except an hour earlier than everyone else."

Cadfan opened one eye. "Really?" He let out a sharp burst of air. "You cannot know how relieved I am to hear that."

"Why not simply dismiss the man?" Evan said. "He had the ability to make a livelihood another way. He didn't have to be a soldier."

"You mean his craft?" Cadfan lifted his chin as he spoke to Evan. "If you've seen carvings—and I admit to his skill with a whittling knife—they were done years ago, not long after you left.

These days, if the man wasn't working, he was drinking. Sometimes he was drunk while on duty. I sent him home to sober up twice in the month before the battle against the Flemings."

That was news to Gwen, and by Evan's expression, news to him too. Still, it was perhaps not surprising, given what they'd learned of Meicol's character.

Evan sighed. "Do you have any insight as to why Meicol would attack Barri at the celebration?"

Cadfan's eyes were closed again. "They hated each other from an incident that happened years ago when you were here. Beyond that, your guess is as good as mine."

At a sign from Saran, the companions filed from Cadfan's room and returned to the courtyard so as not to talk among the sick in the barracks.

Hywel gave a grunt of displeasure. "Unfortunately, we can't pin any of these deaths on anyone as of yet. And even if we could, we need irrefutable proof—preferably a confession—to take a trusted member of the king's court before the king and accuse him of murder."

"But who do we accuse?" Gwen said. "We know there are two types of murder: crimes of passion and desperation—which Sir Robert's killing felt like—and those that are planned in advance, like the poisoning. It's one of the reasons I think we have two murderers, not one."

Angharad was looking into the distance, but Gwen didn't think she was seeing the interior of the castle so much as thinking—which a moment later proved to be the case when she spoke: "One thing seems clear from our work today. If Meicol hadn't ended up dead himself, everyone would have been perfectly happy to pin all the deaths on him."

21

Gareth

Gwen had gone up to the castle to poke around with Hywel, which was as good a way as any to get both of them into trouble. Thus, before he left the monastery, Gareth made arrangements for the men of Hywel's teulu, whom he commanded, to treat Dinefwr Castle as if it were Aber. After the poisoning, the men had been up all night with Gareth, but they'd taken turns sleeping yesterday. With the new day, most were now able to concentrate on their duties again.

Gareth sent Goch of the red hair and large feet with ten of the company to scout the area around the castle. With so many of Cadell's men down, that duty was sorely neglected, and Gareth had not yet ruled out an attack from an outside force. An enemy—perhaps even Walter FitzWizo, who was loyal to King Stephen—could have orchestrated all of this. Gareth hadn't forgotten those three men killed on the road the night of the feast either. They'd been up to something, but as they were all dead, nobody knew what that had been.

He charged Rhodri with leading the rest of the men, who would remain inside the castle, to fill in where Cadell's men could not. Lord Maurice had men in the castle too, of course, as did Richard de Clare. It could be they'd end up tripping over each other in their attempt to keep the residents of the castle safe, but that was better than not being safe. Admittedly, it was also a bit like locking the barn door after the horse had escaped, but Gareth was doing the best he could with the resources he'd been given.

Because he wasn't putting in an appearance at the castle at all, Gareth didn't have to explain himself to Prince Rhys or Richard de Clare. Last night, he had diverted them in advance by suggesting that this morning they ask among their men if anyone had seen or heard anything unusual or relevant to the investigation and report back. Truth be told, that questioning needed to be done, and Gareth hadn't had time to do it, which was also why he'd suggested Angharad and Evan help too.

Aside from the fact that he and Gwen liked the way the pair looked together, time was running short, and it wasn't only Cadell who was impatient for answers. Gareth needed to find the poisoner and the murderer. It was incredibly irksome that he didn't know how many culprits there were, much less *why* they'd struck in the first place. It made it a little hard to predict when they might strike again.

This ride from the monastery was becoming as familiar to Gareth as the road from Aber through the pass of Bwlch y Ddeufaen in Gwynedd. As they rode along, he noted the familiar landmarks: that old, gnarled tree, the start of a stone wall, the same three cows in the field before the village, and the series of potholes to be avoided as they reached the bottom of the hill up to the castle. It was reaching a point where he knew the road well enough that he could have traveled it without a torch, even were it dark and stormy. Likely, the killer could say the same.

The thought prompted him to speak out loud. "He has to be a member of Cadell's court."

"What's that?" Gruffydd was riding to Gareth's right, and had remained silent up until now to allow Gareth space to think.

Gareth turned to the Dragon captain. "Whoever killed Sir Robert did so in the church graveyard, which is out of the way and not a typical place to meet anyone by accident. Furthermore, Robert was killed from behind, indicating he'd been followed or awaited. The killer knew his victim—and even more, knew his potential movements." He clenched his hand into a fist and pounded it onto his thigh, finding himself frustrated as usual by what he didn't know. "Along the same lines, even with the large number of people at the castle for the celebration, whoever poisoned the pie had to have been known to the kitchen staff. A stranger couldn't have passed through that kitchen without someone remarking upon him."

"You are right on all counts, which means we need to know more about our suspects." Gruffydd barked a laugh. "It would be helpful to *have* suspects."

They were passing through the village now. As with the road, Gareth was becoming familiar with the faces that turned to look at him as he went by. Here in the south, people weren't comfortable with strangers. It was all the more reason to think the killer was one of them. Even with all the comings and goings of the army, the people of Dinefwr's village would notice a newcomer who wasn't a soldier, and while they might not have come forward to tell Gareth, they might speak to the abbot or someone in authority they knew. So far, they had not.

The company arrived at Alban's manor to find two village boys, the eldest perhaps having achieved manhood, industriously chopping at the overgrown grass along the roadway with long knives. It was about time. Perhaps when Alban had been only a steward, he hadn't felt the need to maintain the property, but now with Robert's death, he was the lord of the manor. As Gareth himself could attest, ownership changed a man's perspective.

Gruffydd, who by then had been riding just ahead of Gareth, motioned that the five Dragons (the company was lacking Evan) spread out to have a look around the estate. Gareth himself approached the manor house, and, for the second time in two days, walked in on a fight. This time, to Gareth's complete lack of surprise, it was between Alban and Caron. The pair were so loud, Gareth opened the door and stepped inside the house without them noticing. It turned out they were in the back, all the way through to the kitchen where Gwen had met with Caron.

"You spent it?" Caron was shouting. "How could you? We agreed you wouldn't!"

Gareth was completely happy to eavesdrop on the argument and to have a moment to himself inside the manor. Now that he could name Meicol as the master carver and had a more complete perspective on the man himself, he was able to better admire what he'd done here. And it occurred to Gareth that Meicol had done it for Robert, not Alban.

He rubbed his finger along the arm of a chair, carved to look like a paw. It was one of twelve that sat around the long table. All of the edges, legs, and arms were elaborately decorated. He could almost picture the bear that had been the model crouched on the other side of the table. Meicol might not have been deemed reliable anymore and might have been drinking too much, but Sir Robert had seen his worth and employed him at length. It seemed amazing to Gareth that Cadell hadn't done the same. And now it was too late.

"Do you like the table?" The little girl he'd seen with her nanny earlier stood at the bottom of the stairs, her hand on the railing.

"I do." Gareth swept his fingers along the smooth finish.

"Uncle Meicol made it." She made a sad face. "He's dead now."

"I know. I'm sorry."

She walked forward. "Can I show you something?"

"Of course." He reached out a hand and tugged on one of her pigtails. If he wasn't mistaken, she was going to grow up as beautiful as her mother. The cliché *I don't envy her father* passed through his head a heartbeat before he realized someone might say the same thing about him. He had a daughter too, younger than this girl, who was utterly beautiful. And he didn't think it was just fatherly pride saying so. Woe betide any future young men who attempted to woo her before Gareth had assessed them fully and deemed them worthy.

Meanwhile, the little girl dropped to her knees and crawled under the table. “Come here.”

Half-laughing, he got down on his knees and then his rear and scooted himself after her. Instead of four legs on the corners, the tabletop was supported by two pedestals attached to one another by two thick crossbeams running between them. The little girl put her finger to her lips and then reached up and touched one of the knotholes in a pedestal. With a click, a drawer popped out. She pushed it back in, pressed the knot again, and it popped out again.

Gareth’s eyes were bright. There really was far more to Meicol than met the eye, and they would all be wise to remember it. “Is there anything inside?”

She nodded solemnly and pulled out a carved cat the size of Gareth’s pinky finger “Meicol told me if I ever had something I didn’t want my brothers to steal, to hide it in the drawer. My doll doesn’t fit, or I would leave it here so my brother can’t hurt her.”

“I’m sorry about your doll. I have a little girl too, and she would not be happy if someone hurt her doll.” Children could be—and often were—cruel if left to themselves. He slid out from underneath the table. “Meicol was a good friend to you.”

The girl followed, still holding the carved cat. “Do you think he’d like it if I brought the cat to his funeral?”

“I’m sure he would, but don’t leave it on the grave. He carved it for you because he wanted you to have it.”

She nodded again, the cat clenched in her little fist. By now, the fight in the kitchen had died down, and it was time to make himself known to Alban and Caron. Then the front door opened, and Llelo, who again was tagging along, poked in his head. "Remember what Evan said about comparing this house to the barn at Aber?"

Gareth raised his eyebrows. "I do."

Llelo nodded. "There's something Gruffydd wants you to see."

22

Gareth

Alban entered the room before Gareth could leave. "Why are you back?"

Gareth spun around, having just related to Llelo the finding of the secret drawer under the table. He assumed Alban knew of it, even if the little girl thought otherwise. Still, Gareth wasn't going to be the one to tell him. "We have more questions."

Alban folded his arms across his chest. "Such as?"

Gareth eyes went to the door, expecting Caron to come through it at any moment, but she didn't. "Ones that haven't yet been answered." He paused. "When was it that you beat Meicol?"

Alban's jaw dropped. Gareth had deliberately asked the question in such a way that assumed Alban had done it, and he obliged by not denying it. Instead, he let out a puff of air and turned towards the fireplace, putting his forearm on the mantle and leaning into his arm. "The day before he died." He looked up. "But I didn't kill him! He didn't even fight back. The man was so pathetic, after a few blows, I stopped, and what I did to him was hardly enough to kill him."

Gareth well remembered the bruises on Meicol's torso, but he also remembered what had transpired in the great hall at Dinefwr. It had been Meicol who had taunted Barri, and also Meicol who'd swung the first—and only—punch. That wasn't the behavior of a pathetic man who wouldn't fight back. Then again, Meicol had been drunk, and Barri had been an equal, while Alban was his superior. "What did you confront him about?"

Alban's chin went rigid, and for a moment Gareth didn't think he was going to answer, but then he took in a breath and half-laughed. "If you must know, he was behaving in a manner which was too familiar with my wife."

Gareth managed to keep his face blank. Somehow, from what Evan had said about Caron, he couldn't see her giving Meicol the time of day. She hadn't when she'd been a youth. It was bizarre that she would now as a married woman. "She is with child. Did you think the baby was his?"

"No!" Alban scoffed. "I didn't say she returned his interest."

"Did he touch her?" Llelo spoke urgently from behind Gareth. They'd already had the conversation about how Llelo, as a man, was larger than almost all women. He needed to monitor his physical proximity to them at all times and to make sure he didn't use his greater size and strength to intimidate when he didn't mean to.

Alban glanced at him. "She says no, just that he was too forward. I didn't like the way he was always snooping around anyway, so I decided to give him a lesson he wouldn't soon forget."

Gareth took in a breath through his nose. He couldn't argue with what Alban had done, if, in fact, Meicol had offended his wife. The fact that Alban hadn't killed Meicol then and there, however, indicated Alban might even be telling the truth—because why beat a man half to death only to poison him the next day?

"May I speak to Caron about this?"

Alban frowned. "I would rather you didn't. What with the baby and the death of Sir Robert, she hasn't been feeling well at all."

Gareth lifted his chin to point to the kitchen doorway. "I overheard you two arguing just now. Something about spending money—perhaps money you don't have?"

Alban's face went completely blank.

Gareth almost rolled his eyes. Alban might be guilty of wrongdoing, but if so, he wasn't an expert criminal. If he had been, he would have been prepared for questions, rather than acting surprised every time Gareth asked them.

"What was it about?" Gareth urged.

"It was nothing. Just household concerns." Alban recovered enough to shake his head and smile ruefully. It was a good attempt, but Gareth didn't believe him for a single heartbeat.

"Are you a gambling man, Alban?"

He shrugged in attempt to convey casualness. "Dice with the men on occasion." Then he looked fiercely at Gareth. "What passes between me and Caron is a private matter and none of your concern."

"It is my concern if it pertains to murder."

"It doesn't!"

This was the most emotion Alban had shown, far more than he'd displayed at the loss of Sir Robert or any of the people who'd died at the castle. Gareth hadn't known any of them himself, but he didn't live here. These were men Alban lived and worked with, and yet he'd mentioned none of them.

"We spoke with Meleri, your cousin."

Now it was Alban who rolled his eyes. "I'm amazed she talked to you. She's simple, you know."

"We noticed." Gareth studied Alban for a few heartbeats. Then he said under his breath to Llelo, "Is what you found something Alban can help us with?"

"I don't see why not."

Gareth turned back. "My son says we have something to show you. Will you come with us?" Without waiting for a response from Alban, he turned on his heel and followed Llelo out the door. Alban did, in fact, exit the manor too, and when Gareth glanced back, his brow was furrowed. "Where are we going?"

"Over here," Llelo said mildly. He led them around the back of the house to a narrow cart path, half the width of the one that led to the house. The wheel ruts were evident, however, even if the vegetation overhung the path on both sides. It hadn't rained in several days, but the ground was still fairly damp under the trees, and boot prints were evident in the dirt. As Gareth's own men had been down here and back, he didn't try to read anything into them.

"Really, Sir Gareth. This is absurd," Alban said from behind him, having come to a halt at the start of the track.

Gareth turned to look at him. "I have the full confidence of King Cadell to follow where this investigation leads me."

From beside him, Llelo didn't scoff, though he'd probably had to swallow down his instinctive denial. Still, Gareth hadn't actually lied. He *had* been charged with the investigation, but *full confidence* was something of an overstatement. Gareth deliberately hadn't told Cadell he'd returned to Alban's house.

Then Llelo put into words what had been at the back of Gareth's mind since they'd arrived, though he hadn't managed to articulate it. "Why aren't you at the castle seeing to your men, Alban? Here it is noon already, and you haven't been there since the celebration. Shouldn't you be with them, especially since your captain is ill as well?"

Alban's mouth opened, closed, and then opened again. This question, like all the others, had surprised him, maybe especially coming from a fifteen-year-old. But then he shrugged and answered. "Caron was unwell yesterday, and I had Sir Robert's affairs to attend to. I sent one of my servants to King Cadell to tell him I would come when I was free. When you arrived, I was just about to leave to ride to the castle."

Gareth accepted the explanation for now, but like practically everything that had come out of Alban's mouth, it raised Gareth's hackles.

Llelo knew it too. "It's still odd," he said in an undertone.

"You're not wrong," Gareth said in the same low voice. He himself was Hywel's captain and knew intimately that the obligations of a man of Alban's stature, even if he wasn't captain of the teulu but second-in-command, as Evan had been, were numerous and daily. As Llelo had pointed out, his obligations should be all the greater with Cadfan ill and unable to see to his men.

In addition, Gareth was landed, having been given an estate by Prince Hywel upon his marriage to Gwen. But even with the honor, rarely had he been given leave to see to his own lands on Anglesey. Gareth had a trustworthy steward who did most of the work, but Alban seemed to run things here himself. The difference couldn't even be that the manor was close to the castle or that Alban wasn't often called to leave the vicinity of Dinefwr. Every king moved around the countryside from castle to castle or royal *llys*. It was how he kept an eye on his people and his land. When he went, his teulu went with him. That meant Alban went with him.

As Llelo had said ... *odd.*

Deciding to leave the matter for now, Gareth and Llelo continued to lead Alban down the path a good quarter of a mile until they reached a ramshackle shed. From its size and the fact that it was still standing, despite the tree that had fallen on it, the shed had once been well built. Even with the tree, the roof was intact, and although the exterior hadn't been whitewashed in at least a decade, the cracks between the boards had been filled in recently.

As they arrived, Iago pushed open the big double doors, which created an opening large enough to allow a horse and cart to enter. The hinges didn't squeak. "Come see what we found."

The cart path continued past the shed and headed off to the right. It had the look of looping behind the manor house before returning to the main road. Gareth would send someone along it in a moment if Gruffydd hadn't done so already. He probably had, being thorough and committed to his position as leader of the Dragons. In fact, Gruffydd, like Evan, had become far more content, if not happy, since taking on the position. Life wasn't the same without Rhun, but it could be lived.

The shed proved to be dry storage for hay, and a glance up at the ceiling confirmed Gareth's initial guess: the roof had not been breached. Iago didn't stop to inspect the interior but moved between the mounds of hay to the back of the shed where a cart was parked. Aron was sprawled on his stomach underneath it, with the upper half of his body disappearing through a trap door in the floor. At Gareth's approach, he popped out his head and grinned.

Another pair of doors allowed access to the cart path from this side of the shed, and Gruffydd opened them while Iago and Steffan hauled the cart out of the way of the trap door. Gareth walked to the hole and looked into it.

"We thought you might like to take a look for yourself, seeing how much you like cellars and trap doors." Aron was trying not to laugh.

"You're lucky Prince Hywel isn't here this time. He'd wipe that smirk off your face." Gareth tried to come off as stern, but he couldn't maintain it. He laughed along with Aron. The rest of the Dragons looked at him with varying degrees of amusement, pleased with themselves for the joke they thought they were playing on him.

Alban, who'd entered the shed as well, looked from one man to the other, not understanding what they were jesting about. Of course, there was no way he could know about the number of times Gareth had been captive in a cellar. Though it had been more than once, if a man couldn't laugh about pain, then he shouldn't have Gareth's job.

"I don't know what you're so concerned about," Alban said. "Sir Robert used this place as storage, but it's too close to the river, and everything becomes too damp if left in the cellar for any length of time."

Gareth glanced back at Alban. "What kind of things did he leave here?"

Alban shrugged, implying unconcern, but his jaw was tight. "I don't know. This was before my time, you understand."

"Who might have been down here recently?"

Alban shrugged again. “How should I know? My duties have kept me busy, and it’s far enough from the house that you can’t hear anyone in the shed or along the track.”

“If you had to guess,” Gareth said.

“Children playing, perhaps. I could ask my farm hands.”

Gareth tipped his head. “Please do.”

Alban folded his arms and leaned against one of the posts that supported the roof, affecting a casual attitude. “I can’t understand why you are suspicious of me. I have nothing to hide.”

Gareth eyed him. “You were Sir Robert’s steward. I would have been neglectful of my duty if I hadn’t questioned you. As it is, I won’t keep you any longer.”

Alban appeared to snort under his breath, though he was quiet about it. He gestured towards the cart, which the Dragons had moved outside. “Please clean up after yourselves before you leave.” He stalked away and didn’t look back.

“He’s hiding something,” Aron said matter-of-factly.

Gareth watched him go, and then he turned to Steffan. “Follow him up the track, will you? I want to make sure he really rides away.”

“Yes, sir.” Steffan headed away after Alban.

Gruffydd rubbed his chin. “It’s hard for me to see the boy Evan describes in the man he is now. What happened to him?”

Iago shrugged. “He’s discovered he will never achieve what he’d hoped. I imagine that wife of his isn’t letting him forget it either.”

Gareth studied his men. “Is this really what you had for me? An empty cellar?”

“Someone has been here recently.” Cadoc scraped his foot across the floor, sweeping aside the loose hay. “There’s fresh dirt everywhere.”

Aron copied him, brushing aside more of the hay. “There’s more on the rungs of the ladder. That’s why we didn’t go down it.”

Gruffydd leaned close to Gareth and said in a low voice. “They’re catching the fever, Gareth. If you don’t look lively, they’ll be going off on their own next.”

“They wouldn’t be the first,” Gareth said, though at that point his smile turned a little sad because one of those who’d become so afflicted had been Prince Rhun.

“After you.” Gruffydd lit a lantern that had been resting on a hook by the front door.

Gareth took it and started down the ladder, noting, as Aron had pointed out, the fresh dirt clinging to the rungs. Alban’s denials aside, his men were right that someone had been down here very recently.

However Alban hadn’t lied about the cellar being empty. When Gareth reached the bottom and raised the lantern, he revealed ... nothing.

Gruffydd poked his head into the hole. “Anything?”

“Uh ... not much.” Gareth beckoned with his hand. “Come on down.” He might have preferred to have Evan at his side, but Gruffydd had done some investigating in his time, and he was an excellent tracker.

A slight tremor crossed Gruffydd's face. "I don't like enclosed spaces." But he turned himself around and came down the ladder anyway.

Meanwhile, Gareth crouched to the floor. Now that his eyes had adjusted to the dim light, he could clearly see footprints and tracks in the dirt. "Pretend this is the woods. What does the ground tell you?"

His brow furrowed, Gruffydd began to move carefully around the room, trying not to mar the footprints, though that was difficult because they were everywhere. "I see the prints of many shoes, though—" He bent down and studied what was in front of him. "Alban might not be wrong that children were down here. Roughly half the prints are too small to be a man's boot."

"Could be several small men," Llelo said from above them.

Gruffydd grunted his agreement. "Hard to tell. Let's just say they belong to people smaller than any of us here." He swept his hand through the dirt and rubbed it between his fingers. "Not all the dirt is native to this cellar either. Several of these clods are of the same type of soil as on the rungs of the ladder and on the floor of the shed."

"And vice versa." Llelo's head was back in the hole. "The dirt down there is reddish, very fine, and not clumped."

Aron crouched beside Llelo. "Somebody went in and out of this hole more than once."

"Several someones, I'd say." Gareth pointed to the side wall four feet away. "A large chest sat there. You can see the outline on the floor and the wall." He turned slowly on his heel. "This room was at one time full of chests and boxes."

"And crates." Gruffydd indicated a crisscross pattern in the dirt by where he was standing.

"Chests and boxes aren't exactly farm equipment," Aron said.

Gareth laughed. Evan had spoken to him of Aron's wit. It wasn't so much that he had an off-kilter way of looking at the world, though that could be useful, but that he saw to the heart of a matter and had the ability to point it out. "You two can come down if you want to."

Their heads disappeared instantly, to be replaced by Llelo's feet and then his whole body as he came down the ladder, followed by Aron a few steps behind. Gareth could hear the rest of the Dragons moving about the shed, their feet clumping on the wood of the floor, which was the cellar's ceiling. In his experience, most buildings that stored hay had some kind of crawl space at the lower level, or at the very least a wooden frame, to keep the hay off of the dirt. Hay needed the circulation of air to stay dry and not mold through the winter. Whatever had been stored down here couldn't be damaged by water either, or hadn't been stored here long.

"What's right there?" Gareth pointed to the far corner. "Something just glinted in the lantern's light."

Llelo cat-walked to where Gareth indicated and crouched to the ground. He swept away some loose dirt with his finger and then drew in a breath. "You have good eyes, Father." He held up a coin, his own eyes brighter than ever. "Gold."

Gareth risked marring the floor with his own boot prints and crossed to see for himself. Llelo kept scraping away dirt, at first desultorily and then more enthusiastically, ultimately revealing a leather sack the width of a man's hand. Mouth wide, Llelo opened it and proceeded to pour gold coins into Gareth's palm. They came so fast, he cupped both hands to hold them all.

Llelo stopped pouring with the bag still more than half full, and then opened the top wider so Gareth could pour most of them back in. Gareth kept a few, however, to examine. They weren't all the same, with some ancient and others newer, but they all were gold. One in Gareth's palm showed a double-headed man on one side and half-naked soldiers on the other with the word *Roma* written underneath.

His mouth went dry as he contemplated the wealth before him. People kept leaving coins for him to find, but these were unlike any he'd ever seen. Few Welsh kings had the wherewithal to mint their own coins. King Owain hadn't done it. But these were Roman and ancient and a long way from home. No stretch of the imagination could justify their presence in the cellar of a minor lord's shed in Deheubarth.

Gruffydd and Aron had come over too, of course, and they looked at the gold in Gareth's hand. Aron took one of the coins and held it up to the lantern light. "What have we stumbled onto?"

Gareth shook his head. "A treasure, clearly, but whose it is or where the rest of it has gone—and what it has to do with these murders—is yet another mystery."

23

Hywel

Hywel signaled that the men should spread out. At one time he might have resented not being able to go anywhere without a dozen men around him, but he felt less distaste these days—especially here in Deheubarth where they were surrounded by enemies and former enemies turned temporary friends. Gareth had sent Steffan back to the castle to ask Hywel and Gwen to come to him.

Unusual as that request had been, it was even stranger for Hywel to find himself in a barn adjacent to the Towy River, west of the castle and one of the many properties belonging to St. Dyfi's monastery. The building was in fine condition, as the cracks in the walls were newly daubed and whitewashed, and the thatch roof was whole and looked new too. Abbot Mathew, as Hywel would have expected, saw to the proper care of his holdings.

"I'm not sorry to leave the castle," Gwen said as they reined in. "I feel like everybody's watching me all the time, waiting for me to announce some new finding that will indicate the investigation is over."

"They want answers, and they think you have them—or might have them. And it just may be that we will have more in a moment," Hywel said.

"Poor Angharad is now going to be barraged with questions in our absence," Evan said.

Gwen smiled. "I'm pretty sure she's used to the complexities of Deheubarth's court, and it won't be the first time she hasn't told the whole truth to her uncle."

Evan grunted. "It would be nice if it were the last, however."

That was enigmatic, but Hywel didn't pursue what was happening with Evan's personal life—not yet anyway—and lifted his chin to point to Gareth, who'd come out of the barn to greet them. "Why are we meeting here?"

"I don't trust anyone in the castle," Gareth said without apology, "particularly not with this."

He helped Gwen from her horse, and then they moved into the barn, empty for the day except for doves cooing among the rafters. At night, the barn would house cows, pigs, and sheep, all of which were either in an adjacent pasture or rooting their way around the muddy stockade. Twenty men on horses were entirely out of place in such a setting, but the water trough was full, and there was feed for the horses, so Hywel wasn't discontented.

Once inside, Gareth went straight to his saddlebag and pulled out a heavy leather bag, tied at the top. Its contents clanked a bit in a fashion Hywel had come to associate with money, though he hadn't ever seen such a large moneybag before.

"More to the point, I didn't want to be walking around the castle with this in my possession." Gareth held it out.

Hywel looked around at the Dragons, who were the only other people in the barn, since Hywel had left his teulu outside. The men weren't exactly grinning, but their eyes were alight with expectation. That made Hywel almost more wary, and he eyed Gareth as he took the bag from him. It was even heavier than he'd thought, and he weighed it in his hands while Gareth helpfully untied the string at the top.

Hywel took out a coin and held it up to the afternoon sunlight coming through the open doorway, which faced west.

"The sack was buried in the dirt in a corner of an otherwise empty cellar underneath one of Alban's ramshackle sheds." Gareth gestured to his son. "Llelo dug it up."

"Only because you saw one of the coins glinting from the dirt, Father."

Gruffydd moved to stand beside Gareth. "The shed hasn't been standing empty for long. At some point recently, maybe as recently as yesterday or the day before, it contained many boxes and trunks. We could still see the impressions they'd made in the earth floor. Fresh earth clung to the rungs of the ladder and was scattered on the floor of the shed."

As Gareth and Gruffydd related what they'd seen and discovered, Hywel found himself in that uncomfortable moral gray area where what exactly was the honorable thing to do was less than clear.

Gwen had been uncharacteristically silent up until this moment, but now she frowned. "Did Alban know you were in his shed?"

"Yes," Gareth said. "He came with us and showed no concern at all that we were there. In fact, the only thing he seemed to care about was that we put his cart back in place when we were done."

"Was he there when you found the gold?" Gwen said.

"No," Gareth said. "He left before we went into the cellar, though he knew we were going to."

"I'm thinking he knew something had been there," Aron said flatly. "Alban didn't care that we looked in the shed because he'd already moved what was inside."

"But he wasn't the one who buried the gold." Gwen bit her lip, her expression pensive. "If he had, would he have walked away?"

"No, he would not have," Iago said. "No man would have. He would have stayed to protect it. If you'd found it, he could have claimed it for himself."

Hywel weighed the bag in his hand. "Are you thinking this gold is one piece of a larger treasure? That this is a small fraction of what was there that has since been moved?"

"I hate to speculate," Gareth said. "If Alban is involved, and how could he not be, that would explain why he didn't care that we went down there."

"What was in the cellar doesn't have to have been valuable," Gwen said. "If the items were really farm equipment or household goods—it makes the place all the better to hide something like this bag."

"I would be more likely to agree if the items hadn't been recently removed," Gareth said, "and maybe in a hurry, since whoever did it left the gold behind."

"In which case, the people who moved the rest of the items were not the same as those who buried the bag," Hywel said.

"It was very dark down there. Gareth spotted a coin from across the room, but only because the lantern light hit it at just the right angle. Otherwise, we wouldn't have known it was there." Aron put out a hand to Gareth. "What if it wasn't children playing down there, but women? The feet were booted, not barefoot, as children often are this time of year."

"What's this about women?" Hywel asked.

Gareth turned to him and explained, "Many of the boot prints were smaller than you might expect if they'd been made by men." He looked at Gwen.

She raised her eyebrows. "It wasn't me."

Aron laughed. "We didn't mean to imply it might have been. Would you mind showing me your foot?"

Gwen found a seat on an overturned bucket and stuck out one foot. Then the Dragons gathered around. Hywel laughed at the intensity of their expressions as they studied her boot.

"So what are we thinking?" Steffan said. "This is Caron's doing?"

"Or a servant, or any of a dozen women in the area," Gareth said, frustration in his voice. "The shed is isolated enough that the whole cantref could have had access to it—and Alban and Caron might not even have known about it."

"If not Alban, could the gold have belonged to Sir Robert?" Llelo had been quiet throughout most of the conversation, perhaps feeling as if he didn't really belong, even though he'd dug up the bag. "He could have buried it and told no one."

"At which point, with his death, it belongs to Alban," Iago said.

But Gruffydd shook his head. "You forget that a few coins were left loose within the surface dirt. The sack was buried hurriedly, recently, and not well."

Steffan tapped a finger to his chin in mimicry of Hywel. "Why would that be?" He was not much younger than Gwen and a proficient swordsman (and knifesman), but that devotion to his art had been somewhat at the expense of a study of the way people thought.

Aron snorted. "Because whoever buried them wanted to keep the gold a secret from his partners."

Gruffydd rubbed his chin. "If a man finds a penny beside the road, to whom does it belong? Clearly the true owner is the one who lost it, but how does he find that man, and how would that man ever prove it was his?"

"And what if he's dead? Or stole that penny in the first place?" Aron said.

"Here's what I know—" Hywel motioned that his men should gather around him. "I swore to you when I brought you together that the tasks I laid upon you would never compromise your honor or mine. You would be soldiers more than spies, and if I asked you to spy, it would be for Gwynedd, not for me. But I find myself in a quandary as to the right thing to do here."

"With the gold, you mean?" Evan said.

Hywel nodded. "My impulse, of course, is to keep it; to hide it. Certainly, in no way do I want to bring it to the attention of Cadell or any of the other lords here."

There was silence for a moment, and then it was Cadoc who spoke. He was normally not one to involve himself in strategy or politics. He shot his arrows where Hywel pointed and protected his brothers. Anything else he viewed as not of his concern. "It doesn't matter to whom it once belonged. It's yours now. You should send it home to Aberystwyth today. We know the gold isn't Cadell's. It certainly isn't Alban's rightful property—nor Sir Robert's for that matter. That makes it fair game, no matter whose land it was found on."

That was a response Hywel would have expected from Cadoc. A former assassin, he had little regard for anything beyond the practical. But Steffan nodded too. "Cadoc is right, my lord. Wealth is power. You need to keep it. To give the treasure to Cadell serves nobody but Cadell."

"What would be the disadvantage of keeping it?" Hywel said.

"We can't use it as evidence," Gwen said immediately. "We have to pretend you went to Alban's house, Gareth, and found nothing."

"Not nothing," Gareth had spent the last few moments with his back to the group, looking out the doorway. But he'd been listening, and now he turned back. "We could say we found one coin in the dirt, which is true as far as it goes, and there is ample evidence there was more at one time. Even one Roman coin would be outside Alban's purview."

"Here's a downside, my lord," Evan said. "If Cadell discovers we found more than one coin and didn't tell him about it, it could jeopardize your current alliance."

Gruffydd shook his head. "This alliance is going to last only as long as Cadell sees an advantage to it. He wants Ceredigion and is only biding his time until he attacks us at Aberystwyth." He gestured to the five other Dragons. "We all know it."

"Gareth is right, however, that we should say we found a coin. Two or three might be better." Evan was tapping a finger to his lip while staring at the sack, which by now Hywel had closed and tucked in the crook of his arm. "This is a murder investigation, and I don't think we should hide the fact that something is very much not right at Alban's estate."

Hywel scratched the top of his head. The Dragons were confirming what he wanted to do, but that didn't mean the decision wasn't of dubious morality. So he turned to the personification of his conscience. "What do you think, Gwen?"

She spread her hands wide, but didn't articulate an answer.

"You don't disagree?"

"Even if I do, it doesn't mean I have a better idea. The coins were stolen from someone who can't be Cadell—and, quite frankly,

I find it hard to believe that such an individual would be an ally of Gwynedd."

Gareth looked at his wife. "You sound more sure of that than any of us. Why?"

She laughed. "Cadell would hardly have entrusted you with any investigation if he knew Alban's cellar contained enough wealth to build a castle. Or three."

"As usual, you speak good sense." Hywel jerked his head towards the horses. "Gruffydd, Steffan, I want you to take the gold and ride home to Aberystwyth."

The men nodded their acceptance. Hywel's decision might be entirely misguided, but at least he and his closest companions were unified around it, and today it was the only decision he could make. "But first—" He reached into the sack and pulled out a handful of coins. Then he went around the barn, giving one to each man, including Llelo, who took his and clenched it in his fist without looking at it or Hywel.

Gruffydd, however, wasn't so quiet, and he tried to give back the coin Hywel had forced into his hand. "What is this for, my lord?"

"No more and far less than you deserve. I believe in rewarding men when they excel at their work. I haven't always had the means to do so as I would like. Today I do." He looked around at all of them. "You each gave me your opinion with honesty and without expectation of gain for yourselves. You, individually and together, are worth more to me than fifteen sacks of gold."

Then Hywel turned to Gwen and dropped a coin into her lap, and when she looked up at him, brow furrowing, he said, "Don't argue with me."

Their gaze met for another few heartbeats, and then she nodded. "No, my lord. I won't."

Hywel turned back to Gruffydd and handed him the bag. "If you leave now, you can reach Ceredigion by morning. Best you don't stop unless you have to."

"You have my word," Gruffydd said.

"Thank you. Cadell notices everything, but given the upheaval in his household, he can hardly question me about the whereabouts of my men."

"If you show him the coins, it will distract him—especially when you suggest there might be more." Gruffydd moved to put the sack of gold into the pack on his horse's back while Steffan mounted his own stallion.

But before Gruffydd could buckle the straps closed, Gareth said, "Wait." He put out a hand to Gwen, "Give me your coin." Gwen obeyed, and then Gareth went around to each of the others and took their coins too.

Such was the trust among Hywel's men that they gave them to Gareth without hesitation. He dumped them all back in the sack, fastened the buckle on the saddle bag, and finally turned to Hywel, who'd watched him without intervening, but without understanding either. "We appreciate the gesture, my lord, and we aren't throwing your generosity back in your face, but imagine Cadell's response if he discovered a gold coin on any of us."

Hywel's expression cleared. "He'd be apoplectic. He certainly would think there were more and know I'd lied to him." Then he laughed. That had been a close call.

With a wave of his hand, Hywel sent Gruffydd and Steffan on their way, finding himself filled with a sense of equanimity. He could trust both men, and that trust was not to be undervalued, which was why he'd given each man a coin in the first place. When a man was well-paid, he was less likely to resent the wealth of another and certainly less likely to be bought by an enemy. Even the newer men to Hywel's service would be confirmed in their belief in Hywel's loyalty to them—and reward him with their own.

"I suggest you gather Cadell, Rhys, Maurice, and Richard together so you can tell them about what you've found all at the same time," Gwen said.

Hywel swung around to find her looking at him with smiling eyes.

"How mischievous of you, my dear," he said.

"Mischievous?" Llelo asked. "Why?"

Gareth guffawed and answered for Hywel. "Because if Hywel tells Maurice and Richard about the treasure at the same time he tells Cadell, then it can't be kept a secret. Knowledge that more may be out there will untune the harp, as my father-in-law says. It will create discord and put every man against the other."

It had been some time since Hywel had knowingly caused trouble for others. At least in this instance, it wasn't entirely for his own amusement, though he had no regrets about discomfiting Cadell. More importantly, Gruffydd was right that it was only a matter of time until Cadell turned his attention on Ceredigion. The alliance to attack Wiston was an interlude only. War was coming. By keeping the coins, Hywel deprived Cadell of great wealth—a wealth that might have one day been used to attack Ceredigion.

Now, Hywel would be able to use that same wealth to defend it.

24

Dinefwr Castle

February 1143

Gareth

Four years ago ...

"My father should have chosen Rhun for this task." Hywel stood with his hands on his hips, staring out the window of his chamber.

Gareth had known from the first moment that King Owain had asked Hywel to go to Deheubarth that Hywel resented the duty. In fact, this was the third time in as many days that Hywel had proclaimed Rhun as more suited to the task than himself.

"But he didn't, my lord. Your father is suspicious of Anarawd and his motives, and he thinks you will be less trusting and drive a harder bargain than Rhun will." Gareth sat with his long legs stretched out in front of him, his chair tipped back against the wall, and his arms folded across his chest.

They'd been waiting for nearly an hour for King Anarawd to see them, which didn't bode well for the final negotiations regarding Anarawd's marriage to Hywel's sister. If all went well, the wedding would take place in six months' time. From the look on Hywel's face, however, he'd prefer the six months were six years. Or maybe never.

Gareth didn't know what was going on in his lord's head, and while it was completely like Hywel to be secretive, it wasn't like him to be secretive with Gareth. Gareth had given up trying to pry what was bothering Hywel out of him, however. His lord would tell him—or he wouldn't—in his own time.

Hywel brought down his head. "It is true I am less trusting than Rhun, but if my father was so suspicious of Anarawd, it makes me wonder why he agreed to this marriage in the first place."

"He is the King of Deheubarth and an important ally. Besides, your sister is in favor of the marriage."

"She wants to be a queen." Hywel scoffed. "She is a child."

"Elen is your favorite sister. You want what is best for her, but since you can't dissuade your father from this wedding, you will drive as hard a bargain as you can." Gareth indicated the half-closed doorway behind Hywel that led to Hywel's bedchamber. "Did the girl you bedded last night give you any useful information?"

"No." Hywel eyed his captain suspiciously. Gareth made sure to look innocently back. "She was lovely, but not bright."

A knock came at the door, and then one of Hywel's soldiers poked his head into the room. "A messenger has ridden into the castle from the east, my lord. I thought you would want to know."

"You are right. I do."

Hywel was out the door before Gareth had dropped the chair's front legs to the floor. A messenger from the east meant one thing: news about the war between King Stephen and Empress Maud. The fighting between these two royal cousins had been going on for four years. For the most part, anarchy in England had not spilled over into Gwynedd, but there were many more Normans here in the south, and the kings of Deheubarth had been constantly at war with them.

Mostly, in Gareth's experience, the lords of Wales supported whichever side was losing because unrest and chaos in England meant they were left to themselves. Anarawd was supporting Stephen at this moment because here in southern Wales, Robert of Gloucester, Maud's brother, was in close confrontation with Stephen's ally, Gilbert de Clare, the Earl of Pembroke. Anarawd's brother, Cadell, had taken a host of men from Deheubarth in support of Clare, and thus King Stephen, who, last Gareth had heard, had settled in for a long siege of Empress Maud's castle at Oxford.

Now Gareth hustled after Hywel, as anxious as his lord to hear the outcome of that battle. There was no point in complaining that it had taken nearly six weeks to hear any news. The roads into Wales had been made impassable with snow and ice—and then runoff—since the Christmas feast.

Once in the great hall, he pulled up just within earshot of King Anarawd, who'd been holding court around the fire from an ornate chair. He rose to his feet at the sight of the messenger coming towards him. The man's cheeks were wind-chapped, though the weather was finally warming and the snow was gone.

"My lord, I have news from England."

Anarawd motioned with his head that the messenger should follow him into his receiving room. On occasion, a lord wished to hear news in private before disseminating it to the residents of the castle, and this appeared to be one of those times. Without asking permission, Hywel followed—and thus so did Gareth.

The only other person Anarawd was allowing to hear the news was his steward, who carefully shut the door to close the room off from the great hall.

The messenger bowed before speaking in a strangely squeaky voice. "King Stephen has taken Oxford, my lord."

"And Empress Maud?" the king said.

"She escaped."

Anarawd pursed his lips. "When?"

"At Christmas."

Anarawd took in a breath and turned towards his chair, which, like in the great hall, was placed close to the fire blazing brightly in the hearth. "My brother?"

"Sends his regards. He is coming." And before the king could sit, the messenger put out a hand. "There is more, my lord."

Anarawd raised his eyebrows, but didn't speak or make any other motion to tell the messenger to continue. The man understood anyway, and as Gareth watched the exchange, he understood why King Owain had agreed to marry his daughter to the King of Deheubarth: Anarawd was a force to be reckoned with. He ruled with a strong hand, didn't suffer fools, and expected to be obeyed without having to actually give commands. He might even be a good king.

"My lord, your brother asks me to inform you that Maud's treasury did not make it to Devizes with her, and rumor says it entered Wales."

*****

That lost treasure was at the forefront of Gareth's mind as he stood with Hywel in the very same receiving room where they'd faced Anarawd four years ago. Gareth was not a very good liar, but Hywel was excellent at it, so it was fortunate he was doing all the talking.

Richard, who'd deferred his departure because of Sir Robert's death, prowled around the room, glancing every so often at Hywel and Gareth. Maurice Fitzgerald stood by his brother, William, who had risen from his bed and seemed in better health than Cadell. The two brothers looked much alike, with dark hair that could have been Norman or Welsh, long noses, pointed chins, and pale skin. It was easy to see their kinship to Cadell, though the king's hair was lighter in color—and further along towards going gray.

Gareth had always thought Cadell looked nothing like his brother, Anarawd, but as he sat in his great chair by the fire, his fist to his chin, he very much resembled the dead king. He held the three coins Hywel had given him, turning them over and over in his fingers.

Maurice stepped closer to Cadell and held out his hand to his cousin. Mutely, Cadell relinquished one of the coins. Gareth didn't know what kind of response he'd expected from Cadell, but silence definitely wasn't it. Then again, silence was exactly what Anarawd had given the messenger four years ago when he'd announced in this very room that Maud's treasure might have come to Wales.

There must have been something about the coins that demanded the owner continually touch them, because Maurice began rolling his coin between his fingers in imitation of Cadell. Gold had been driving men mad for as long as there had been men. Greed was an ugly emotion—but it was also one of the best motives for murder Gareth knew, and he saw it in the faces of the lords before him.

Only Rhys, who was turned away towards the window, showed no such interest beyond a cursory glance at the coins his half-brother held. As always, there were undercurrents here Gareth didn't understand, and it seemed to him, as with Anarawd and his messenger, that the men in the room were speaking to each other without words, and Gareth wasn't privy to their silent language.

He cleared his throat. So far he'd done nothing but bow, leaving the narrative to Hywel. Nobody had mentioned Gruffydd, who'd returned to Aberystwyth with Steffan and thus couldn't be produced, or Llelo, who had actually dug up the coins. The less these lords knew about the specific circumstances of the find, the better.

Maurice and Cadell exchanged another long look, one that again Gareth couldn't interpret, except that it was meaningful. Hywel shifted from one foot to the other. The silence was becoming awkward, and the longer it went on, the clearer it became to Gareth that these lords had something to hide. They *had* been astonished to learn the coins had been found in Alban's shed, but the idea of a treasure in Deheubarth was not a surprise to any of them.

Then the door to the receiving room opened, a boot scraped in the doorway, and Gareth turned to see who had entered. If looks were arrows, between Hywel and him, Anselm would have had several sticking out of his chest. Cadell's spy lifted his hand slightly, as if in greeting, even though they were glaring at him. Then, half-sheepishly, half-amused, he sauntered his way to Cadell's chair. With his short stature, unmuscled form, and sharp mind, Anselm had made a credible prior, which was why Gareth hadn't questioned his identity until it was too late.

At Anselm's arrival, Cadell's eyes flicked to the men from Gwynedd for an instant—so quickly Gareth almost missed it—and then he sighed and motioned that Anselm should speak. "I didn't expect you to return so soon."

"I heard about what happened here and came as soon as I could."

Gareth found himself suddenly furious—at Anselm, of course, but also at Cadell, at these arrogant southern lords, and at himself for being duped by them—and his hands clenched into fists. Meleri—and Gwen before her—had said she could see his anger in his body, so he knew he was giving himself away. He forced himself to relax and breathe more easily.

Beside him, Hywel stirred and flicked out a hand. Gareth subsided further. Hywel was smiling that smile of his that many saw as amused but Gareth knew to be predatory. Fortunately, Gareth himself managed to clear his emotions from his face, if not his body, by the time Cadell answered Anselm. "I assure you it wasn't necessary. As you can see, we have the best investigator in Wales among us."

Anselm's eyes brightened as he looked at Gareth. No longer remotely embarrassed, the amusement had won out. "So I see." He turned back to the king. "And yet, I bring news you will want to hear." He gestured to the two coins in Cadell's hand. "And I see this is a timely moment for it." His hands clasped behind his back, Anselm said, "For many years I have been tracking rumors of a treasure."

Gareth's hands itched to throttle the spy for his arrogance and insolence, and he didn't trust himself to speak.

But Hywel canted his head. “Empress Maud lost it after Oxford.”

That got Anselm’s attention, and his eyes narrowed. He didn’t look quite so pleased with himself as he had a moment ago, a fact which gave Gareth no end of satisfaction. “How did you hear of it?”

Cadell sighed and answered for Hywel. “Prince Hywel and Sir Gareth were here when I sent my brother word of it. Anarawd swore the messenger to secrecy.” He pinned Hywel with his gaze. “My brother hoped Gwynedd would be equally discreet.”

“We were,” Hywel said softly. This prince of Gwynedd didn’t get angry often, but Gareth could hear the wrath in his lord’s voice, even if nobody else knew it was there. This alliance had started out as good politics, and Hywel had gone into it with his eyes open. The fight against Walter FitzWizo couldn’t have gone better, but if accord with Anselm was a required part of the pact, the men of Gwynedd weren’t going to be so amenable to Deheubarth’s wishes as they’d been up until now.

Anselm, being a spy, was more perceptive than Maurice or Cadell, and he pressed his lips together for a moment before facing his king again. “As you know, we had thought the treasure might be in FitzWizo’s keeping.”

Maurice and William behaved as if this wasn’t news to them. No lord looked directly at Hywel or Gareth—which Gareth had to think was deliberate. Then he spied Rhys out of the corner of his eye. For once, he’d been completely silent, a skill Gareth hadn’t thought the boy knew, and he’d allowed everyone else to forget he was there. He was watching everyone, however, having positioned himself in such a way that he was in the shadows, but could see the faces of his brother and cousins.

Half an eye on him, Gareth took a chance. "That's what Sir Robert was looking for, of course, in Wiston's keep."

William rose up onto his toes and settled back down again. "Of course."

A mutual sigh seemed to pass around the room. If Cadell believed Gareth had figured this all out earlier, rather than after Anselm's arrival, Gareth wouldn't be sorry. At times it was useful to be underestimated, but today wasn't one of them.

In addition, any niggling sense of guilt he might have had about giving these lords only the three coins instead of the whole bag was gone. Hywel's supposed allies had been searching for the treasure while keeping him in the dark about their motives. And it was clear they'd had every intention, if they found it, of keeping it for themselves. If the Dragons hadn't found the coins and given a few of them to Cadell, Gareth and Hywel would never have learned anything about Cadell's quest for the treasure at all.

King Cadell looked at Gareth. "Where is Alban now?"

"He should be here. One of my men saw him mount his horse and ride from the manor. He said he was headed to the castle. With Cadfan ill, leadership of your teulu falls to Alban."

"Find him now." Cadell grimaced as a pain in his stomach, which up until now had let him be, overtook him. "And get me some answers."

25

Gwen

It was evening now, and the hall was warm, though not uncomfortably so. Gwen put the back of her hand to her mouth to cover a yawn she couldn't swallow down. She was glad her father had made do with Hywel as a singing partner and let her stay at her table. She could tell Meilyr was feeling Gwalchmai's absence keenly, which was probably good for both of them, and she hoped her brother was getting on well with all of the responsibility of entertaining King Owain.

Gareth had led a search for Alban throughout the castle but hadn't found him anywhere, and nobody had seen him that day. Once Gareth reported this, Cadell asked Prince Rhys to take a company of men to Alban's house to bring him to Dinefwr for questioning, forcibly if necessary. From what little Gwen had seen of Alban, she knew him to be talkative and not by nature one to disguise his emotions or thoughts. She hoped—for his sake and theirs—that he wouldn't hide the truth of his involvement in whatever was happening here.

If she had been allowed in Cadell's receiving room, she would have suggested they bring Caron in too. Her behavior needed a closer look: Gwen had questions about the multiple accusations that she had betrayed Alban with another man, her fighting with Alban, and what, in fact, she had been doing with Meicol that had prompted first Cadfan and then Alban to beat him for it.

At the same time, Gwen didn't see how the accusations of infidelity could be true. Even if she was irritated with Alban much of the time, Caron was proud of her station as Robert's niece and pleased to be lady of the manor. She hadn't shown she was as unhappy with his lack of advancement as everyone else seemed to be. Gwen wondered if the common disrespect for Alban had come first, or if it had come after he'd failed to be accorded the rank he'd aspired to and the one everyone had assumed would one day be his.

"May I sit down?" Anselm, of all people, was standing opposite her and indicating he wanted to sit at their table.

Gwen despised the man to such an extent that she had to prevent herself from shuddering at the sight of him. He was a snake on a different level from almost anyone she had ever met. While Prince Cadwaladr was amoral and self-absorbed, he justified his actions to himself and didn't think of himself as a villain. By contrast, Anselm was clear-eyed and calculated about what he did: he was doing evil, and he *knew* it.

"Of course." Gareth gestured that Anselm should pull out the bench. Since Gwen and Gareth had arrived at the table first, they were sitting with their backs to the wall, and Gwen felt a vindictive pleasure in knowing that if Anselm was to sit, his back would be to the door. No man—warrior or spy—liked that.

"I know you don't like me or trust me." Anselm settled onto the bench with a casualness that was extremely irksome. He had changed from his traveling clothes, which had been mud-spattered and common, into a green tunic of fine weave, and his undershirt was embroidered at the collar and on the sleeves, as on a woman's gown. His boots were knee-high and polished until they shone, which Gwen could see because his breeches were tucked into them like a Norman's might be. All the more reason not to like or trust him.

"We don't," Gwen said.

Anselm wobbled his hand back and forth as Normans did to imply doubt. "I was serving my lord as he asked me to. You do the same every day."

"My job doesn't require me to deceive everyone around me," Gareth said.

Anselm snorted and leaned back a bit. He'd been leaning forward, his elbows on the table, in a behavior meant to imply intimacy and that the three of them were co-conspirators. Now he abandoned the pretense and slapped his hand once on his thigh. "Fine. I have been ordered to tell you what I know."

"We're listening." Gareth was delightfully unforgiving.

Anselm rolled his eyes, prompting stifled laughter from Gwen. She hadn't wanted to show any emotion, but Anselm was so obviously frustrated by their obstinacy, and they just as determined to keep it up.

Unfortunately, her laughter prompted him to grin. "As you know, Empress Maud's treasure went missing after the siege of Oxford. We always suspected it might have come to Wales, but more specific rumors surfaced earlier this year that made us sure of it. King Cadell sent me in pursuit of them."

"That can't be why you were in St. Asaph," Gwen said. "St. Kentigern's monastery was never rich."

"No," Anselm said shortly. "Hardly. My duties are many and varied. Inquiry into the whereabouts of the treasure was just one of my pursuits. Rumor said it had come north. Some even reported Earl Ranulf had it, which was how he was funding his wars against Gwynedd and King Stephen."

Gareth grunted. "You weren't wrong to be concerned. Ranulf is unpredictable on his best day, and we have all wondered if he was stripping his treasury in his quest to maintain his independence."

"I was also on the trail of Prince Cadwaladr." Anselm looked at them with dark eyes. "King Cadell is concerned about what he might do next—or what he might convince King Stephen to do, if it is true he has sought refuge in the English court."

"We all have been concerned," Gwen said.

"It may be, however, that he has gone to Bristol," Anselm said.

Their heads came up at that. "Earl Robert would not harbor him, not with what he knows about his exploits," Gareth said.

"In the past, Earl Robert would not have, but he is ill, and his son—" Anselm paused, "—well, you know."

"We do," Gareth said.

"We understand Earl Robert has a wasting disease," Gwen said.

Gareth sighed. "He is a good man. He would have preferred to die on his feet."

"Wouldn't we all." Anselm took a drink of mead from the cup in front of him. He'd brought it with him, as Gwen and Gareth had brought theirs, tapped from a new barrel in Cadell's cellar over which one of Hywel's men was standing guard. Trust in Dinefwr's kitchen was still a long way off.

Gwen could see why Anselm was so good at his job. He was endeavoring to warm them to him, and she was succumbing to his charms, listening and talking to him as if she didn't hate him. It was irksome to find herself manipulated so easily. She hardened her chin. "What does any of this have to do with the treasure?"

"As we know, Robert's son, William, is not the man his father is. He cares little for who wears the crown and much more about his own position in whatever regime ultimately wins this war. He knows Maud's claim to the throne of England will be much weakened once his father dies. He is secretly currying favor with King Stephen behind his father's back."

"You can hardly blame him," Gareth said. "Many men joined Maud's cause for Earl Robert's sake rather than for hers. Nobody likes her."

"That is an understatement. She's arrogant and vindictive," Anselm said. "There is even rumor that she sees her defeat on the horizon and will soon return to France."

"That will embolden Stephen," Gareth said. "I can see why William might be worried about his future."

Anselm canted his head. "And then there is Maud's son, Henry. He is cast more in the vein of Robert himself. He could be king—and a good one. As evidenced by his invasion a few months ago, he is not ready to give up."

Gwen's eyes widened as she realized what Anselm was saying. "Is William thinking that by reacquiring the treasure he might buy his way into Henry's court?"

Anselm looked at Gareth, his eyes twinkling. "She's a clever one, isn't she?"

"I'm right here," Gwen said, relieved in a way to be irritated again.

Then she felt Gareth's hand on her thigh, and she subsided.

Gareth, meanwhile, was looking directly at Anselm. "Such a gift could fund Henry's military campaigns, as he is ever short of money."

"It could."

"Are you surmising, with all this talk of politics, that William of Gloucester has had a hand in the murders here?" Gareth said.

For once, Anselm showed uncertainty, and he shrugged. "Everything I've told you so far is my understanding of the current political situation in England. We have Ranulf doing his best to carve out a kingdom for himself in the north, Earl Robert holding much of the west, and King Stephen centered in London. If these coins you found are really part of the vast treasure that was lost, the discovery of the rest of the wealth will change the balance of power in the whole country." He leaned forward again. "Don't you understand yet? *Everyone* is seeking it."

Gwen forced herself not to think of the bag of gold coins making its way even now to Aberystwyth in Gruffydd's saddle bag. She didn't dare show anything on her face except interest in Anselm's story, and she prayed she was a good enough spy after all these years not to give anything away she didn't mean to.

Gareth was doing the same, though he still had a hand on Gwen's thigh. "If the treasure was really in Alban's shed, we will squeeze him until we find out where he moved it to. That's the easy part."

Anselm harrumphed. "I am not so sure. He can't have been working alone, and he may not readily give up his partners, not if he thinks he can stall us or if there's any chance of keeping any part of it for himself."

"Meicol and Sir Robert are dead," Gwen said. "He could have killed them to keep the secret."

Anselm shook his head. "I know Alban. He might have murdered Sir Robert, but he wouldn't have poisoned the pie, and he certainly isn't a master thinker. My sources say the treasure was initially in the charge of a woman Maud trusted. She took it out of Oxford, and then it disappeared without a trace."

"A woman? By herself?" Gareth said.

"The treasure was guarded by men, of course," Anselm said. "I have tracked the rumor from Oxford to Chepstow to Chester to here. The only thing that is clear is that none of the men who might have been involved in its capture made it home again."

"They could have been killed in the fighting with Stephen," Gwen said. "Maybe there never was a treasure."

Anselm looked at her intently. "It is your husband who found the coins."

Gwen's lips twisted. She had to grant him that.

"Could Caron be this woman we seek?" Anselm said.

"I was thinking earlier that she has to be involved," Gwen said, "but she was never Maud's maid."

"I didn't say *maid*," Anselm corrected. "The woman was high born, a lady-in-waiting."

Gareth scoffed. "Those aren't exactly thick on the ground in Deheubarth."

"Caron was Sir Robert's niece, but she has never left Deheubarth," Gwen said. "She has birthed five children!"

"That is a problem." Anselm tapped a finger to his lips. "And then there's FitzWizo's spy, whomever he might be."

Gareth paused in the act of drinking from his cup. "You know of one for certain?"

"His existence is why Cadell was so careful to keep secret his plans for Wiston. That he was successful tells me the spy is not as highly placed as he'd feared."

Gwen shot a look at her husband. "In other words, that spy wasn't Sir Robert or anyone else in Cadell's inner circle."

Gareth gestured with his cup to draw their attention to the main door to the hall. "Prince Rhys is back."

Anselm turned on this bench to look where Gareth indicated. The young prince strode through the doorway. He was in full armor, his left hand resting on his sword and his helmet tucked into his right elbow. His face was uncharacteristically grim, however, and at the sight of it, Gareth rose to his feet.

Rhys saw him and detoured towards him rather than heading straight to the receiving room at the back of the hall. Cadell was still too ill to sit on the dais, which was occupied at the moment only by the Fitzgerald brothers and a few of their men. Unsurprisingly, most everyone had chosen to eat sparingly tonight, and the benches were more than half empty.

Rhys came to a halt at the end of their table. "He wasn't there, and Caron is indisposed, vomiting continually, so she could not be questioned, other than to say she didn't know where her husband was. She claims he rode to the castle."

Anselm slammed a fist onto the tabletop, revealing an underlying temper Gwen hadn't known was there. "He's fled, then."

Rhys shook his head. “I wouldn’t say so, Anselm. While we were there, his horse arrived back at the manor. It still wore a saddle, but it was riderless.”

26

Evan

One of the sayings Evan remembered well from his time under Sir Robert's tutelage was the adage that *motion was almost always better than no motion.* It was a style of fighting he taught to all of his students, one that relied on quick, consistent thinking and action.

The basis of all sword fighting was a series of movements so prescribed it formed a ritual at times in its precision. Each swordsmaster took the same basic framework and embellished and added to the steps. Each had signature moves a keen observer might recognize as the foundation of his students' style—and know who had taught them just by watching. Some might promote a cool stillness followed by sharp, quick movements before a return to stillness. Others preferred pure aggression, and still others considered wasted any move that wasn't meant to kill.

Sir Robert had constructed a system to bring down an opponent that went three or four moves beyond what might be necessary if victory was quick, but he had pounded into Evan's head that thinking three moves in advance wasn't enough. He wanted six, and he wanted his students to be able to complete all six without stopping. His students were to be relentless.

And as Evan rode away from Dinefwr Castle yet again, it occurred to him that whether or not he was physically moving, the idea applied equally to murder investigations. It was, in fact, Gareth's hallmark too. Evan wondered if someone looking at him, if he knew Gareth, would recognize Gareth's training in him.

He glanced up at the sky. Clouds had begun to move in over the course of the evening, and he put out a hand as the first drops of rain fell. He instantly stopped feeling sorry for Angharad, who'd been left behind. He had given little thought over the course of his life to the lot of women, but he found himself missing her and said as much to Gareth, who was riding beside him.

Gareth chuckled. "Those are words I'd almost given up hope of ever hearing you say."

Even more oddly, Evan was completely unembarrassed. "I'm surprised myself." He frowned as he turned to his friend. "Do you think she'll have me?"

Gareth's eyes were bright. "It isn't Angharad I'd be worried about. It's whether her uncle will let her go, and to Gwynedd yet again."

"I'm going to have to beard the lion in his den, aren't I?"

"I'd say so. And you'd better do it before you talk to Angharad."

"How?"

Gareth laughed and shook his head. "Best walk straight up to him and ask him."

They had come down the hill from Dinefwr, following in reverse the path Alban might have taken from his manor. It was only three miles, and the way was straight, as Evan knew well by now, but there were many side tracks to hide a fallen man if his horse had spooked and thrown him.

Before they'd left the castle, Hywel had urged King Cadell to send only a handful of men, in addition to the Dragons, to look for Alban, but the king wasn't viewing this quest to find Alban as a search party so much as a manhunt. He wanted Alban in his custody, and he didn't care how much of any crime scene got trampled in the process.

Evan motioned to the remaining three Dragons. With Gruffydd gone, command had fallen to him. "The three of you stick to Prince Hywel like a burr. Don't let him out of your sight even for an instant. Llelo and I will ride with Gareth."

Gareth scoffed. "This worrying about me has gone a little too far, don't you think?"

"Alban's horse came back riderless. His absence could be the result of an accident, but I don't like the odds of him coming to harm the very day he's questioned about his activities. Mark my words, this is going to turn out to be another murder. Nobody is riding alone in these woods, least of all you, the man charged with finding the killer." Evan snorted. "We haven't forgotten, even if you have, the incident at Aber when you almost died in a ravine. Gwen would have my head if I let anything happen to you."

"Let them guard you, Gareth." Hywel grinned. "It will be good for you to have a taste of what my life is like all the time."

Gareth's chin had a stubborn set to it, but he didn't argue anymore. Evan was right, and they all knew it, even Gareth.

"We'll go this way." Gareth jerked his head to indicate a path to the north of the road.

The track was one Evan had not yet ridden along, but once they'd followed it a hundred feet or so, they heard voices up ahead. Then they rounded a bend and found Barri and two of Lord Maurice's men standing in the middle of the road, having dismounted from their horses. They were arguing.

From a distance, Evan wasn't able to make out what they were saying—just that they'd raised their voices—and at the sight of the newcomers coming towards them, the three men stopped talking.

Gareth's horse danced a bit as he reined in. "What seems to be the trouble?"

The rain was coming down harder now, and the torch Llelo carried flickered mightily in the rising wind. It was made of oil-soaked cloth, however, so it wouldn't go out unless they doused it in the river or stamped it out in mud. He had a second one strapped behind him on his saddle bag for when this one expended its fuel.

One of Maurice's men, Henry, whom Evan knew, spoke first. "We found something, my lord, though Barri thinks it's nothing." He augmented his last comment with a sour look at Barri.

"Show me." Gareth dismounted and tossed his reins to Evan, seemingly intending, despite Evan's lecture of moments ago, to head off alone with men not of his own faction.

Evan tipped his head to Llelo, telling him to go with Gareth and Maurice's men. Evan himself wanted to stay with Barri, who showed no sign of entering the woods and towards whom Evan had been feeling more and more distrustful with each passing day.

"We found some crushed leaves and blood." Henry pointed to the ground. "I think these tracks could be from a body being dragged." He headed off, followed by Gareth, Llelo, and the second of Maurice's men. Barri remained in the path, reins in one hand and a torch in the other, looking more disgruntled by the moment.

Evan dismounted too, but instead of following Gareth, he halted in front of Barri. "What's going on?"

"Nothing is going on," Barri said. "All this suspicion and hate circulating through the men is making me more ill than a castle full of poison ever could. Alban didn't do anything wrong, and I don't like that he's being treated as if he did."

"Gold was found in his shed."

Barri tsked through his teeth. "That could have been there for years. It's undoubtedly Sir Robert's."

"Who's conveniently dead and can't tell us anything," Evan said. "How well did you know Alban?"

Barri gave him a baleful look. "I hadn't seen him in two years before our recent alliance." He frowned at Evan. "Did someone say otherwise?"

"Who's the father of Caron's child?"

Barri looked first discomfited and then alarmed. He leaned in to Evan and spoke in a voice so low it barely carried the few inches between them. "How did you know about that? Nobody knows about that."

"You obviously knew."

"Who told you?" Barri urged. "Was it Anselm?"

That came from out of nowhere, but was perhaps one of the most disconcerting things Barri could have said. "I can't say."

Barri snorted his disgust and kicked at a rock in the road. "It serves no purpose to speak of it. It was a long time ago, and Caron has always been Sir Robert's heir anyway. Why does it matter that she bore his child?"

Suddenly Evan felt he'd lost the thread of the conversation. If Caron was newly pregnant with Sir Robert's child, relations between them had not taken place a long time ago. Barri was talking about something else entirely. Evan decided to take a leaf from Gareth's book and remain silent, in hopes that Barri would be made so uncomfortable that eventually he *had* to speak.

Meanwhile, Barri paced around the narrow cart track, not looking at Evan, until finally he grabbed his arm and yanked him closer. "All of this is Anselm's doing. If something happens to me, you remember that!" And at Evan's nod, he added, "I will tell you everything, but not here." Voices could be heard coming back to them. "Meet me at the monastery when we're done."

With these words, it occurred to Evan that Barri trusted him, even thought of him as a friend, and he had a pang of guilt that Barri might have thought more highly of him all these years than he'd ever thought of Barri.

Llelo popped out of the woods. "We found him."

"Is he—" Barri's eyes went wide.

Llelo nodded. "I'm sorry. He's dead."

After that, Llelo volunteered to be the one to return to the castle and notify King Cadell of Alban's death, and Barri went with him as part of his duty to Lord Maurice. Evan let him go, unable to keep him. The rest of them took Alban back to the monastery to lie next to Sir Robert. Both the monks whose job it was to prepare the bodies and the gravediggers had worked nonstop for two days getting ready for the funeral, which would take place tomorrow. Truthfully, those who'd died the first night at the castle should have been in the ground by today, but the abbot had decided out of respect for the dead that he could put it off for one more day until those who had lived—particularly the king—were well enough to attend.

Evan stood in the doorway of the little room off the cloister, watching Gareth examine yet another body. As he watched, he found Barri's accusation of Anselm replaying over and over again in his head. He had half a mind to speak to Barri further, as he'd requested, before he told Gareth anything about it. If Anselm had something to do with any of this, Gareth would be furious. Though Gareth wasn't hot-tempered normally, premature words or actions would do nobody any good. And they might break apart this fragile alliance of lords.

But then Gareth glanced up at him and asked, perceptive as always, "What's wrong other than the obvious?"

"What do you mean?"

Gareth tipped his head to Alban. "He was your friend."

Evan pushed away from the doorframe. "Not so much. I didn't know any of these men half as well as I thought I did."

"Men grow up. They change."

"Do they?" Evan said. "Does anyone ever really change?"

"Some do."

Evan turned to find Abbot Mathew behind him, and he moved out of the doorway to let him in. Vespers had come and gone, so Mathew should have been in bed, seeing as how dawn came early this time of year. "Someone who allows Christ into his heart can become someone different than the man he was before."

Gareth pulled the sheet over Alban's head, calling an end to his examination. They'd known as soon as they'd seen the body what had killed him: his head had been smashed in, much as Sir Robert's had been, a similarity that was impossible not to remark upon. His neck was also broken, however, so it was possible his horse had spooked and dragged him through the woods to where they found him, some fifty yards off the road. Otherwise, they were looking at foul play again.

"Most don't change, however." Gareth moved closer. "Most people fundamentally don't want to."

Abbot Mathew gently turned back the sheet to expose Alban's face. "He was a good man."

"Was he?" Gareth said. "How many would agree?"

The comment prompted Mathew to look at Gareth with some intensity. "I admit he was prideful and arrogant." He waved a hand at Evan and Gareth. "It's hard to find a soldier who isn't. But he loved his wife, and he did his best. He turned a blind eye to the sins of others."

Evan took a chance. "Like Caron's?"

Mathew froze. "Why would you say that?"

Gareth melted backwards towards the wall, out of the torchlight, such that when Abbot Mathew turned around, it might even have seemed that he and Evan were alone.

"We have heard from several sources that Caron has had relations with other men," Evan said.

"If that is true, it's the first I've heard of it."

"Some say the child she bears is not Alban's; others that her infidelity began with her eldest."

Mathew shook his head with vigor. "No. You have been misled."

"Are you sure?"

"Why would you even suggest such a thing?"

Evan tried to speak matter-of-factly to ease Mathew's apparent uncomfortableness with the conversation. "This is what we do. We ask questions, and sometimes we don't like the answers."

Abbot Mathew's brow remained furrowed. "While it's true Caron was pregnant when she married Alban, the child is his." He sighed. "They're hardly the first couple to have their first child eight months after their wedding. There's no mystery here, and I don't know why you've heard differently."

Gareth straightened from his position against the wall. "We have heard three different stories from three different people about Caron's lack of fidelity to Alban."

"How pure are the motives of those who speak thusly?" Abbot Mathew said somewhat tartly.

That gave Evan a moment's pause, and he frowned, realizing that all three stories had been told specifically to him. Was it because he was a known quantity to the people of Dinefwr and they trusted him, or because they knew him and thought he could be easily deceived?

"Alban had fired the undercook, who resented the loss," Gareth said, "and Cadfan had been promoted to captain of King Cadell's guard over Alban."

"And Barri—" Evan pursed his lips, trying to think what Barri had to gain by casting doubt on Caron and Alban. He felt a pang of guilt at his own role in the accusation. Perhaps Barri wouldn't have said anything at all if Evan hadn't brought it up.

"Alban suggested Barri as a man from whom we'd find answers," Gareth said. "Perhaps Barri is seeking to distract us."

"A man's reputation is all, even more so when he is dead and cannot defend himself." Father Mathew shook his head. "This is a bad business, my sons. I am praying every hour that you bring it to its conclusion quickly."

27

Gareth

After Abbot Mathew left, Evan explained more about what Barri had told him, little as that was, and his vague accusation of Anselm. It was Barri's words, coupled with the bits and pieces they'd acquired along the way, that had given Evan the knowledge to question Mathew, and for that Gareth was grateful. He did lament the foul layer that seemed to underlie Dinefwr, much of it just below the level of villainy. Unfounded accusations and gossip appeared to be a way of life.

It made him wonder if there was something unusually wrong with the moral fiber of the people here. Was it due to a general disregard for right and wrong that started at the top with the king, or was Aber no different, and Gareth was so used to encompassing the misdeeds of the people of Gwynedd that he couldn't see it? He was, however, perfectly happy to indict Anselm, sight unseen, for everything that had happened at Dinefwr. Unfortunately, if he was to do so in the presence of King Cadell, he needed more than Barri's word.

"Where did Barri say he would meet you?" Gareth said.

"Here at the monastery." Evan frowned. "I didn't think too much about the specific spot."

"Let's have a look around, shall we?" Gareth grabbed a torch from a sconce outside the church door and walked across the courtyard with it. Evan had a lantern of his own, and he followed Gareth towards the graveyard. Sir Robert had met his killer there, and despite that fact, it was still a good place to meet someone after hours.

Gareth took a few steps past the gate and slotted his torch into another sconce by the entrance.

Evan handed Gareth the lantern and then crossed his arms and leaned against the post. "I'll wait here. That way I can see anyone who comes through the main entrance or out of the cloister." The rain had let up, and he pushed back his hood. "I know you've been wanting to have another look at the cemetery when nobody else was about."

Gareth lowered the lantern to a few inches above the grass. When he'd been murdered, Sir Robert had fallen between two gravestones, surprised from behind by his attacker. Gareth began to circle the area, not necessarily looking for anything specific, but looking for *something*—anything—that would give him a perspective on the killer. With both Robert and Alban dead, plus the poisoning, the death toll had risen to such a height that he was surprised Cadell hadn't picked a man out of the crowd and hanged him just to be seen to be doing something.

Of course, that didn't appear to be the way he worked. Gareth had to respect him for his patience, though that didn't lessen the pressure on Gareth himself to find answers where up to now he'd found none.

The graveyard was in the form of a triangle, since the road that ran by the church didn't run exactly north to south but off at an angle, and the church itself had been oriented east to west. An oak tree the builders had chosen not to cut down took up the far western corner, with enough room between the trunk and the wall for a man to fit, were that man looking to hide. It was as good a place as any to start, and Gareth moved behind the tree, bending to shine the lantern deep within the grass, hoping to see footprints or a token to indicate a man had stood there.

"I wouldn't have said it was a nice night to be standing in a graveyard." The voice was Anselm's, and he wasn't talking to Gareth, hidden as he was behind the tree, but to Evan. If the fact that Anselm was in the graveyard at such a late hour wasn't bad enough, the second question, following hard on the heels of the first statement, raised Gareth's hackles. "Are you alone?"

"I'm here to meet someone," Evan said.

"Is that so." It wasn't a question.

"Not you, obviously," Evan said.

Gareth doused the lantern and eased further behind the tree as silently as he could while still making sure he could see Evan and Anselm. He'd kept the lantern low to the ground because he'd been looking for boot prints, a fact for which he was grateful now since the grass and the tree had hid the light from Anselm's eyes. There had definitely been boot prints in the earth too, making him think his guess about where the killer had stood was right. If not for Anselm's arrival, he would have taken a measurement, but instead he stayed still and listened.

Anselm looked right and left. "I don't see anyone."

Evan eased into a more ready stance, even to the point of dropping his left hand to his sword. "He's late."

Anselm spread his hands wide. "There's no need for that. I am not your enemy."

"How do you figure?"

"Your prince allies with my king. Thus, we are allies ourselves. Who are you waiting for?"

Gareth noted Anselm's habit of tagging a question onto the end of an otherwise innocuous string of thoughts. It was an interesting technique for catching a suspect unawares.

And, with a start, Gareth realized that's exactly how Anselm was treating Evan—as if he was a suspect and someone to interrogate.

Evan, who may or may not have realized himself what was happening, answered calmly enough. "Barri."

"Maurice's man. Why?"

"I'm not sure that's any of your business."

Gareth swallowed down a laugh. If the shaking of Anselm's shoulders was an indication, he was amused too, but what he said next was not so amusing. "Then perhaps you won't be pleased to hear that I saw him taking the western road not a quarter of an hour ago."

Evan frowned. "What do you mean?"

"As I reached the bottom of the castle hill, I saw Barri riding past on the main road, coming from the east. He kept going, however, so if you were thinking to meet him tonight, I suspect it will be a lengthy wait."

Evan looked at Anselm for a long moment. He held himself so still Gareth wasn't sure he was even breathing. Anselm's back was to Gareth, so he took a chance and showed himself for a heartbeat, signaling to Evan that he should go. Evan made no sign of recognition that Gareth could see from this distance. But then he scoffed, turned on his heel, and stalked away, back through the gate. At first his footsteps resounded on the cobbles of the courtyard, and then they faded away.

Gareth himself moved back into hiding the instant Evan departed, retreating behind the tree and barely daring to breathe.

Anselm stood silent for a moment, letting Evan get out of sight, and then he shoved the gate closed, turned, and began to walk deeper into the graveyard, towards the several dozen newly dug graves that men had spent all day digging in preparation for the funeral tomorrow. He passed Gareth's position, though still fifty feet and many gravestones away from him, and then finally stopped, facing away from Gareth, his hands on his hips. "I know you're here. You can come out now."

Gareth didn't move.

A few heartbeats later, he was glad he hadn't. Barri himself straightened from where he'd been hiding behind a stone crypt. He came out slowly, almost haltingly, while Anselm waited for him, still amused. Fortunately, the distance and angle between their two hiding places meant Barri couldn't have seen Gareth when he'd shown himself to Evan.

"What game are you playing?" Barri said.

Anselm scoffed. And then, before Barri knew what was happening, the spy had swept Barri's legs out from under him, landing him face first in the grass. With his knee in Barri's back, Anselm pulled on Barri by his ponytail, lifting his head and chest off the ground, and put a knife to his throat. It was a series of moves Gareth had never seen done so well—and so quickly Gareth himself had hardly been able to keep up with the steps.

"You might want to save your thanks until after you tell me what I want to know. Where's the treasure?"

"I don't know!"

"Try again." Anselm jerked harder on the ponytail. For a small man, he had a startling ability to be menacing. "You are at the heart of this. You killed Sir Robert, and then you killed Alban. Why?"

"I didn't! I didn't!"

"It had to be you. There's nobody else it could be."

Barri was trying desperately to hold his neck away from the knife, but Anselm gave no quarter. He tugged once, and Barri screamed. From where Gareth crouched, he couldn't see what Anselm had done, but whatever it was, it had been painful. If Barri had been Gareth's own man, he would have intervened, but he didn't trust either of these men.

"I have no problem slicing your throat and leaving you to bleed out right here."

Barri screamed again and then with gasping breaths said, "All right! All right! I killed Alban. But he's to blame for Sir Robert's death."

Anselm didn't ease up. "Keep talking."

"We did have the treasure, stored in the cellar of Alban's shed, just like Sir Gareth thought. We've been quietly selling it, a piece at a time, for years."

"How did you come by it?"

"We were both at Oxford, on Stephen's behalf. We caught Maud's men after they sneaked the treasure across the river. They were supposed to take back roads and meet Maud at Devizes. She got away, but the treasure couldn't move as quickly."

"Surely the two of you didn't do all this yourselves?"

Barri didn't answer immediately, but then the scream came again. Gareth couldn't see from where he crouched what Anselm was doing to Barri, but it was enough to keep him talking. Barri was in genuine fear for his life. Even if Cadell chose the Norman punishment of hanging over the Welsh practice of *sarhad*—payment to the victim's family—death later was better than death now by Anselm's hand.

"Not at first." Barri's voice trembled. "We-we killed everyone else in our company."

"That sounds like you, not Alban."

"It was my idea," Barri said sulkily. "Alban went along with it because of the gold."

"Why were you not caught?"

Barri's voice came a little stronger, now that he was speaking the truth. "It was such chaos and confusion after the battle that once the men who helped us were dead, it was easy to hide the treasure and return to our respective companies. A bleeding head wound can explain a day's absence."

"What was Sir Robert's role? Was he there that day?"

"No. But somehow Cadell and Maurice learned the treasure hadn't made it to Devizes and had come to Wales instead." The words tumbled over themselves. "They began to openly look for it, and Robert was getting too close!"

"What about Alban?"

"He was losing his nerve. Those men from Gwynedd don't back off for anyone. I knew Alban was going to betray me, so I followed Robert to the church and killed him before Alban could tell him the truth."

"Why not just kill Alban then and save yourself the trouble?"

"Alban is never alone. Besides, if Alban died, Robert might return to his manor. I couldn't risk him searching the property. Of course, while I was in the graveyard here, someone was moving the treasure from the cellar."

"Who?" The question came with a jerk of Barri's head.

"I don't know!"

Evan had spoken of Barri as clever and secretive, and his plan had been just that. It was disconcerting that he and Alban had managed to keep it a secret all this time, right under King Cadell's nose.

"What about Meicol?" Anselm said.

"I don't—I don't know anything about why he died."

Anselm didn't believe him, and more screams erupted from Barri but no more answers. The rain had started to fall again, and the water and blood ran together down Barri's neck.

"Where is the treasure now?"

"I told you the truth!" Barri was sobbing. "Don't you think I would tell you if I knew? It was in the cellar of the shed, and then it wasn't. Someone moved it, but I don't know who. Neither did Alban."

"So say you! What if he lied to you? You've killed him, and now we'll never find it!"

In that moment, Gareth really thought Anselm was going to slit Barri's throat. Throughout the interrogation, Gareth had been watching Anselm's face more than Barri's, and it was terrifying in its coldness and certainty. He could have been whitewashing a house, so little did what he was doing to Barri affect him. And still, Gareth had to admit that without Barri's confession, they might never have discovered the truth about the murders or that the treasure had been moved on the night of the celebration.

The question, of course, which Anselm had already asked, was *by whom*?

What was also clear to Gareth was that all Anselm cared about was the treasure. He had no feelings one way or the other about the murders. Information about them was a means to an end. It also occurred to Gareth that were Anselm to silence Barri, it would leave the spy to pursue the treasures himself, for his own gain.

Truth be told, Gareth had learned as much about Anselm in the last quarter of an hour as he'd learned about Barri.

Anselm finally seemed to accept that Barri could tell him nothing more, and he came off Barri's back. Barri collapsed onto the grass, weeping.

Anselm turned his head and looked directly to where Gareth was hiding. "Did you get all that?"

Gareth laughed under his breath, though entirely without humor, and stepped out from behind the tree. "Yes."

From his pocket, Gareth pulled the short length of rope he always carried, the one he could have used to measure the length of the boot print. With Barri's confession, that was no longer necessary. Kneeling, he tied Barri's hands behind his back and then lifted him to his feet.

Turning him, he held him by the upper arms. He had looked into the eyes of many murderers over the years, but few showed as little regret about what they'd done as Barri. He regretted being caught, certainly. He regretted losing control of the treasure. But he didn't care a silver piece for the deaths of Sir Robert or Alban, his co-conspirator. Admittedly, Alban himself had sold out Barri earlier in the day.

"Do you know what Robert was doing here that night?"

"No." Barri spat on the ground. "And I don't care. It's just my bad luck you didn't take the bait."

Gareth's eyes widened briefly as he understood what Barri meant. "You planted that signet ring to make us think Robert was spying for FitzWizo."

Barri tsked through his teeth. "Why didn't you believe it?"

"We're asking the questions." Gareth had no need to explain himself or his methods to Barri. Though the truth was, with Robert dead, pursuing that lead hadn't seemed important. It did mean that if there was a spy within Cadell's domains, he was still out there. "How did you come by it?"

Barri's scorn was tangible. "I pulled it off one of FitzWizo's men. How else?" He had poured out his guts to Anselm, but now that the pain had ended, he could be disrespectful to Gareth.

"If he wasn't a spy, why was Robert here?"

"How should I know?"

"Guess."

"The stables at the castle are full, so he left his horse here. He'd done it all week. Alban said Robert was seeing a woman."

"Why would Alban care who Robert saw?" Anselm said.

"If they married and had a child, Alban would lose everything." Barri sneered. "We had more than enough gold to see us through, but Alban wanted the status and land he would get through Robert upon his death. He wanted respect."

"So you got it for him—for all of a single day before you killed him too." Gareth found himself sickened and disheartened. Gone were the days when men like Barri could spark a righteous anger in him. Now they just made him want to sleep for a week. "Do you know where this woman lives?"

Barri jerked his head to indicate west. "Somewhere that way. I don't know her name. Nobody does."

Gareth eyed his captive. A thought had just occurred to him, and he wanted to speak of it now, since he feared the moment he gave Barri to Cadell, he would lose access and control. "Were you the one who spread the rumor that Walter FitzWizo had the treasure? You're Maurice's man, so you could have done it easily."

Barri had the conceit to look proud of himself, but it was Anselm who answered. "Walter FitzWizo is a supporter of King Stephen and a far more loyal one than the Fitzgeralds and the Earl of Pembroke have ever been. If the treasure had come to Wales, Wiston was a logical place to have stored it until it could be safely transported to Stephen's treasury in London."

Gareth nodded to himself. "And the reason it wouldn't have been transported already is the miles of territory controlled by Earl Robert of Gloucester between here and there."

"Indeed. It was sound logic, just not what happened to it." Anselm began to walk away, not towards the monastery courtyard, but out the other side of the churchyard.

"Where are you going?" Gareth called after him. "This is your arrest, not mine."

Anselm waved a hand above his head without looking back. "You heard everything he said. I don't care to waste any more time with a murderer and thief." Then he paused as he reached the last gravestone, finally turning his head to look at Gareth. "The treasure is out there, and I am going to find it."

28

Angharad

"Uncle, I would speak to you."

When Angharad had first come to Dinefwr after the death of her father, she had been afraid of Cadell, fooled by how calm and collected he remained at all times, thinking it was the outward manifestation of a deeper wisdom.

No longer was she that girl, nor even the one who'd fallen in love with the handsome Prince of Gwynedd. Time and grief had taught her to question, to consider, and most importantly, to apply what she knew to what she saw and make her own assessment of a man's character.

For example, she'd decided upon meeting Prince Rhys, even at thirteen, that he would grow to be a man to be reckoned with. At the moment, he was lounging on a bench against the wall, eating slices out of an apple he was carving with his belt knife. The implications of the conversation they'd just had with Sir Gareth and the traitor, Barri, meant nobody was going back to sleep easily anyway.

"What is it now?" Cadell didn't look up from the paper he was reading. It was a deliberate ploy to intimidate her, to let her know he was a busy man and not to waste his time.

"When Prince Hywel's men return to Aberystwyth, I would like to travel with them."

Silence. The king continued to read, leaving Angharad standing before him. It was only with great effort that she refrained from shifting from foot to foot. After a count of ten, Cadell looked up, his expression bored. He leaned back in his chair, putting an elbow to the arm and a finger to his lips. "Who is it?"

"I-I don't know what you mean." It made her angry that he could see right through her and that he didn't mind making sure she knew it.

"Just tell him, Angharad." Rhys had finished his apple and drawled out the words. "Regardless of who it is, you should let her go, brother."

Before Cadell could answer, someone knocked at the door, and at Cadell's summons, entered.

It was Evan himself, though he paused on the room's threshold, clearly somewhat taken aback by the scene before him. "I'll return later."

"No, no." Rhys waved a hand airily. "Come in. This concerns you, I think."

Cadell barked a laugh. He didn't look angry, however, which boded well for the future. Evan stopped beside Angharad, and before he addressed himself to Cadell, he looked at her. "Are you well?"

Angharad knew this was the moment to speak of what she'd come to talk to Cadell about, but she found her words catching in her throat, so instead she nodded numbly.

Rhys, who seemed to be finding the entire scene delightful, said, "She was just inquiring of the king if he would give her permission to travel to Aberystwyth with your company when you leave."

Through several heartbeats, Evan gazed at Rhys with a completely blank expression, and then he turned deliberately to Cadell and bowed. "I came to inquire on the same matter. If Angharad would like to come, Gwynedd would be delighted to have her."

Cadell rested one hand on his belly and put the other to his chin, rubbing at the two days' growth of beard he hadn't felt well enough to shave as yet. His eyes were fixed on Angharad's, and she lifted her chin, forcing herself not to look away.

"This is what you want?" He tipped his head to Evan. "You're sure you want to be a soldier's wife?"

The occasion called for brazenness, and she didn't hesitate. "Yes."

Cadell scoffed and turned his attention to Evan. "You can support her?"

"I am a knight."

Cadell's lips twisted sourly, and he studied them for so long Angharad feared he would say no. But then he nodded. "Gwynedd it is."

By comparison, getting permission from Prince Hywel was a matter of a raised eyebrow and a nod, after which Evan led Angharad out of the hall. They ended up in the shelter of the blacksmith's works. The banked fire was warm, and they stood close to it, their only other light a torch Evan had brought from the hall and put in a sconce attached to a nearby post.

"I apologize, Angharad, for how this fell out tonight. I was trying to do the right thing in the right order, but it got turned around all wrong." Evan blew out a breath. "I never asked you to marry me."

Angharad's color was high, and she was grateful Evan couldn't see it in the relative darkness. "I only intended to wrest permission to ride with you to Aberystwyth. I never meant to hurry you or—" She swallowed hard. "I don't want you to think my interest in you is only because I want to escape Dinefwr."

Evan was gazing at her with those green eyes of his and with as serious an expression as she'd ever seen on his face. "So ... you don't want to marry me?"

Angharad found a joyful laugh bubbling up in her chest. "I'm quite certain you still haven't asked me."

"You already answered your uncle, but I have to ask again. Are you sure you want to be a soldier's wife?"

"I was always going to be a soldier's wife, even had I a married a prince." Best to begin with honesty, and Evan didn't balk at the reference to Prince Rhun.

"As long as you're sure." From an inside pocket of his leather coat, which he wore against the rain tonight instead of full armor, he removed a small bag, and from within its depths, he pulled out a ring. It was golden and narrow, meant for a woman. "This was my mother's." Before Angharad realized what he intended, he went down on a knee before her and held up the ring. "Angharad. *Cariad.* Will you marry me?"

She gazed down at him, finding tears pricking the corners of her eyes. When she'd entered the hall for the celebratory feast, she'd had no future beyond the castle's walls. But here she was, three days later, with her life was turned upside down. Before she thought any harder about it, she bent to Evan. Because he'd made no attempt to kiss her himself, she put her hands on both sides of his face and pressed her lips to his.

She'd surprised him, but he warmed to the kiss, putting his own hand behind her neck to hold her to him while at the same time rising to his feet.

It was a life he was offering her, and though it wasn't the one she'd at one time thought she'd have, it was one worth living.

29

Llelo

Llelo's heart had leapt when his father had suggested the previous night that he be the one to ride west in search of Robert's mysterious woman. First light hadn't come soon enough for him, and his father had found him in the monastery stables in the murky dawn for a few last instructions.

"This is an information-seeking quest only. You are not to take risks. You are not to confront anyone or bare your sword. You understand?"

"Yes, Father." Llelo tried to tone down his excitement and look at his father with calm eyes and a mature demeanor. But from that very first quest back at Newcastle-under-Lyme, when his parents had taken him and Dai in, he'd wanted to learn everything about this job they did. Anyone could be a soldier, but it took a great man to bring a murderer to justice—and behave in a just manner while he did it.

"I don't think I have to impress upon you the importance of this task. I have too much to do and too little time to do it in, and I have everybody watching me. Whoever this woman is, Sir Robert kept her a secret for a reason. I will honor that choice until I have reason not to."

"Yes, sir."

"Your mother does not know I'm sending you, so don't make me regret it." He handed Llelo a sketch of Sir Robert. "This woman we're looking for may not even know Robert is dead."

Llelo sucked in a breath. "I'll have to be the one to tell her."

His father put a hand on his shoulder. "Are you sure you're ready for this?"

There was hardly a question his father could have asked that could have done more to straighten Llelo's spine. "Yes. You can count on me."

His father's expression softened. "You have nothing to prove, Llelo. You are my son, as surely as the child in Gwen's belly. I am already proud of you."

Llelo nodded jerkily and then turned to mount his horse. He did believe his father. Or at least Llelo believed that his father believed what he said—and that he would continue to love Llelo even if this unborn child was a boy. Llelo's advantage was that he was fifteen now. A man. And the more that he behaved as one, and the more his father relied on him to do a man's job, the more permanently he'd be established in everyone's eyes as Gareth's son six months from now. And six years from now. The new baby wouldn't be a man for fourteen more years. Llelo would be nearly thirty by then, with a family of his own. He'd be a knight in his own right.

And the best chance for all of that to happen began with doing what his father needed done right now.

"One last thing." Gareth reached up and handed Llelo a slim iron key. "It fits none of the possessions Robert brought with him. Maybe there's a box at Alban's house I don't know about, but in the meantime, when you find her, maybe you'll find what it goes to."

Llelo took the key. "Yes, sir."

And he was off. He rode along the road heading west, which happened to be the same one they'd traveled along to get to Dinefwr so innocently four days ago for the celebratory feast. Nobody was talking about the alliance much now, not like they had been. If his father didn't solve these murders, it could soon be dead, the fractures caused by the deaths too great a chasm to leap across.

Bearing in mind the stories his father had told him about searching for culprits during past investigations, Llelo stopped at the first hut he came to. It was early morning still, but farmers and herders rose with the dawn, as had Llelo himself, and a young woman was drawing water from the family's well. He dismounted and walked over to her, very conscious of the sword at his waist and trying to keep his expression sober.

She looked at him, at first absently, since she was hauling up a full bucket of water, and then with interest. His face flushed before he could stop it, and he covered up his embarrassment by grasping the rope and helping her pull up the bucket the last few feet.

"I can manage," she said, taking the handle from him.

He wanted to be helpful, but she was determined and didn't want his help, so he stepped back. "I don't mean to offend." He pulled out the sketch his father had drawn. "Do you know this man?"

The girl, who couldn't have been more than a year or two older than he was, tipped her head to study the paper. "That's Sir Robert."

Llelo's expression cleared. "You know him?"

"Of course I know him. He is one of King Cadell's men. I have offered him water many times."

Llelo found himself disbelieving, but he tried to keep the skepticism out of his voice. "It is my understanding that he hasn't been to Deheubarth in some time."

The girl frowned. "Whoever told you that wasn't speaking the truth. I've seen him several times a month this whole past year. He doesn't always stop, but he always waves."

"He was riding from the castle?"

"Not always, though most recently he came down the road same as you."

That could have meant he was coming from the monastery, as he'd been doing the night he was killed, but Llelo didn't comment upon it. "When was the last time you saw him?"

Her brow furrowed as she thought. "A week ago?" She spoke uncertainly. "He'd ridden by daily for a week, but I haven't seen him since—" She stopped, her expression filling with horror. "Is he among those who died at the castle?"

Llelo took in a breath. “He wasn’t poisoned.” But then before her face entirely cleared with relief, he had to add, “He is dead, however. He was murdered that same night.”

Now her expression crumpled, and she put her face into her apron, not wanting Llelo to see her tears. He stood in front of her awkwardly, uncertain if he should pat her shoulder or simply ride away. He opted for clearing his throat. “I am so sorry.”

“Do you know who killed him?” she said from underneath the fabric.

“We do.”

She pulled down the apron so he could see her face again. “Good.”

Llelo moved on to the next croft and the next. The response to Sir Robert’s death was the same from everyone. Llelo’s parents had dealt with many murders over the years, and few victims had been so universally beloved. Llelo began to feel he was doing something wrong, and he hoped his father wouldn’t be too disappointed in him.

But he soldiered on. Close to a dozen farmsteads dotted the landscape within five miles of Dinefwr to the west, each family blessed with a field for their own foodstuffs, some of which would be tithed to the king, and then common pastureland for their cattle and sheep. This was rich country—far richer than Gwynedd, which was rockier. His birth father had been a wool merchant, and Llelo wasn’t so far removed from that life that he didn’t recognize the value of the coats on the sheep, which would be sheared in another month.

He had forgotten to ask the first girl *where* Sir Robert might be riding to along this road, and at about the tenth household, he began to realize that there was something underhanded about people's answers. Several simply refused to say anything at all. When yet another man skated his eyes to the left, Llelo's heart began to beat a little faster. He pressed the man, but then had to give up when he abruptly turned away towards his barn.

Llelo let him go, realizing he needed to come at this from a different direction, particularly if he was speaking to a woman. He'd discovered during this expedition that girls and women responded to him better than men. He would have to ask his mother about it, but he thought it was because he was young: his age made him unthreatening to women but not worthy of respect to men, despite the sword he wore belted at his waist.

The next house was down a side track from the main east-west road. The property was well-tended, if small, and a woman was trying to juggle a baby on her hip while still hanging her laundry on a line. Llelo scooped up the caterwauling baby, who was so surprised to find himself in the arms of a total stranger that he stopped crying.

"Thank you! If I put him down, he eats rocks, and my mother is tending to my sister's child."

"What about your husband?"

"Ach." She motioned dismissively with a momentarily free hand. "He's off at the castle. Seems they've had some trouble up there and needed an extra hand in the smithy."

"You didn't go with him?"

"Heavens no!" She looked at Llelo between two garments she was hanging on the line. "Poison, wasn't it, that did them all in? He said he'd send for me when he was sure it was safe."

Llelo smiled to himself. Prince Hywel would be pleased to learn of the distrust the poisoning had created among Cadell's people. Llelo's task, however, remained ahead of him. "Do you recognize this man?" He held up the sketch of Sir Robert.

The woman peered at it, catching her son's hand as she did so, since he was trying to snatch the paper from Llelo. "That's Sir Robert! I've never seen such a likeness." She met his eyes. "Did you draw this?"

Reluctantly, he shook his head. "My father. But he's teaching me."

"It's a fine skill to have. My older boy is good with his hands." She pursed her lips. "Why are you asking about Sir Robert?"

"We are trying to retrace his steps. His woman lived near here, but I need someone to point me to the correct house."

The woman's brow furrowed. "Why are you asking?"

Llelo met her gaze. "Ma'am. I'm sorry to tell you, but Sir Robert is dead."

She put her hand to her mouth, gasping a little. "No! We hadn't heard that he was among those poisoned!"

"He wasn't poisoned."

Tears leaked out of the corners of the woman's eyes, though she wasn't overtly sobbing. "Poor Jane."

Llelo gave her a moment while he considered how to ask without asking what he wanted to know. "Can you take me to Jane so I can tell her in person that he's dead?"

"Of course." She gestured down the lane, which continued past her house. "She lives another half-mile that way." Then she put her hand to her mouth again, and her eyes widened over it. "Oh no! The babe!"

Llelo swallowed. "She's with child?"

The woman nodded, still with her hand to her mouth. Then she heaved a deep sigh and reached for her own baby, who'd been occupying himself with the brooch on Llelo's cloak.

"The child is Robert's?"

Again the nod. "He was fixing to tell the king that he was marrying, but he wanted to finish out his service against the Flemings first."

"Would you mind coming with me to see her?"

The woman sighed. "I'll have to, I suppose. She won't understand you otherwise."

"Why would that be?"

"Well, you see, she's Norman."

30

Gwen

It was a relief to know who had murdered Sir Robert and Alban, but it made Gwen sick to think that Barri might have been in the graveyard not to confess to Evan but to kill him. It was the only sensible reason that he'd asked Evan to meet him there. When she'd said as much to Gareth, he'd just stared at her. Apparently the thought hadn't occurred to either of the men. No matter how many times the threats against them were pointed out, she could never convince either her husband or his friends they were really in danger.

Meanwhile, the issue of the poisoning and the poisoner remained unresolved, and Gwen was unsatisfied with their progress. Questioning the residents of the castle had not achieved much—certainly not the identity of the culprit. Thus, the next course of action was to go through everything again.

The men had been called in to speak to King Cadell. Although he'd been walked through Barri's confession last night, he had insisted on going over it all again this morning, this time in the presence of the Fitzgeralds and Richard. Up until now, Cadell had been a man of relatively even keel, but when Gwen had passed by the doorway on her way to check in with Saran, it sounded like a chair had hit the wall of Cadell's private audience chamber. He was revealing his distant kinship with King Owain.

For once, she was glad that the men from Deheubarth didn't consider a woman important enough to be present. Evan, meanwhile, was occupied with Angharad and her preparations to leave Dinefwr for good. As a woman in love herself, Gwen had itched for years to find a woman for Evan. It was even better, though, that he'd found someone on his own, and Gwen was particularly pleased she would have a new friend and companion in Angharad.

"What are we looking for exactly?" Saran tossed another blanket towards a large pile forming in the middle of the barracks common room. Other women were rolling up pallets and scrubbing down tables and chairs. Not everyone had recovered from their sickness yet, but enough were on their feet to return the room to its original purpose.

"Some clue or indication of who might have poisoned the pie. We're really to the point where we just want a list of names of people who *could* have."

"Well, for starters, where did the poison come from? As I said over Meicol's body, it isn't as if processing poison can be done in any kitchen. Besides which, the plant has to be grown first."

"I knew I came to you for a reason," Gwen said. "Obviously, there are gardens in every household from here to Gwynedd. The murderer could also have bought the poison and transported it here. In that case, we will never find the source, but if he didn't—"

"Exactly," Saran said. "But if he didn't, then the poison was grown locally, and we should look for it. It is a rare plant. Not to boast, but if it were one of the common ones, I would know it."

Their first stop was at the castle's kitchen garden. Like Old Nan's garden, Gwen had already given it a cursory going over, but the whole point of the day was to go over everything again. The garden's position on the south side of the castle made the most of whatever sunshine managed to make it through the twelve months of clouds that were the weather in Wales.

Gwen followed Saran through the rows, but this garden was entirely devoted to vegetables. The garden outside the castle walls was accessed through the postern gate, and it proved not to be any more informative. Not only was monkshood entirely absent (a relief in a way), but so were hemlock, foxglove, and wisteria. In fact, lack of abundant herbs for healing (or flavoring food) was some indication as to why the castle's healer was so bad at his job.

"Where is the healer, anyway?" Gwen asked Saran, having returned to the courtyard of the castle.

"He remains ill." Saran shrugged. "I suppose I shouldn't be surprised. He is quite fat, and the pie did look delicious."

Gwen couldn't help but laugh.

"That is unkind, I know." Saran patted Gwen's shoulder. "You might think I wanted his job, which I don't!"

Their next step was to ride the short distance down the hill to the monastery. Abbot Mathew was just arriving at the castle as they were leaving, and though he gave Gwen a piercing look, she merely sketched a wave. If he'd been Abbot Rhys from St. Kentigern's, she would have valued his participation in whatever they were doing, but they were in Deheubarth, and she didn't know him well—and didn't know if she could trust him. It was a mutual loss.

The monastery's kitchen garden was located to the west of the church, though far closer to the main buildings than the barn in which they'd met yesterday to discuss the gold coins. Gwen stepped into the herbalist's hut and sniffed the air, finding herself immediately comfortable. The sentiment was even more true of Saran—who greeted the elderly monk with an embrace.

"You look fine, my dear." Siawn was his name, and he beamed at her. "Marriage suits you."

Siawn himself seemed to be well suited by his profession. His face was weathered from so many years spent in his garden, his stomach somewhat rotund as befitted his age, and his eyes were bright. They gleamed, in fact, with interest and intelligence.

Saran introduced Gwen, prompting Siawn to take her hands. "I wasn't here for the dreadful goings on up at the castle as I was tending to several sick children over the hill a ways." He lowered his head and gave her a piercing look. "But my abbot mentioned you to me when I returned home this morning. He thinks very highly of your husband." Then the monk bustled straight for the door. "Let me show you my garden."

Walled only on the north side, which was where the most delicate plants were grown, the garden was like the others in that it made the most of whatever sun was available. Brother Siawn led them along a path, pointing out his prized plants, and ended up in the northwestern corner where the brick wall met a thick shrub. A chest-high wooden fence surrounded a plot of land, fifteen feet on a side, setting off this small portion of the garden from the rest.

Siawn gestured with his head to the fenced area. "Medicinals grow here." He canted his head. "And poisons."

With Siawn's permission, Saran opened the gate. Gwen remained outside. The two healers didn't need her ignorance interfering with their work and the space was small enough that she would probably just get in Saran's way. Instead, she leaned against the fence and watched them move among the plants, talking softly to each other.

"Looking for clues, are we?" Anselm's voice came low in Gwen's ear.

Gwen spun around, instantly angry that he had snuck up on her and wanting to smack that sneer off his lips.

He knew it too, because he took two hasty steps back and spread his hands wide. "I mean you no harm. I'm just doing my job, same as you—though, if our jobs are the same, yours is an unseemly one for a woman."

"This is the woman who uncovered your plot in St. Asaph, so don't mock." Gwen knew that she should keep her mouth shut and not rise to his bait, but she couldn't help herself. She was terribly annoyed that it had been Anselm who'd coaxed—or tortured, if Gareth's description was accurate—the truth out of

Barri. Not that Barri deserved her sympathy, given that he'd killed two people.

"What are we doing here?" Anselm lifted his chin to point to Saran and Siawn. Saran was still bent among the plants, but Siawn was giving Anselm something of a beady eye.

"*We* aren't doing anything," Gwen said.

Anselm scoffed at Gwen's obstructionist attitude. "I will rephrase. Why are you watching them grub among the plants?"

Gwen frowned. "The man who poisoned your lord is still out there. Nobody should be pretending the danger is over."

Anselm snorted. "You are reading too much into this. The food had gone off. That is all."

Gwen found her breath steadying. "How can you think that?"

He shrugged. "Even if everyone was poisoned, what good does finding the plant do you? Anyone could have crept in here and taken it."

"Not just anyone would know how to prepare it, however," Gwen said.

"I heard you don't even know what plant you're looking for." Anselm's lips twisted in disdain.

"If you care so little for the source of the poison, what are you doing here with us? I thought you had gone off seeking the treasure."

Anselm looked away, appearing somewhat discomfited for the first time that Gwen had seen.

Gwen's eyes widened. "You thought we were here for the treasure! Did you think we'd found it buried in the garden?" She laughed mockingly. "Not doing too well on your own, are you?"

"It is somewhere," Anselm said stiffly. "It is only a matter of time until I find it, but you aren't in a cooperative mood today. I will take my leave." He gave her a short bow, one she couldn't interpret as anything but mocking, and departed.

Gwen tapped her knuckle to her upper lip as she watched him go. If she never saw him again it would be too soon, but she probably wasn't that lucky. Still ...

"You know, Saran," Gwen said over her shoulder, "for all that Anselm is a snake, he does have a point. Barri moved freely within the monastery grounds."

Siawn came to the little gate. "I assure you no treasure is buried in my garden." He gestured expansively to include the whole of the space. "The earth is full of new plants, and I haven't turned the soil in weeks."

Gwen swept her gaze around the garden to see that Siawn was right. He had new plantings of all kinds, but no plot had just been turned over. She chewed on her lower lip, recalling the visit to Old Nan. "What might you plant from seed during the first week in June?"

Siawn was still at the gate, his hands tucked into the sleeves of his robe. "Late season carrots and peas, perhaps? April and May are the best time for planting, and I've done all of mine already. If you've waited until June, you will need to get the seeds in the ground immediately to give them the most time in the summer sun and hope you haven't started too late."

Gwen thanked the monk, but she didn't say what she was thinking. The treasure had caused enough deaths so far. There was no reason to endanger Siawn with more knowledge than he needed to have. In fact, the more she thought about it, the less she wanted to speak of what was in her mind to anyone but Gareth.

Saran had finished her inspection and came to stand beside the monk. "You grow an amazing variety of plants, Siawn."

He beamed. "No doubt the sin of pride will be my undoing, but I have some of the best specimens in all of Deheubarth, though Old Nan's garden runs a close second."

"What does she have that you don't?" Gwen said.

"She grows more flowers than I do, of course, and her roses—" He shook his head, marveling. "She also has the finest specimen of Lady Laurel I've ever seen. It only grows in the mountains usually."

"Lady Laurel?" Saran gazed across the fence at Gwen.

"Is something wrong?" Gwen said.

"Lady Laurel is also called Daphne, Gwen. I've never seen the plant myself, but I've heard of it."

Siawn nodded sagely. "Even a twig would be dangerous for you, my dear Gwen. Its bark causes miscarriage. If ingested fresh, a single berry can blister the mouth and cause vomiting and death."

Gwen found herself gasping. "Why didn't you say something sooner?"

Siawn blinked. "I-I only arrived home today." The monk looked from one woman to the other. "There are so many poisons, I didn't think to privilege one over another."

"The people who were poisoned had blistered mouths, Siawn," Saran said.

"I'm sorry. I didn't know." He swallowed. "Does it help if I tell you that just touching it can cause rashes and weeping sores?"

That caused Gwen to draw in a breath too. "May the Lord have mercy on us!"

"What was that?" Siawn said.

"It doesn't matter." Gwen motioned to Saran and Siawn. "Come with me!"

They had no time to lose.

But as they reached the monastery courtyard, Gwen discovered that the events of the day had overtaken her. As she rounded the corner, she was faced with a host of men, including King Cadell, Prince Hywel, and her husband. Gwen's eyes widened. She had completely forgotten about the funeral for everyone who'd died.

The Dragons were all here too, and they'd spread out around the courtyard in such a way as to appear randomly dispersed, but they weren't fooling Gwen for an instant. They were on guard, as always. Hywel and Gareth were near the church steps, in a circle that included Cadell and the Fitzgeralds. Everyone was dressed formally except for Gwen.

Embarrassed to still be wearing her third-best dress, she found Evan near the corner of the church, not far from the cemetery gate. "How long before the funeral?"

"It starts at noon, Gwen."

She glanced upwards, checking the location of the sun, which was high in the sky. "I need Gareth."

Evan looked down at her, his interest sharpening. "Why?" He'd been watching the lords desultorily, bored with the proceedings as were all the Dragons. They seemed to have two ways of being: action and sloth, motion and no motion, with hardly anything in between.

Gwen pursed her lips, not answering in part because she didn't know what exactly she should say without talking to Hywel or Gareth first. She trusted the Dragons with her life, but she'd reconsidered her suspicions of where she might find the treasure and was halfway to convincing herself that her idea was absurd. It was offensive to even think Meleri or Old Nan had anything to do with any of this.

On the other hand, both were vulnerable women in their own way. Perhaps Meicol had convinced them to help him steal the treasure, bury it in the garden, and then poison the castle as a distraction...

Her thoughts stopped there, since it was Meicol who'd ended up dead.

31

Gareth

Gareth held his tongue. It would do no good to castigate Gwen for going off on her own (even with Saran) while he was busy with King Cadell. It was a topic for another day, after all this was over. She had accused him of being cavalier with his safety, and here she and Saran had done exactly the same thing. The last two days, Llelo had taken it upon himself to keep an eye on his mother, but Gareth had sent him off on an errand, leaving Gwen unprotected. So really, this was all Gareth's fault.

The fact that Brother Siawn was involved at all was disconcerting too. All things being equal, Gareth would have kept whatever questions Gwen had about the poison plant within Gwynedd. Though he hadn't dismissed his wife's concerns, the idea of Meleri or Old Nan having anything to do with murder was absurd.

And yet ... Gwen's instincts were usually good, and he'd be a fool to ignore them. Especially if she turned out to be right.

"I can't leave. Cadell will notice."

"Why would he?" Gwen's eyes were on Hywel, who'd remained on the steps of the church next to Lord William. "Prince Hywel and my father are going to sing something beautiful, and nobody will be wondering what happened to the captain of Hywel's teulu or the Dragons."

"We're lucky nobody has yet wondered why there aren't six Dragons," Gareth said, feeling sour.

"We keep moving so nobody can count us," Evan said in all seriousness.

"Has Angharad said anything about where Gruffydd and Stephen have gone?" Gwen asked him.

"She noticed they were missing, of course, but I told her I would tell her everything when we reached Aberystwyth."

Gareth laughed. "And she's newly in love enough to have accepted it."

"Have you seen Old Nan?" Gwen stood on her toes to look for herself, but there were too many tall men around her to see much of anything.

"No, but I saw Meleri," Evan said.

Gwen glanced again to Prince Hywel, who'd been joined by Angharad. The girl's eyes were on their little group, but Evan gave her a quick shake of his head, and she stayed where she was.

"Can we go now?" Gwen asked her husband.

"I still don't have a good idea as to how. My horse is in the stable, as is yours."

"Ours aren't," Evan said. "We'll ride double."

It wasn't that Gareth didn't want to pursue Gwen's idea. He wanted nothing more. But his—and now Gwen's—encounter with Anselm had made him very wary. What's more, he didn't see Anselm here, which meant he was out there, somewhere, causing mischief. Gwen might be right that the treasure—or even the poison—could be found in Old Nan's garden, but if Old Nan was there alone, she would be vulnerable to Anselm. The spy was up to something, and all day Gareth had felt as if at any moment he might find an arrow between his shoulder blades.

Evan motioned with his head and, without having to do anything more, caught the attention of the other Dragons.

Taking Gwen's arm, Gareth led her around the edge of the crowd, which was growing larger by the moment as everyone from village, castle, and farm arrived for the service. A mass would be sung, they'd bury the dead, and then attend another meal up at the castle—though Gareth didn't know how many people would actually eat. He still hadn't eaten anything produced by that kitchen other than bread. But perhaps everyone would come anyway, trusting, as they had to, that their king would keep them safe.

Fortunately, Hywel had far more men to guard him than just the Dragons. As the captain of Hywel's teulu, Gareth had fifty men at his disposal, and he found Rhodri and Goch near the stable. "Prince Hywel is in your hands."

Rhodri narrowed his eyes. "Anything we need to know about?" His tone was so flat it almost wasn't a question.

"Not yet."

The corner of Rhodri's mouth twitched. "We'll take good care of the prince."

"I know you will."

They had to fight against the flow of people in the courtyard in order to reach the main gate. Gareth had caught Hywel's eye before heading out, and he could see the frustration in the prince's face that Gareth was going and he wasn't. In the end, the size of the crowd turned out to be an advantage because there were just too many people to keep track of, and they arrived on the road where one of the stable boys was standing with the Dragons' horses without being hailed or stopped.

Except by Prince Rhys, who stepped out from behind a tree and glared at them. "What do you think you're doing?"

"Solving your brother's problems for him, that's what." Gareth wasn't feeling particularly charitable to Rhys at the moment, though in truth he liked this young prince. "You can come if you promise not to get in the way."

The look of surprise on Rhys's face, in and of itself, was almost worth any inconvenience having him along might cause. Gareth grinned, turned to boost Gwen onto a horse, and then mounted behind her. Siawn and Saran shared a mount, and then the Dragons shared the final two horses. Cadoc and Aron rode off at a canter, soon disappearing around a far bend. They were the advance guard, few as they were.

Two miles later, the rest of them turned into the yard in front of Old Nan's house, only to hear screeches and shouts coming from behind the garden wall. Gareth hastily dismounted from his horse and ran to the entrance to find Old Nan, a shovel raised above her head, raging at Aron, who'd fallen on his back in the dirt. Before she could bring the shovel down, Gareth caught the handle just above where she held it in her fists.

"What is going on here?" He looked into her eyes and saw rage looking back at him. Gareth was shocked enough to step back, but not so much that he released his hold on the shovel.

"He attacked me!"

Aron gasped. "I found her digging up that patch. There's silver in there." He pointed with his chin to a wheelbarrow set to one side of the garden plot where a silver candlestick stuck up from the dirt.

"The boy doesn't know what he's talking about," Old Nan said. "All I was doing was digging in my patch, working the soil, when he grabbed me from behind!"

Between one breath and the next, Old Nan had wrapped herself up again in her cloak of blindness.

But Gareth couldn't forget what he'd seen in her eyes. She'd *seen* him. "Who are you, really?"

"I'm Nan." The reply was tart, and she stared at a point over his right shoulder, just as she'd done the day they'd met.

Gareth set her on her bench by the wall while the Dragons set to work on the garden plot, working quickly to haul silver pieces and gold plate out of the ground.

Before Prince Rhys could get to work too, Gareth pulled him away from the treasure. "How long has Old Nan lived two miles from Dinefwr Castle?"

"I don't know exactly. I do know that her sister lived here, and she came to stay with her before my stepbrother died," Rhys said. "Her sister died at some point later, and she stayed on."

That was not very specific, but Gareth left the prince overseeing the treasure and found Gwen, Saran, and Siawn standing in front of a two-foot-high bush growing behind a row of trellised beans.

"That's Daphne?"

Siawn sighed. "Indeed."

"I suppose it wouldn't have made a difference had anyone remembered it sooner." Gareth stared at the plant, trying not to sound accusatory. "It's really that poisonous?"

"In my defense, it is rare." Saran approached the plant and reached down to feel the soil. "Does it look to you like someone tried to dig it up recently and gave up?"

Gareth bent and ran his fingers through the earth as Saran had done. Like the plot where the treasure had been hidden, the soil was freshly turned. "Perhaps halfway through trying to remove it, the murderer decided it was best to leave it where it was rather than risk the attention caused by its absence."

Then Gareth looked to where Old Nan was sitting, up against the garden wall but fifty paces away. "She has to be fooling us. She can't really be blind."

"She seems blind, Gareth," Gwen said.

"You didn't see the way she looked at me earlier when she was in a rage."

"She's very protective of her garden." Gwen took in a breath. "You have to admit that if she can see, she has maintained an incredibly convincing act for many years. Why would she do that? Why would anyone?"

Gareth looked at his wife. "If she can see, it's an incredibly effective front. She can go anywhere, do anything, everyone is solicitous, and nobody questions her or her motives." He was suspicious enough of Nan at this point that he was considering the idea she'd been sent into Deheubarth on the trail of the treasure all those years ago—by Empress Maud perhaps, or Earl Robert, or even King Stephen in the same way Anselm spied for Cadell or Gwen for Hywel, though Gareth would never put his wife in the same category. A blind old woman was the perfect disguise, allowing her a freedom of movement afforded to few others.

Gwen still looked uncertain—and maybe even a little concerned about Gareth's sanity.

"It has to be her," Gareth insisted. "She's a more likely candidate than Meleri!"

"I don't know, Gareth—"

"Let's find out." He cast around for something to throw that had weight to it, but not so much it would hurt. He came up with a round seed pod and walked to within ten paces of Old Nan. He studied her for a moment, and then called her name, "Old Nan!"

As her head swiveled towards him, he threw the pod towards her face. Old Nan's hand came up in an instinctive move only a sighted person would make. As she caught the pod, her face was again transformed by hate—and then she made a dash for the door.

32

Gwen

While Rhys stayed behind with Iago, Aron, and Cadoc to finish digging up the treasure, Siawn, Saran, Gareth, Evan, and Gwen took Old Nan back to the monastery. Gwen was relieved the mass hadn't ended, so they didn't have to bring Old Nan through a crowd.

Once inside the main gate, Gareth and Evan led Old Nan towards the guesthouse, which had a large common room that would serve as their interrogation chamber for now, and Gwen ran to the entrance to the church. The vestibule was deserted except for men of Hywel's teulu, and she approached Rhodri, who was standing guard at the entrance to the nave. "I'm looking for Meleri."

"Who?"

Gwen gritted her teeth in frustration. Most of the people from Gwynedd who'd met Meleri yesterday had been left back at Old Nan's place. Then Gwen spied Richard de Clare, who was standing just inside the entrance to the nave, rather than up at the front with the other lords. She sidled up to him. "Have you seen Meleri?"

Richard raised his eyebrows, giving every indication that he was ready for adventure once again, and tipped his head to the right. "She's standing among Dinefwr's servants."

This group was clustered at the back of the nave, the few of them that were still alive, since their ranks had been hard hit by the poison. Gwen didn't see Meleri at first, but then she turned her head, in the way people do when they're being watched, even though Gwen had done nothing to draw attention. At the sight of Gwen, Meleri smiled beatifically and waved like Tangwen might.

Gwen waved back, motioning that Meleri should come to her, and when she reached Gwen, she whispered. "Do you like my dress? Caron gave it to me."

"It's lovely," Gwen said sincerely. There was no point in disturbing Meleri's equilibrium and a great deal to be gained by keeping it. The mass was ending anyway, and as Meilyr raised his voice in song, the people began to follow Abbot Mathew and a line of monks out the door that led to the graveyard rather than the courtyard. Gwen caught Meleri's elbow. "Come this way with me."

Meleri followed happily, crossing the courtyard to the guesthouse. Her cheerful demeanor remained until just across the threshold, when she faltered at the sight of Old Nan sitting in a chair pulled out from the long table.

Gwen, who was holding Meleri's elbow, spoke to her gently. "It's all right. She can't hurt you."

Old Nan glared across the room at Meleri, proving without a doubt she could see just fine.

"What's going on here?" King Cadell spoke from behind Gwen.

Gwen turned to see the king with Richard, who gave Gwen a sheepish look, implying it was his fault the lords were here instead of at the burial.

"We've found your murderer, my lord," Gwen said, moving with Meleri to one side to allow him to enter. "You're just in time to hear the story."

A quarter of an hour later, the guest hall common room was full of angry men suffering through various shades of disbelief as Gwen and Gareth took turns relating each step of the investigation, up to the finding of the treasure in Old Nan's garden. Siawn, backed up by Saran, even came forth and spoke of the Daphne, the nature of its poison, and what would have been needed to turn the berries to poison.

All the while, Old Nan glared at all and sundry in angry defiance.

Cadell planted himself in front of her. "Who do you work for?"

She laughed up at him. "Wouldn't you like to know."

Cadell backhanded her across the face, an act that was met with shocked silence by everyone else in the room. She was a murderer and a liar, but everyone had spent years thinking of her as a blind old woman. "Tell me!"

Old Nan pressed her wounded cheek to her shoulder and didn't answer. Her hands were tied behind her back, but if they hadn't been, Gwen was sure she would have made a rude gesture at the king.

Gwen had sat Meleri in a chair by the fire, and after Siawn had finished his part of the story, he'd hurried off to his workshop to find the salve for her rash that Gwen had promised her earlier. Even Cadell, whose face was as red as the fire, knew better than to shout at Meleri, and so he allowed Gwen to put the first questions to her. "How did you hurt your hands?"

"There was a plant," Meleri said immediately. The exchange between Cadell and Old Nan had widened her eyes, but the display of violence directed at Old Nan appeared to have made her less afraid of the older woman rather than more. "Old Nan had me help her collect the berries. She didn't want to touch them."

Gwen could see why. "What did she do with them?"

"I don't know."

"Did you do other things for her, Meleri?"

"I put a vial in Meicol's pack." She smiled, proud of herself. "And I gave him a tart."

"A tart Old Nan made?"

She nodded. "I told him I made it, though."

"Why would you tell him that?"

"Old Nan told me to."

Gwen glanced quickly around the room. Several of the men were standing with their hands to their chins, well aware of the significance of what Meleri was telling them. "Did Meicol know about the treasure, Meleri?"

She frowned as she thought. "I don't know."

"How did Old Nan find out about it?"

"I don't know." Then Meleri smiled sweetly. "I did a good job helping her move it though." She looked up at Gwen, her eyes bright. "She's not really blind, you know."

"So we gathered," Gareth said dryly.

Gwen shot him a quelling look and then turned back to Meleri. "I'm sure you were very helpful. This was from Alban's cellar to her garden?"

Meleri nodded. "So many pretty things." She brightened again. "She gave me my own tart as a reward, but I don't like currants, so I didn't eat it."

Gwen's breath caught in her throat, knowing how close to dying Meleri had come.

Meleri went on, unaware of the horror in the room. "I didn't tell her because Caron says when you tell people you don't like something they give you, it makes them feel bad."

"Caron is right."

"She also says it's wrong to take other people's things or reveal their secrets." Meleri smiled up at Gwen. "I keep everybody's secrets, don't I?"

"You do."

Meleri's innocence was unfeigned and had all the men in the room believing every word she said. Her story, though very different from Barri's, made perfect sense.

Then Gwen saw Gareth whisper in Evan's ear. Evan nodded and left.

What they needed now was Old Nan's story, and maybe that would finally tell them why Meicol had died. Barri hadn't even known he was involved. To that end, Cadell planted himself in front of Old Nan. "We have enough to hang you now, and believe me I will if you don't talk."

"You will anyway."

"Perhaps." Cadell canted his head. "You are a spy, and if your master wants you badly enough, I might have the need to ransom or trade you instead."

Equally with hanging, that would be a Norman thing to do. Rhys moved to his brother's side. "Tell us what you did, Nan. You kept yourself hidden all these years for a reason. For someone. Who?"

Nan's eyes narrowed at the young prince. "I've always said you were too clever by half."

"So are you, apparently," Rhys said. "Come on. What do you have to lose? Tell us what you did and what you planned. Let us see how clever you were. You certainly pulled the wool over our eyes all these years."

Nan laughed mockingly. "I did that." Her eyes went past Cadell and Rhys. "Where's that smart young man from Gwynedd?"

Gareth raised a hand from where he was leaning against the wall, out of the way. "I'm here."

"You're the only one who guessed. Are you proud of yourself?"

"People are dead. Are you?"

Old Nan burst into laughter. Then she gestured with her head. "Look at all of you. So serious! So blinded! Yes, I gave the tart to Meleri to give to Meicol. Yes, I poisoned a castle full of people. Is that what you wanted to hear?"

"We want to know why," Gwen said from beside Meleri.

Old Nan snorted. "Because I could! I volunteered!"

Gareth unfolded his arms and came closer. "Who do you work for?"

"Who do you think? Walter FitzWizo!" Then she cackled at the looks of consternation that crossed the faces of the people looking back at her. "You didn't see that coming, did you? I was sent to spy on you, Cadell. And I did."

Cadell lifted his chin. "You couldn't save your lord from defeat."

For the first time Old Nan deflated a little. "You kept that close to your chest, didn't you? Brought in men from the outside to do your dirty work and put out that you were off to Chepstow."

"I knew I had a spy in my midst. I just didn't know who."

"You should be dead."

Cadell ran a hand through his hair. "When did you learn about the treasure?"

"Meicol told me. He followed Alban to it. He wasn't sneaking around Caron." She snorted. "He found the treasure and stole some coins he hoped wouldn't be missed. He gave a few to me out of pity. Pity!"

Gareth stepped closer. "Meicol told you about the treasure, and you poisoned him and everyone else for it. Why didn't you leave with it the night of the feast?"

"I meant to." She spat on the ground in disgust. "I'd arranged with Lord Walter for three of his men to help me move it, but they never arrived."

Gwen's eyes widened. "You overheard Prince Rhys telling me about their deaths. That's why you left when you did."

"Smart girl." Old Nan nodded. "Instead, I fetched Meleri from where she was hiding, and we moved the treasure to my garden that night. I didn't dare take it farther, not with so many patrols on the road." She canted her head. "Besides, I wanted the rest of it."

Cadell's eyes narrowed. "What is that supposed to mean?"

"Silver and gold plates and candlesticks are all well and good, but where are the gems? The coins?"

Cadell turned to look at Gareth. "You found none?"

"Not in the garden," Gareth said (disingenuously). "If there was more at one time, it's gone now."

"Perhaps Caron can tell us what happened to it." Evan strode through the doorway with Caron in tow. Her eyes were puffy from weeping, though it was unclear whether that was from her husband's burial service or from being hauled to the guesthouse for questioning.

Evan led her towards a seat near Meleri and sat her in it. She didn't look up, instead gazing steadily at her hands in her lap.

"Where's the rest of the treasure?" Cadell was clearly fed up.

"What are you talking about?" Caron's eyes were wide.

With more patience than Cadell, Gareth related how they'd arrived at the conclusion that there was more wealth than what Old Nan had buried.

"I don't know! I mean—" Caron hunched her shoulders, "—we took a few things and a few coins, but not many. It's like Barri and Alban agreed from the first: we had to manage it."

"How many coins were there last you saw?" Cadell said.

"A king's ransom." She shook her head. "So I was told. I never saw any for myself. Alban didn't like me to look at it. He was afraid someone would come upon it by accident, so he allowed the shed to decay and went there rarely, usually just to make sure it was still there."

"And gems?"

"A hundred?" She frowned. "That's what Alban said. He made a necklace for me out of one." Caron brought it out on its long chain and showed it to Cadell.

He harrumphed and turned away.

Caron looked pleadingly at his back. "You think it was easy, acquiring that kind of wealth? How does one keep people from knowing? It was a bigger burden to sell it than to keep it a secret all these years. Every new dress I wore was talked about from here to Aberystwyth! Barri spent most of his share on clothes and that dagger." Then her rising defiance was dispelled by a sudden burst of tears. "Did he use it to kill Sir Robert or my husband?"

"No," Gareth said. "Neither was stabbed, and Barri was wearing it when we captured him. He prized it too much to murder Sir Robert with it."

"We've heard rumors that he is the father of your child," Gareth said.

"Who, Barri?" Caron's head came up at last, horror in her eyes.

Gwen scoffed. "Not Barri. Sir Robert."

Caron gaped at her. "He was my uncle! What do you take me for?"

Gwen let it go. It was the least of their concerns. "Could the men have buried some of the treasure elsewhere and not told you?"

"If so, I don't know where." Caron glared at Meleri. "I can't believe you took it without telling me! I can't believe you didn't confide in me at all! You ungrateful wretch! After we took you in and everything."

Meleri cowered before Caron. "Old Nan told me not to tell anyone, so I didn't."

Caron sniffed her disapproval. "Look where listening to that woman got you."

33

Llelo

Llelo spoke both French and English, in addition to Welsh, but he decided not to take offense at the presumption that he spoke neither. "I don't need you to translate, but I would appreciate the introduction. I don't want to scare her."

"You are bringing her bad news. Today won't be a good day no matter how you try to soften the blow." The woman bobbed a curtsey. "I'm Alus and this is Rory. I'll take you there now."

Llelo chucked the baby under the chin. "I appreciate your assistance."

They set off at a walk, Llelo leading his horse while Alus wrapped Rory and herself up in a long cloth and tied it at her shoulder, allowing her to carry the baby on her hip without using her arms. Before becoming part of his new family, Llelo had spent absolutely no time thinking about women and babies, but he knew them now, with Tangwen born after he'd come to Gareth and Gwen, and now with the new baby due in the autumn.

As the woman had explained, they didn't have to walk far down the road before a house came into view. Unlike Alban's manor, Jane's house was rigorously maintained, with grass cropped so short Llelo assumed a goat had eaten recently. The trees and hedges were neatly trimmed, and the one-story house was newly whitewashed and thatched. As they approached, a woman exited the front door. She was middle-aged, but even Llelo's young eyes appreciated her dark curly hair that couldn't be tamed by any scarf, gray eyes, and red lips that looked naturally colored.

At the sight of Llelo and Alus, she came forward. "What is it?"

Alus gestured to Llelo and said in halting French, giving the impression that she had learned it specifically to speak to Jane, "This is a man-at-arms from the castle. He asked to speak to you."

Llelo put a hand on his chest. "I'm Llelo ap Gareth. I have been sent to trace the movements of Sir Robert this week, and I understand he was your friend."

To Llelo's dismay, Jane leapt at him, grabbing him by the shoulders and shaking him. "Where is he?" She was panicked already, and he hadn't yet told her the bad news. "You said *was*. He's dead isn't he?" And right there in the garden, Jane began to sob. "I knew it the moment his horse arrived without him."

Alus pulled Jane away from Llelo and put her arms around her shoulders, though not without a glare in his direction.

Llelo drew in a breath, pleased at least to have solved the little mystery of the horse as well. "I'm sorry, madam."

"Was he among those poisoned? Is that why he didn't make it? He fell ill on the road? I've been worried sick for the last three days."

"Why didn't you come to the castle to see for yourself?"

"He told me never to go there. We were keeping our relationship a secret, you see, until he could speak to King Cadell about it." She pressed her fingers to her eyes, and her sobs lessened. He sensed that his news was no more nor less than what she'd expected and feared, and the outburst of pain had been building for three days.

"Madam—" Llelo brought out the key his father had given him. "Do you recognize this key?"

Jane reached out a trembling hand. "It's Sir Robert's, of course." Before Llelo could say anything more, Jane put a hand on Alus's arm. "Thank you for bringing this young man and the news of Robert's death. I know you must get back to your own hearth now."

"But—" Alus wanted to stay, but she couldn't argue with Jane's gentle dismissal. "Of course."

Alus tightened the cloth at her shoulder, hitched the baby higher on her hip, and set off back down the road to her house. Jane watched her until she was out of earshot, and then she turned back to Llelo. "He left me a strongbox and a key of my own. The box can only be opened with both keys." She looked up at him with the saddest eyes Llelo had ever seen. "He is really dead?"

Llelo nodded. "I'm sorry."

Jane sighed and started to walk away. "Come. If he died, I was to use the keys."

Llelo tied his horse to a post by the door. "What's in the box?"

She didn't answer, and he didn't press the matter, because it seemed he was about to find out, since she led him inside her house. Such was the wealth of Sir Robert—and this woman—that she had a fireplace built into the side wall rather than a central hearth with a hole in the roof to let out the smoke.

This time of year, the fire was not lit. Jane crouched to the stones that made up the base of the hearth and pulled them from their places, revealing a hole underneath. From the hole, she hauled a foot-wide chest and then lugged it to the well-scrubbed table. One glance told Llelo the table was also the work of Meicol, given the carved edges and paws for feet.

Then she went to the sideboard and pulled open a drawer. Taking out a key, she brought it to the trunk and placed it in the lock. There were holes for two keys, and with a nod from Jane, Llelo inserted the key that had been Sir Robert's into the second slot. On the count of three, they turned the keys, and the chest opened. Inside were a bundle of papers and two leather bags.

Jane turned away as if she wanted nothing to do with it. "See for yourself."

So he did. Each of the letters was signed and sealed by Sir Robert himself, and the two bags contained gems and gold.

Llelo swallowed hard to see the coins. "This is Sir Robert's wealth?"

"It is mine."

Llelo fingered one of the coins. It was a match to the Roman coins he'd found in the dirt. "Why show it to me?"

Jane gave him a long look and then gestured that he could sit. "You are from Gwynedd?"

"Yes, madam. My father is Gareth, captain of Prince Hywel's teulu."

"The man who saved the life of Prince Henry?"

Llelo smiled. "The same. I was there that day too."

Jane looked down at her clasped hands, and was silent long enough that Llelo worried he was dismissed, but then she lifted her head and spoke, "Four years ago after the siege of Oxford, Robert found me wandering beside the road, beaten and battered—and with no memory of my name or where I'd come from. I have never remembered."

"You had this wealth on you at the time?" Llelo asked, and at her nod, he added, "How is it that you weren't robbed of it?"

"The coins and jewels were sewn into my skirt."

Llelo wondered privately how hard Jane and Robert had looked for the person she'd been, since they might have thought they'd find an abusive Norman husband at the end of that quest, whose gems and coins these were. Robert obviously hadn't wanted that. Llelo gestured to the chest. "And those papers?"

Jane touched them gently. "A letter confirming Caron as his heir; another acknowledging that the child I bear is his; and the deed to this land, which he leaves to me, as separate from the manor for Caron." She picked up the first document and handed it to Llelo. "Show that to the king, if you think it's necessary."

"What about you? Aren't you coming to the castle with me?"

"Please tell the king that if he would like to speak to me further, I will be here, but I will not go there. This is my home." She gestured around the room. "I see no need to leave it."

Llelo stood, deciding in that moment he had no need to force her. He closed the lid of the chest over the gems and coins, carried the box to the hearth, and hid it again in its hole.

Then he turned back to Jane. "I will convey your regards. Thank you for the truth."

"The truth is always best, don't you think?"

"Unless it isn't."

Jane glanced at the repaired hearth before looking back at Llelo. Their eyes met, they both paused, and then she nodded. "Unless it isn't."

Llelo was convinced he'd found Maud's missing lady-in-waiting, the one who'd been charged with conveying the treasure out of Oxford. But as he bowed his way out the door, his thoughts churned over what he was going to say when he returned to the monastery. He would tell the truth to his parents, as Jane had suggested. But it occurred to him that this might be another story King Cadell need not hear in its entirety.

34

Gwen

Tonight they had forgone the hall up at Dinefwr and chosen instead to dine in Hywel's pavilion, set up in one of the fields adjacent to the monastery. It was private, and they had the pleasure of Hywel's voice, even if Meilyr was still tasked with singing to entertain the other lords at the castle.

Evan and Angharad were both there too, at her uncle's request, since it was her last night at Dinefwr. He had given her a small bag of silver coins as dowry, but her inheritance from her father was actually an estate in Ceredigion, which he'd lost when Gwynedd had annexed the region. Thus, it fell to Hywel to award it to her—an odd circumstance for the niece of the King of Deheubarth, but somehow appropriate too, since she would now be in his retinue.

Contented from a full meal cooked over an open fire by Hywel's own men, Gwen put down her empty cup. "Meicol should have said something to someone other than Old Nan."

She had seen what they'd collected from Old Nan's garden. Having dug a pit ten feet on a side and six feet deep, as if it were a large grave, Meleri and Old Nan had placed crates of valuables in it and then covered the whole thing with dirt. Nobody would have ever found it, especially once Old Nan started her plantings.

"He had spent many years feeling unhappy and unworthy. The beatings Cadfan and Alban gave him may have confirmed his decision that he couldn't go to them about the treasure." Gareth's long legs were stretched out in front of him. "Meicol had nobody he could trust."

"Unlike me." Having finished singing for now, Hywel sat beside his captain, his arms folded complacently across his chest.

Gwen rested her head against her husband's shoulder. She could fall asleep at any moment. "Are we thinking Meicol was the one who buried the coins, to be retrieved at a later time?"

"That is very a good question, Gwen, and not one we should be asking out loud before we reach Aberystwyth." Gareth pulled her closer. "The location of the rest of the treasure is King Cadell's problem now. He will find answers or he won't."

"And we aren't going to help him anymore. Though I never thought I'd say it, good luck to Anselm." Hywel raised his cup in a toast and took a long drink of mead. He was always careful not to let down his guard, but he was drinking a little more freely tonight. The mead had come from a barrel they'd brought from Aberystwyth.

"Even without FitzWizo's men, Old Nan should have run. She was a fool to stay." Llelo was half asleep on the other side of the table with his head resting on his arms, but by speaking he showed he was listening.

Gwen was immensely proud of the work her foster son had done, proving Gareth had been right that he was a good choice to follow in their footsteps. Some might think it foolish to trust someone so young with such a big secret, but by now Llelo had earned their trust.

"She thought she was smarter than everyone else. She'd fooled everyone for this long. Why not a few days longer?" Hywel set down his cup. "As your father also says, Gwen, *at the end of the song comes payment*. The thief will pay in due time."

"Does that mean we will too?" Gwen said softly, though nobody but Gareth heard her.

Then a horse whinnied at the entrance to the pavilion, and they turned to see Prince Rhys dismounting. He entered the tent and, at Hywel's gesture, found a seat on the bench beside Llelo. "So where is it?"

Gwen narrowed her eyes at the young prince. "Where is what?"

"The rest of the treasure." Rhys's lips twitched. "Nobody survives around here without identifying who knows things others don't." He bowed from a sitting position in Hywel's direction. "My lord. Please. I know you told my brother that you and your men are leaving in the morning, but I would ask you to stay."

Hywel unfolded his arms. "I'm all ears."

Rhys put his elbows on the table, the endearingly eager expression that he'd worn often in the last few days filling his face. "How did you know the treasure was buried in Old Nan's garden?"

"We didn't. It was a hunch." Gwen canted her head. "As it turned out, it was a good one."

"And that Old Nan wasn't blind?"

"It was the only thing that made sense," Gareth said.

Rhys nodded. "I want to go back. I want all of you to go back with me."

Gareth let out a *pfft* of air. "We ransacked the garden, the hut, her house, Meicol's house ... there are no trap doors and no secret compartments. That we haven't found it is not from lack of trying."

"It's there. I know it. We've missed something. Old Nan didn't know about it because Meicol hid it from her."

"Based on what evidence?" Gwen said.

"It makes sense, doesn't it?" Rhys was growing agitated, and he leapt up to pace back and forth in front of the table. "What would you have done if you'd found it? He gave a few coins to Old Nan and kept nothing for himself?"

"He would have taken what was easily portable," Gwen said.

Rhys nodded. "The missing gold and jewels are somewhere close. They have to be. It's the only explanation."

Hywel rubbed his chin and looked at the others. "What does your gut tell you, Gareth?"

Gareth pushed to his feet. "I'll get the others."

Prince Rhys put out his hand before Gareth could leave. "Not too many. I'd like to limit the number of people who know about this. It's why I came here alone."

Gareth gave him a long look, and then he nodded and headed out.

It was nighttime. Gwen was exhausted. But she certainly wasn't going to be left behind. She looked at Rhys. "You don't trust someone at the castle?"

He shrugged.

"Is it your brother?"

"I don't trust anyone." He glanced at Hywel, who was watching them closely. "That's the first lesson you learn as a younger son, is it not?"

Hywel gave a low laugh, but then he sobered and leaned forward, his eyes intent on Rhys's face. "You have to trust somebody sometime." He glanced at Gwen out of the corner of his eye. "Believe me when I say it can make all the difference."

Once back at the little steading, they dismounted: Hywel, Rhys, Gwen, Gareth, Llelo, Aron, Iago, and Cadoc, though the archer instantly headed into the woods. In turn, Iago nodded at Gareth and set off in the opposite direction with Aron. "We'll establish a perimeter."

Gareth looked at Gwen. "Would you like to start with the garden?"

"The three of you go on," she said, referring to him, Llelo, and Prince Hywel. "I'll stay with Prince Rhys."

Gareth gave her a look not unlike the one she'd received from Abbot Mathew earlier in the day, but he nodded and strode towards the garden door.

Rhys remained where he was, and she turned to him. "What is your gut telling you?"

"Why are you asking me? You were the one who realized that the treasure could be buried in Old Nan's garden. Nobody else had got that far."

"But you are the one who brought us here."

"I did. I hope I'm not wasting our time." Rhys pushed open the door into Meicol's house ahead of Gwen—and pulled up on the threshold. Meicol's tools were scattered all over the floor. The figures and carvings had been knocked over, and his mattress had been pulled apart, so there were feathers everywhere.

"If we needed proof that someone else was involved, we have it now," Gwen said.

Rhys made a rumbling sound deep in his chest. "Someone obviously had the same idea we did, and he's none too happy about not finding what he was looking for."

A boot scraped behind them, and both she and Rhys jumped. Anselm leaned against the frame of the door. "You're right about that at least."

Gwen glared at him. She despised him on principle, and nothing he'd done—not even getting Barri to confess—could make her think well of him.

Anselm put up both hands, palms out. "I'm just trying to find the truth, same as you." He gestured to the ransacked house. "The treasure isn't here."

"We can see that." Rhys spoke through gritted teeth. "How do I know you didn't find some of the treasure and keep it for yourself?"

Anselm grinned. "Would I have made myself known to you if I had? I'd be halfway to Bristol by now."

He had a point, though Gwen had learned not to trust a man who answered a question with a question. Anselm was unpredictable. She didn't understand him—and really didn't want to.

Rhys snorted and gestured with his head. "Be on your way."

Anselm's smile was just short of insubordinate. "Yes, my prince." He bowed. "As always, I am at your service." He left.

Gwen started to move about the room, discontent rumbling in her own chest at what Anselm had said and done.

"We might as well go, Gwen," Rhys said from behind her. "He's right that there's nothing here."

Gwen looked back at the prince. "Is he really gone?"

Rhys poked his head out of the door and then pulled back in, nodding as he did so.

"Shut the door."

He obeyed with a click of the latch. "What is it?"

"There are bits of this investigation Anselm doesn't know about."

Rhys's expression lit. "Good to know."

"From the start I thought the bed was far too grand for a man of Meicol's station, but of course he made it himself, so he could do what he liked." She touched one of the posts, which had been carved as if real vines snaked up it.

"I'm listening."

"Meicol had more work than perhaps the men up at the castle knew. For starters, he did all the woodwork in Sir Robert's house. That includes a great table in his hall. Alban's daughter showed Gareth a secret drawer underneath it, hidden in one of the table's pedestals."

Rhys took a step forward. "You think that he made one for the bed?"

"If so, Gareth couldn't find it." She began running her hands along the headboard. It looked and felt solid to her, as it should. She pressed every knothole, but there was no accompanying *click*.

Rhys joined her enthusiastically at first, but after he too found nothing, his interest began to wane. Gwen harrumphed and sat on the edge of the bedframe.

Rhys sat down beside her. "I was really hoping we had something here."

"Me too." She put her chin in her hand, her eyes scanning the room. A nearly life-sized cat lay on the floor close to her foot. On impulse, she picked it up and shook it, but nothing rattled. It was as solid as the bed. Still, she turned the cat over in her hands. "Who inherits all of Meicol's animals, my lord?"

"My brother, naturally, as Meicol's liege lord."

"What will he do with them?"

Rhys shrugged. "They're beautiful. He could sell some, but he has spoken with admiration of Meicol's handiwork, and more likely he will eventually give them away as gifts." He pointed with his chin to a cluster of several more. "The dragon has always been his favorite."

"As well it should be." Handing the cat to Rhys, Gwen darted forward to pick up the dragon. It too appeared solid, but she began running her hands all over the creature anyway.

"There's nothing here, Gwen."

"I'm sure you're right—" She broke off at the *click* that sounded in response to a hard thumb on the dragon's eye. At first she didn't know what she'd accomplished, but she held the neck tightly and twisted, and the whole head turned and came off. A seam had been hidden by the dragon's collar. Wool was stuffed into the neck and body, and she pulled out one tuft after another. Inside each little ball Meicol had place a gem, and one by one she dropped them into Rhys's lap.

35

Gareth

"Sir Gareth!"

Gareth turned, interested to see Prince Rhys coming towards him across the monastery courtyard. As had been the case last night, Rhys had no guard, and the way his hair stood up on end indicated he might have just woken up.

Gareth left the adjusting of his stirrups to Llelo, and walked towards the gatehouse to intercept Rhys. "May I help you, my lord?"

"Walk with me, if you will."

"Of course."

The young prince had the long legs and short torso of a man who hadn't quite reached his full height and weight, which was unsurprising in that he was fifteen. The two men headed across the courtyard towards the graveyard, which wouldn't have been Gareth's first choice as a place to talk, but it seemed Rhys was yet another resident of Deheubarth who viewed it as the perfect spot. As they walked, Rhys kept his head down, as if he was still thinking about what he wanted to say.

Once near the oak tree behind which Gareth had hidden to witness Anselm's questioning of Barri, Rhys put out a hand to stop him. Then, all alone, he did a circuit of the perimeter, making sure nobody was hiding behind any tree or gravestone, before coming back to stand in front of Gareth.

"I have a favor to ask of you." And then, even before getting confirmation from Gareth that he would actually do this favor, he reached into an inner pocket of his jacket and came out with a small bag, which he held out to Gareth. "I want you to keep these for me."

Gareth stopped himself from taking a step back, and he didn't take the bag. "What are you asking of me?"

"Please do not be offended." Rhys reached for Gareth's wrist, forcing his hand up and the bag into it. "This is not a payment for services rendered now or in the future. I genuinely am asking you to hold these for me until the day I need them." Rhys wrapped Gareth's fingers around the bag before releasing him and stepping back himself.

Gareth weighed the bag in his hand, his eyes on Rhys. "I don't understand."

"I cannot trust my brother or anyone in his court, and there may come a day when I will have to face him. Wealth of my own will help towards that."

Gareth opened the bag and dumped the contents into his hand. Sixteen gems of various sizes and weights lay in his palm. "Did your brother give you these?"

"I removed them from the collection before we gave it to him."

They'd loaded all of Meicol's carvings into garden sacks and carried them up to the castle. The find had included coins as well as gems, and Cadell had actually been generous, giving out shares of the wealth to Maurice, William, and Hywel, as the three lords who'd brought men to fight against FitzWizo. All three had already received some spoils from the sacking of Wiston Castle, and the haul was more than enough to have made the conquest extremely profitable for everyone.

Hywel had accepted his bag of coins and gems with a complete absence of guilt, for which Gareth couldn't blame him. Like Rhys, he knew his alliance with King Cadell could not last, and he had every intention of making the most of it while it did.

Gareth poured the gems back into the bag. "A devious man might give these to me so you could later accuse me of theft."

"You mean someone like my half-brother. Or Anselm."

"I didn't say it."

"But you thought it. That's not why I'm asking this of you."

"I will have to speak of it to Prince Hywel."

"I would expect no less. It is not my intent to buy your loyalty."

Gareth tipped his head. "What is it, then, that you think you've bought?"

"Time."

Gareth grunted. He'd been impressed with Rhys's intelligence from the first day they'd met, but the boy had grown up in the intervening weeks. Murder and intrigue had the tendency to do that to a man.

"I have no place to put these where they cannot be found," Rhys continued, "and there is nobody in Wales with more honor than you. If Sir Robert were still alive, I might have entrusted them to him, but he is not."

A vision of Hywel's bag of gold flashed before Gareth's eyes but he blinked it away. "I will keep these safe for you." He tucked the bag inside his coat.

Rhys watched him, but didn't move to leave.

Gareth looked at him sideways. "Was there something else?"

"You aren't asking for anything in return? A gem for yourself, perhaps?"

Gareth laughed. "Does it make you uncomfortable that I would do this for you without reward?"

Rhys swallowed. "I said you were honorable, and so you are, but—" He looked down at the ground and didn't say more. Gareth waited through a count of ten, uncertain if the audience was over or what he should say or do. He had accepted the gems out of compassion and instinct, not because it was a sane request.

Finally, Rhys looked up again. "When my brother decides his alliance with Prince Hywel is at an end, I will attempt to give you fair warning."

Gareth studied him. "I would not ask that of you."

"But I will do it anyway." Rhys chewed on his lower lip. "Will you want to give the gems back to me at that point?"

"Not if you aren't ready for them."

Rhys looked away. "My brother, my cousins, or an outsider might think me mad to be trusting a man of Gwynedd."

"Why are you?"

"As your prince mentioned last night, a man in my position has no friends and few allies. Men like Barri or Alban are far more common than men like you." He shrugged. "I don't know any men like you."

"Rhys." Gareth put a hand on the boy's shoulder. "Your world seems that way right now, but when you become king, I want you to remember that it doesn't have to be." He paused. "You might look to Abbot Mathew for help when you need it. I think he is a good man too."

Rhys gave him the kind of look Gareth had come to expect from him: mature for his age, but not yet weathered and hardened. Then he surprised Gareth by bending slightly in a bow, before turning and walking away.

Gareth felt the sack against his breast. He didn't know what he was going to do with the gems, and their weight was far greater than their actual number. Still, he was glad he hadn't said no. He gave Rhys time to disappear around the corner of the church, and was about to head back to the stable himself when Llelo appeared in the gateway.

"Can I ask you something?"

"Yes." It seemed to be the day for conversation with young men of a certain age.

"Why did you send me to search for Jane?"

Gareth studied his son. Though Llelo's expression was mild, but he was looking for an answer, and Gareth wasn't quite sure what it was. So he felt him out a bit first. "I knew you were the right man for the job."

"Why?"

"Because you are smart and capable, and I trust you. And you wouldn't be missed from the funeral rites."

Llelo wrinkled his chin. "You trust Evan. You could have sent him."

"I could have. I chose you." Gareth looked at him a bit sideways as he'd looked at Rhys a moment ago. "What's this about?"

Llelo waggled his head back and forth. He wasn't upset, but it was clear he wasn't sure how to continue. "You sent me only because I'm your son."

"Only?"

"How many other fifteen-year-olds would you even think to send on a task like that? How many would you trust with finding out something so important?"

Gareth put his hand on the gate and carefully closed it to block the view of the men in the monastery's courtyard. Nobody else needed to see this, even if this question was something every son who followed in his father's shoes eventually asked.

"One."

Llelo blinked. His back was to the monastery wall now, and he leaned his head against it. While Gareth wasn't looking, the boy had grown that last inch, and the two of them now stood eye to eye.

"You're asking if I am playing favorites? Do you actually think you didn't earn the task I set you, but I gave it to you, as you said, *only* because you are my son?" Gareth canted his head. "Maybe I did it because I felt pity for you? Or maybe you've decided I thought the task was unimportant, and it was only after you returned successful that I realized how important it had been all along?"

Llelo bit his lip.

Gareth put his hands on his son's shoulders. The knowledge that he had to say the right thing here and the fear that he might not be able to were almost tangible. "Three things. First, I wasn't present at your birth or for the first twelve years of your life, but that matters only because I wish I could have been. I'm grateful to you and to Dai for choosing Gwen and me as parents and for treating me like a father."

"You are my father." Llelo blurted out the words in such a way that implied he couldn't help but say them.

Gareth smiled gently. "And you are my son. Second, because you are my son, I trust you like I trust few men. That means there will be times when I give you tasks that are sensitive. This was one of those times. This is a family business, and you will always have a leg up over other men because of the trust inherent in being part of this family. Families can keep secrets within themselves in a way no other group can."

Llelo opened his mouth to speak but Gareth shushed him before he could. "Third, I meant what I said about you being smart, capable, and completely reliable. Would I have sent Gwalchmai on that journey you undertook?"

Llelo gave a tentative shake of his head.

"No, I would not have. Gwalchmai is neither a soldier nor trained as you are. He has not been following me around in the same way you have done these last three years. Do you know why I brought you south with me?"

"Because Hywel needed men he could trust."

"Yes, that. But also because *I* needed men I could trust. More to the point, you and your brother are not just in training to be knights, in case you hadn't noticed. You are in training to follow in *my* shoes, in a way that only my sons can do. Why do you think I let you tag along behind your mother and me solving murders?"

"So ..." The light was dawning on Llelo. "So I could learn?"

"So you could learn." Gareth nodded. "And what did you learn from that task I set you?"

"How to talk to people. How to get people to talk."

"A task I would not have set you if I didn't think you could do it." Gareth smiled at his son. "And now I have a question for you: do you want to continue?"

"What do you mean?"

"Investigating death is not for everyone. I'm not sure it is for Dai, for all his enthusiasm. Or maybe because of it. I'm not sure being a soldier is right for him either, though I may not know that for certain until he's a little older." Gareth looked at his son gravely. "The fact that you are mature enough to ask me this question only affirms my decision to keep you beside me. You are a man now, and because I am a knight and a prince's companion, you have the right to choose your own destiny. So I ask you again ... do you want to continue?"

The tentativeness of the last quarter-hour was gone, and Llelo's eyes cleared, revealing an almost breathless anticipation. That told Gareth as much or more about what Llelo really thought as his answer.

"Yes!"

The End

Historical Background

The Worthy Soldier was inspired by actual events of 1147 Wales. With Robert of Gloucester in the last year of his life, the war between Empress Maud and King Stephen had reached a new stage involving complex machinations among the lords who served them rather than pitched battles.

Earlier in the year, King Stephen had seized Gilbert de Clare, the Earl of Hertford, and refused to release him until he surrendered all of his castles. Gilbert did so, but as soon as he was released, he joined the rebellion of his uncle Ranulf, Earl of Chester, who had reached a point where he was serving himself more than Empress Maud. Gilbert's other uncle, also named Gilbert de Clare, who was the Earl of Pembroke, demanded that Stephen give *him* his nephew's castles as his hereditary right. Stephen refused, and immediately this Gilbert joined Ranulf's rebellion too, meaning that Stephen had lost control of almost the whole of western England.

Then Cadell, King of Deheubarth and Hywel, edling of Gwynedd, joined forces with Gilbert and his vassals, the Fitzgerald brothers, against the Fleming, Walter FitzWizo. Thus, Stephen lost all of south Wales too.

As to the treasure, Empress Maud had been using Oxford Castle as her seat in the war against Stephen. When she had to flee in the middle of winter—some say in her nightdress—she lost men and wealth, the outcome of which has been lost to time. That Prince Hywel recovered some of it is a product of my imagination.

And yes, it's true: the Richard de Clare in *The Worthy Soldier* is the same Richard de Clare who, in 1169, became the leader of the first Norman conquest of Ireland (see *Outpost in Time* from my *After Cilmeri* series). His vassal, Maurice Fitzgerald, went with him and was the founder of the powerful Irish Fitzgerald clan.

In addition, King Cadell's younger brother, Rhys, who is only fifteen in 1147, in due time becomes the Lord Rhys, ruler of Deheubarth and the most powerful lord in Wales until the rise of King Owain Gwynedd's grandson, Llywelyn Fawr, in the thirteenth century.

To sign up to be notified whenever I have a new release, please see the sidebar on my web page:

http://www.sarahwoodbury.com/

You can also connect with me on Facebook:

https://www.facebook.com/sarahwoodburybooks

About the Author

With two historian parents, Sarah couldn't help but develop an interest in the past. She went on to get more than enough education herself (in anthropology) and began writing fiction when the stories in her head overflowed and demanded she let them out. While her ancestry is Welsh, she only visited Wales for the first time while in college. She has been in love with the country, language, and people ever since. She even convinced her husband to give all four of their children Welsh names.

She makes her home in Oregon.

www.sarahwoodbury.com

Made in the USA
Middletown, DE
13 May 2017